Guardian Angel

By David Trebus

Published by DTstories

Guardian Angel by David Trebus

Dedication

I'd like to thank my friends and family for all their support while I worked on this book. Especially my parents for their faith in me, Nyki for helping me with the mammoth task of editing it without professional support, and Anna/Sara for their lovely cover art.
I'd also like to thank Lynette and my fans for helping me improve this second edition, it's people like you who make it worth writing.

Guardian Angel by David Trebus

Prologue:

Michael opened his eyes to find himself next to Claire and Jazen. They stood on the edge of a rocky cliff with a sea of fire stretching out before them. Molten lava and uncontrolled flames flowed and danced freely all the way to the horizon. In the distance, Michael caught sight of a huge red door wreathed in darkness. He knew instantly that was his destination, straight into the gates of Hell.

"I'm coming for you, Jasmine," Michael whispered. "Please hold on."

Chapter 1: Accident of Design

An urgent beeping startled Michael out of deep, comfortable sleep. He blinked a few times trying to overcome his disorientation, and slowly turned his head to look at the alarm clock. It was still early; he had a good hour to get ready and prepared to work. He hit the snooze button, shutting off the annoying noise at least for a little while longer.

Michael turned his head back and shut his eyes, shielding himself from the harsh glare of the new day that beamed in through the window. London was a dreary place most days, but today the sunshine was all the brighter, shining over the busy, people-packed streets below Michael's small apartment.

He drifted back to sleep, trying to forget the disturbing dream he had just awoken from. Before long, a new dream played out. Michael was walking along a pier with a young, blonde woman. She felt familiar, yet at the same time he had never laid eyes upon her before. She seemed to be surrounded by a shimmering haze that blurred her outline and shone bright like sunshine.

She walked along holding Michael's hand and looking into his blue eyes with a deeply concerned expression. Her touch felt warm and comforting, yet her face was grave and gave Michael a chill. He tried to recall where he knew her from but just couldn't force the memory to the surface of his mind.

"Who are you?" he suddenly blurted out.

The woman smiled. "That's not important right now, Michael. You just need to know I will always be here for you, so don't give up, no matter what happens."

"Huh, what do you mean?" Michael asked feeling confused.

"You need to be careful, Michael. I don't want to lose you." The woman paused, looking up at the sky, as a large cloudbank rushed in from the sea, plunging them both into darkness.

"We have run out of time." The woman continued staring out across the sea. "You need to wake up now Michael, or you'll be late."

"Wait, I still don't even know your name. Who are you?" Michael asked more urgently.

The young woman turned to face him, her bright blue eyes staring into his. She suddenly looked very serious, pulling a stern face.

"No time, wake your lazy behind up! Toodles for now!"

***

Michael woke up with a start. He sat upright with a powerful word on his lips.

"Toodles," he muttered under his breath, without realizing it. He lay back down and looked over at his alarm clock again. It was now 8:30; he had slept for another forty minutes and now only had twenty minutes to get to work on time.

"Oh crap, oh crap, oh crap, not again! Twenty minutes and my ass is toast!" Michael sprang up from his bed, nearly hitting his head on the low hanging-light bulb he couldn't be bothered to fix. He staggered over to the bathroom and ran an electric shaver over his morning stubble, before brushing his teeth in record time. He managed to pull on his suit cursing at his belt which kept catching on the wrong notch.

A glass of water and a banana scoffed down in a hurry were all he could manage for breakfast, as he walked past the kitchen and out into the hallway. Outside, he found himself dazzled by the sunshine, and had to pause for a moment to catch his bearings. "Wow…what a nice day…but why is it always so hot and stuffy in this city?"

Michael worked for a small publishing firm as a deputy manager. The job wasn't a bad one. It didn't pay as much as he wanted but still kept his rent covered, and allowed him some small luxuries. However, it just didn't feel right. He felt he was meant to be doing something different, something better, which was probably why he was often late. He had always dreamed of becoming a writer but, despite some small successes with his work, there'd never been anything big. Sadly, dreams did not pay the bills.

Michael rushed down the steps, stumbling on a loose cobble at

Guardian Angel by David Trebus

the bottom, and out into the street, where he saw a little girl staring up into a tree. He paused for a moment, trying to see what she was looking at. He squinted past the sunshine. Was that a faint outline sitting on a large branch? It looked like a woman, but when he looked closer, it shimmered and disappeared.

The little girl looked round at Michael and said, "Angels Angels, high in the air, Angels Angels, everywhere!" She giggled, before skipping off down the street.

Michael managed a polite but confused smile back at the girl, before running off down the street to catch the bus into work.

***

All around him, the busy city was coming to life. Buses and taxis were ferrying people to shops and work, people were hurrying along the street to their various destinations, and the traditional logjam of traffic was beginning to form, as people struggled to push their way through first. Michael hurried along the road reaching the main street in record time.

Michael was lucky to have an apartment in the city at all, as his company part subsidized his rent. If he lived in the suburbs, he would most likely have been up before the sun had even risen. He did, however, envy those people sometimes, their bit of greenery, the sounds of birds in the morning, rather than cars honking and engines running. The thought felt somewhat lonely; having so many people around always helped him feel less isolated in the world even though those he actually knew would barely fill an elevator.

The high street was packed as usual, even at this time in the morning. Michael dodged the people as he ran along the pavement to reach the bus stop. He still ended up bumping into some, inciting a curse from a businessman and a loud "HMPH!" from a large woman pushing a pram, which she used as a form of battering ram, but most people accepted such things as part of day-to-day life and just kept on going.

Michael threaded his way towards a pedestrian crossing. On the other side of the road, his destination shone golden in the sunlight. If he could just reach it in time, he would only be a few minutes late and could sneak in without anyone being any the wiser. He reached the lights and pressed the button impatiently several times.

To make matters worse, he saw his bus approaching the stop on the other side. It didn't look like more than a few people were waiting for it, and with Oyster cards they could just swipe pay and the bus would be off before he could reach it. Michael uttered a silent prayer that an old granny would muck about with her change or someone would drop a few coins, anything to delay the bus's departure.

The lights finally changed, and Michael almost leapt over the crossing. It seemed his luck was in; the queue of people wasn't moving. It looked as if someone indeed had dropped a few coins and was busy collecting them up off the floor of the bus.

"Seems like lady luck is shining on me today," Michael thought.

Just as he was nearly across the road he heard a loud screech of tyres. He barely had a moment to turn his head before a car came screaming out of a side road. The only thing he saw, before the world became a jumble of confusion, was a young woman driving a car with a mobile glued to her ear.

"I'll…be late for work," was Michael's last thought as he lay on the crossing. Concerned people and onlookers were gathering around him, but he caught one face amongst the crowd, the face of a young blonde woman. She looked concerned, and he thought she was calling out to him. Behind her, Michael swore he could see wings. He tried to listen to what she was saying, but his head lolled back and the world went dark.

***

The driver of the Ford Mondeo had been very busy that morning, meetings to arrange, things to do. So it was no surprise, that she was on her mobile when she came round that corner. What did surprise her were the deafening screams and wails, that emerged

Guardian Angel by David Trebus

from the mobile drowning out the sound of Roland, her assistant. The sounds were like something straight out of a horror movie. They distracted her for a moment, just as a young man began to cross the road. She caught sight of him and struggled to apply the brakes in time, but it was already too late.

The car shuddered to a stop, as the driver dropped her mobile in shock and sat staring at the young man in the middle of the road. All she could hear from the phone was static and the faint sound of laughter. Sitting stunned, she struggled to think of a way she could explain it to the authorities, thinking of what she would tell her husband, praying the man wouldn't be too badly hurt, so her insurance could cover it, and she wouldn't end up in jail.

If the phone going haywire in her ear earlier wasn't odd enough, she swore she could see an outline of bright, shimmering wings leaning over the young man amongst the crowd. Sarah promised herself if everything worked out she would never use her mobile whilst driving again…or at least just use a hands-free.

***

Michael's world was light. It was the only word he could think of to describe it. Light surrounded him; light flowed over him, light even moved through him. He turned what he perceived as his head

Guardian Angel by David Trebus

around, but in every direction only brightness loomed. It was as if he was staring at a spotlight.

Slowly, shapes began to emerge, shapes with elegant white wings. All around him Michael dimly heard a song, a beautiful melodious sound that made him feel strong and confident. Other such songs played all around him, forming one perfect symphony and complementing each other, instead of competing to be heard.

Michael realized the song was somehow part of him, that it *was* him. He tried to understand, to rationalize that a song couldn't be him, that it was impossible, but deep down he knew it was true. Feeling the urge to look down and through the white cloud-like floor, he saw London, the city he lived in.

He saw himself lying in a bed, with people busy around him. What were they doing? What was so urgent that they all had to crowd around him? It was somewhat pleasant in a way, so much attention; Michael didn't get much since he moved away from home.

The notes of his song were playing more urgently. He looked around in confusion, as he felt himself being pulled down towards the city. Part of him didn't want to go; part of him felt like he belonged in the symphony and wanted nothing more than to stay. A light shone on him from above. He understood instantly; it wasn't his time, he had to go back and add his song to the symphony of the Earth. He would get his chance to play in heaven one day, but not today.

Guardian Angel by David Trebus

The pull grew stronger, and the light faded; the clouds grew thinner as he flowed back down towards Earth. Michael's soul was pulled back into his body, as the CPR team brought him back from the brink. Again, Michael swore he could see the outline of a young woman shimmering as she stood over him, but then the world faded again as he returned to his body from what he thought was a dream.

"Time to wake up," a young woman's voice whispered.

***

Michael opened his eyes slowly, squinting at the bright, overhead light. He felt like he had been hit by a bus, and his head throbbed in pain. He turned from side to side trying to get his bearings. On his left sat a machine steadily beeping, and a small display showing different coloured lines. He turned his head to his right and found himself mere inches from the face of a young woman.

She stared straight into his eyes with a concerned but joyful look on her face. She seemed familiar, but Michael couldn't quite figure out where he knew her from. She was beautiful, however, with long straight blonde hair, blue eyes that seemed to shine with inner luminescence, and a cute-looking smile. Then he noticed something else about her: from her back sprouted two swan-like white wings, folded neatly together.

"This has to be a hallucination" Michael murmured, raising his hand to his head so fast he nearly tore the IV out of it. He tried to recall what had happened. He remembered crossing the road, and then…a dream. Michael worked out that he must have been hit by a car or been involved in some kind of accident, ending up in hospital. Then this girl had to be a nurse or some kind of hospital worker. The wings were probably just a trick of the light, a remnant of his dream. Michael sighed as logic took over his confusion, and he turned again to face the girl.

She had moved away from his bedside and seemed to be kneeling on the floor in prayer; the wings, however, had not disappeared as Michael had hoped they would, so he thought he would try a bit of conversation to help shake off whatever was still bugging him. The woman, meanwhile, prayed sending a pleasant almost melodic sounding voice upwards.

"Thank you sweetly for protecting my charge in his hour of need
Thank you sweetly for seeing to his recovery with such speed
I forever will stand by his side; I forever will guide his whole
I forever will sing far and wide, I forever serve body and soul."

"That's a beautiful prayer and a beautiful voice you have there, nurse," Michael commented, a bit taken aback. His head hurt less upon hearing the young woman sing, and he felt more relaxed.

Guardian Angel by David Trebus

"Oh, it's just an old prayer to send thanks into the sympho…" The woman trailed off, then turned round with a growing look of shock on her face.

"*AHHHHHHHH!*" she screamed, jumping back and knocking a small beaker over with her wings.

She recovered herself and returned over to where Michael lay to look into his eyes again. "You…you can see me?" she stammered. "Well, yeah of course, did you think you were like the invisible man? Sorry for embarrassing…" Then it was Michael's turn to trail off as he looked at the smashed beaker. Tricks of light or imaginary wings don't tend to knock things over.

"Those…those wings are *real*?" His head suddenly began to hurt again, and a growing sense of nausea formed in his belly.

His yell brought a nurse running into the room with a half-prepared meal tray. She opened the door almost straight into the face of the winged woman, who stepped aside deftly just at the last moment. The nurse walked straight up to Michael's bed, totally ignoring the woman standing there. She would have been hard to miss. What was going on? It was still possible he was going crazy, or that headache was a sign of something serious.

The nurse went over to the machine and checked the statistics on it, noting Michael's vitals. She then checked his IV and finally turned to him, looking into his eyes before smiling warmly.

"It's good to see you finally awake, you have been drifting in and out for a while now," she said. "I heard you shouting as I was

Guardian Angel by David Trebus

doing the food rounds. Coming out of a coma can be a bit of a shock so breathe deeply and try to relax. Let's get you comfortable, OK?"

Michael felt he had to ask the obvious questions, trying to ignore the winged woman in the corner of his vision. She could, indeed, be just a figment of his confused brain.

"What happened to me? How long have I been here?" he asked as the nurse adjusted his bed slightly allowing him to sit up at a lazy tilt.

"You were involved in a car accident. You were lucky; it could have been much worse. You've been here for three days now. You suffered a nasty knock to the head and a punctured lung, but somehow, miraculously almost, the lung healed itself within a day. The consultant had seen nothing like it. You really are a lucky young man."

Michael nodded in agreement; things were making sense to him now. He sat up very slowly, his whole body aching with the effort and his head swimming. The winged woman was still visible, though she seemed to be hiding in the corner and he had to ask the nurse just to be sure.

"Nurse…do you see anyone else in this room?" He pointed over to the corner as the winged woman waved her hands in alarm, as if to indicate that she didn't want to be given away.

The nurse turned around, then looked around the room. She didn't seem to notice the winged woman at all and turned back to

Guardian Angel by David Trebus

Michael shaking her head.

"Nope, no one else in here. Do you see someone?" She leant down again.

"No-no. I just thought I saw someone out of the corner of my eye," The last thing he wanted was to be taken for a madman.

The nurse hesitated, looking at Michael sternly. "Well, it's probably just your mind playing tricks on you. Do you feel up to something light to eat?"

Michael nodded, feeling as if he hadn't eaten in...well, days. The nurse smiled and left the room. She placed a foldout table in front of Michael with a tray of food on it. The tray had a couple of pieces of toast, jam, butter and a small cup for water.

"Eat slowly and make sure to drink all the water. Your body will need a little time to readjust. I'm going to go back on my rounds now, but if you need anything just push the buzzer there. I'll let the doctors know you are awake and ask one to check on you a bit later. It'll probably be a couple of hours though so just relax," the nurse said.

"It's good to see you awake and again if you need anything just push the buzzer. My name's Sandra,"

She left the room, shutting the door gently behind her. Michael leaned back in his bed, letting the warm soft pillows embrace his aching head again. So he had been in hospital for three days, since a car accident. He couldn't remember much about it just crossing the road, and then dreams. But the winged woman - she felt

Guardian Angel by David Trebus

familiar…and she *still* hadn't disappeared. In fact, while he was thinking she had returned to be inches away from his face.

"AHH…!" Michael yet out a loud yelp, and the woman to stepped back a pace.

"It's true…you can really see me…this isn't good, this hasn't happened before. What do I do? What do I dooo…?" The winged woman was clearly talking to herself as she paced back and forth by Michael's bed.

"This is too weird. I really must be going crazy." Michael sat up, and watched her frantic pacing. In any other situation, she would have looked comical.

Michael pinched his forehead with his fingers, squinting. His headache kept coming and going, either because of the accident, or the mystery woman. Better just to get on with the job of eating his breakfast and worry about his odd situation later. He took a couple of bites, and his body told him it needed more. He devoured the rest of the slice in moments.

The mystery woman meanwhile had stopped pacing and was now staring at him with an odd expression. Michael looked back and shrugged, did he have crumbs on his face? If so he didn't really care.

"What?" he said, mouth half full.

"How can you be eating at a time like this? Aren't you a bit shocked that there's a "*beautiful*" young woman with wings standing in your hospital room? Or do you see Angels every day?"

Guardian Angel by David Trebus

Michael finished his mouthful and washed it down with water before replying.

"Well, considering I've had a knock on the head and I'm in hospital, I just kinda assumed you were a figment of my imagination. Maybe I'm going crazy. Heck maybe I'm even still asleep!"

The woman leaned low over him. She wore a loose fitting white top, and Michael had to try very hard not to accidentally glance down her cleavage. She grinned. She gently placed her hand on the meat of his arm and then pinched it hard.

"*Ouch*". "What the hell was that for?"

"Could a figment of your imagination do that?" the woman countered grinning.

Michael looked at his arm and saw an angry red mark where she had pinched him. He rubbed it to soothe the pain, his mind reeling. She had left a mark; hallucinations couldn't leave marks, could they?

"OK…OK, this is really too much. Maybe I should just go back to sleep. When I wake up, this will all turn out to be some kind of weird nightmare." Michael lay back down shutting his eyes.

"Hmph So I'm like a nightmare! Sheesh, I spend all your life watching you, keeping you safe. I save your life, so your song doesn't join the chorus on High, and this is the thanks I get, called a nightmare!" She folded her arms across her chest and turned her back, looking angry.

Guardian Angel by David Trebus

Michael opened his eyes again, staring at the ceiling. What she had said, petulant though it was, struck a chord with him. Realisation hit him. This woman was the same one in his dream, the same apparition he had seen the night before, and the same woman who had been up in the tree. He had even seen her before the accident. That surely meant she had to be real?

He turned his head slowly, keeping it buried in the pillow against the vertigo of his situation, and he took a long look at her. She was indeed beautiful in a cute kind of way. She looked to be about five-foot-five but her wings made her seem much larger. She had piercing blue eyes, long blonde hair and a pair of red ribbons worked into two front strands. Michael sighed and swallowed his growing anxiety to try and smooth things over with...well, the angel.

"Look, I'm sorry. I didn't mean to insult you, but you have to admit this is a shock to me. I mean, it's not every day you meet an…an angel in a hospital room. It's like something out of a movie."

"This is real, I'm afraid, and I'm not just any angel. I am your angel, your guardian angel. It's my job to look after you, guide you and one day…" The angel trailed off. "Well anyway," she added "I'm just glad you're ok."

"So, what's your name? I mean, you obviously know mine, seeing as you've been with me from day one. Must have been weird seeing me naked all those times, eh?"

Guardian Angel by David Trebus

"My name is Jasmine, and as for seeing you naked, I can't say seeing a tiny winkle was altogether very interesting. But you were a cute baby, I must admit, especially that little birthmark on the back of your thigh. Looks like a little baby sheep,"

This had to be real. No-one had seen that mark, apart from his parents and a few ex-girlfriends. He also felt himself blush at having his joke turned against him. Did she look at him in the shower now he was an adult? No, being an angel he doubted she would do something so improper. Michael decided to accept things as they were, at least for now; if he tried to go against the flow his head might explode.

"So, what happened with the accident? I barely remember it? You must have seen it. After it happened, I saw you in my dreams."

Jasmine's face turned very serious, and she moved to sit by him on the bed. She smelled of the flower she was named after. As she sat on the bed, she barely made an impression, as if she were light as a feather. She placed her hand on the bed to steady herself, then leaned closer.

"You were involved in a car accident, as the nurse told you...but it wasn't really an accident. Someone influenced that driver, distracted her into hitting you. It's the only reason on High let me directly heal you. If it had been natural...I would have lost you." Jasmine whispered frowning.

"Your dreams are how I usually talk to you. The human subconscious is tuned into our songs and sings with us in the great symphony. Dreams are the easiest way for you and us to tap into it, allowing me to guide you, talk to you and comfort you. I was there when your ex left you in the dumps, when you got ill - every time, watching over you and praying you would be OK."

"So. You're saying someone wanted me dead?" a dread grew in Michael's mind.

"Maybe…but maybe not. I mean, the darker powers in the world have many little schemes they like to play out. It could have just been a malicious act…or something more, I don't know. But try not to worry. You're OK now, and I'll be here to keep you safe." Jasmine smiled and placed her hand on top of his.

"You seeing me is something totally different though. I think it's the first time this has happened for hundreds of years." She paused for a moment.

 "Someone's coming. Your doctor. I am going to go on High and try to find out if they know anything. Get some rest. Even from up there, I'll be keeping an eye on you, so try not to worry. If this is temporary, then it was a pleasure to talk directly to you. If not, we can chat when I come back."

   Rising from the bed, Jasmine placed her hands together and raised them above her head. Her wings spread, and a light enveloped her. She sang a few notes and slowly moved upwards in the light. She turned her face down to him, even as her wingtips passed directly through the ceiling. She smiled, pushed one of her hands out towards him and made the peace sign saying, passing through the ceiling in a ring of light and out of Michael's sight.

"What a funny girl." Michael snorted lying letting his head fall into his pillows and trying to comprehend everything that had happened to him, just as the door opened and a doctor came in carrying a clipboard.

"How are you feeling, Michael?" the doctor asked politely. Michael couldn't think of a reply that stated exactly how he felt at that moment that wouldn't make him look like a lunatic. He settled for as good an answer as any.

"Not too bad." he replied nonchalantly.

The doctor checked the machine hooked up to Michael, as the nurse had earlier before looking into his eyes, checking his pulse from his wrist, and listening to his breathing through a stethoscope. He prodded and poked him a few times for good measure, then pulled up a chair next to Michael's bed and sat down placing a medical clipboard on his lap. The angle and the doctor's handwriting made it unreadable.

"Well, Mr Andrews, you're quite a lucky man. When you came in, you had suffered a severe blow to the head, a collapsed lung and some internal bleeding. You had to be resuscitated and went into a deep sleep, or very light coma as we call it. Do you remember anything about what happened?"

"Only rushing across the road to catch the bus, and then a car. Then nothing, until I woke up and saw the nurse."

The doctor nodded. "That's good. No short term memory loss. I don't quite know how but your lung has healed however. I would like to take credit for it, but it is almost miraculous. I expected you to be here in recovery for a few weeks. But, looking at your chart over the last few days and your readings now, I think you should be fit to be released in a couple of days. You must have a strong will to survive."

Michael grinned before he could stop himself. "Or someone looking out for me on high," he thought.

"I guess so, doc," He said aloud "I mean I don't know how, but I just felt protected."

"Well, whoever it is protecting you is doing a good job. I'll be back to check on you again tomorrow, just to make sure everything is OK and there's no unforeseen complications. All things remaining equal, as I said, you should be able to go home the day after tomorrow." The doctor stood up to leave.

Michael nodded, "Thanks doc."

"If you need anything, just ask the nurse. If it's urgent press the buzzer there. Take care, and see you tomorrow, Mr Andrews." The doctor left the room, closing the door gently behind him.

Michael was left alone with his thoughts. He spent the next few hours trying to wrap his head around all that had happened to him. The theological implications alone were enough to blow his mind. Michael had always had faith in a higher power, but to have evidence beyond all doubt slapping him in the face was almost too much to take.

Guardian Angel by David Trebus

He didn't just have faith or belief any more, he had proof beyond all doubt. Well, unless he really was crazy, and it was all some hallucination. He wasn't sure where to go from here. Would he always be able to see Jasmine, or would his ability fade with time? She had said it was abnormal for anyone to be able to see his or her guardian angel. Michael wondered if the ability to see Jasmine would be taken away and his memory of the events erased.

"Could they really do that?" he murmured.

A loud ringing shocked him out of his reverie. A throbbing pain flared up as he looked around for its source and found a telephone beside his bed. He sighed with relief and reached over to pick it up wearily, cutting off the piercing ringing noise.

"Hello…"

"Michael, I've been so worried about you, are you OK? How are you feeling? The doctor just phoned me to say you'd woken up." His mother's voice fired off questions like a chain gun.

"I'm fine mum; the doctor said they should be releasing me the day after tomorrow. They say I've made a miraculous recovery, although my head still hurts a lot,".

"That's good, but they shouldn't be letting you out so soon, you could still have problems. You should tell them to keep you in longer, just in case. I was so worried when they phoned to tell me you were hurt, I almost got on a plane straight away, but all the flights were booked up solid. Has your father been in or phoned

Guardian Angel by David Trebus

you?"

Michael's mother lived in the south of France, where she'd taken a job as an antiques dealer a few years back. She had encouraged Michael to go with her, but his connection with England had held him back; that and his mum's penchant for nagging.

"I wouldn't know if he's been in, I only just woke up. But don't forget he spends a lot of time in America now with his band. Last time I spoke to him, he was somewhere in Arizona. I doubt he would be back in England yet."

The doctor must have phoned his mother to inform her of his condition right after he had left the room. Michael wasn't sure whether to thank him or hate him for it.

"Well I'm going to phone him, his music can sod off. You come first. Let me know if he doesn't ring you. Oh, I'm just so glad you're OK, Mikey, I don't know what I'd have done if you had..."

Michael cut his mother off, knowing she would start crying soon. "It's OK, mum, honestly I'm OK, I was lucky. So stop worrying"

"When you have kids, you'll understand. I'm going to get the first flight I can over there, to check on you, OK?"

"It's fine, honestly mum, I'm fine!"

"Still, I'm flying over first chance I get. It's been months, anyway, and you should have someone with you now." Michael's mother continued ignoring his protestations.

"Listen," she went on, "I have to go now, so you stay safe, sweetie, and I'll ring you when I'm back in the country. Get well soon, love

Guardian Angel by David Trebus

you."

"Love you too mum."

After putting the receiver down Michael let out a long drawn out sign. His mother was very protective, too much so sometimes. Then again, a bit of home cooking and mothering appealed to him after months of bachelor living. It had been over a year since his last girlfriend, and with his parents often, abroad, he did get lonely from time to time. He decided he may as well accept his situation and to look forward to his mother's visit. He lay back in his bed and trying to think again. After everything that had happened since he woke up, weariness overcame him. Michael drifted off to sleep, dreaming of angels and warm, home-cooked meals.

***

Jasmine ascended slowly on her wings of light, leaving the mortal plane of Earth behind. She passed through the various layers of the symphony, perceiving all the different notes and songs as she sought to enter the highest tier of heaven. Every time she returned to heaven, the music always soothed any worries she had and made her feel at peace.

An angel's wings didn't just serve in the traditional sense, letting them fly. They also acted as the conduit or key that allowed entrance to heaven, pulsing with purest light when the angel prayed for entrance, and opening a portal that led to a higher plane. Demons lost this ability upon falling, their wings effectively destroyed and remade into a mocking parody of the form they once held.

Jasmine's thoughts returned, to what lay behind Michael's accident; it was definitely not the work of man. Was a demon was behind it? The thought made her shudder, and she tried to push it aside; hopefully, she would gain the answers she sought when she reached the High seat.

Jasmine was now entering the upper tiers of the symphony; here she could hear the angels' forever raising their voices in praise and love. She slowed her climb and came to a halt, wings beating against the up-draught. Her wings lost their glow and Jasmine stopped, clouds forming beneath her feet and she landed.

To the other angels going about their heavenly business, Jasmine's arrival was just like any other and so they ignored it. Had Jasmine been watching another angel arrive, it would have seemed as if the angel had emerged from a ring of light, much as she had left Earth only moments earlier. One angel, however, did pay attention and ran up to her as she found her feet.

"Jasmine, you are expected." The angel's tone was neutral.

"I am?" Jasmine replied, but then why shouldn't it surprise her that they knew something was amiss?

"Yes, please follow me to the Metatron," the male angel said. "He wishes to hear your story and to help you find your way. Strange events have transpired." He gestured to a golden archway.

The male angel was named Filo. He was of the highest choir and personal attaché to the Metatron, the voice of God. He had a proud bearing and a stern, yet handsome face. His hair was black, where most angels had blond or very light brown hair. His eyes, traditionally blue, glowed with such intensity and faith no one looking into them could fail to be moved.

Jasmine bowed and walked towards the golden archway, which was elaborately decorated, with images of cherubs blowing horns. The space between shimmered faintly as Jasmine approached. Filo fell into step behind her, waiting patiently as she hesitated. It led to the Metatron's private chambers, and usually only, the most important of matters were heard there.

The thought made Jasmine suddenly nervous, a feeling she had not experienced in decades. Angels felt emotions, just like humans, but had a much greater control over them, and could suppress them if the need arose. This time, however, Jasmine lost her usual composure and her hand trembled.

She stepped through the shimmering arch in a brief flash of light and emerged on the other side in a large circular chamber. Pillars of glass, which contained musical instruments that sat suspended in the air, surrounded the chamber. At the far end, a large, wooden chair stood, unadorned but regal in its appearance. By its side, a desk was strewn with parchment and a small electronic device, and

Jasmine's allowed herself a small grin even the angels weren't immune to progress.

In the centre of the room, the Metatron kneeled with his head bowed and hands before him. His majestic wings were neatly folded upon his back, though their span was such that the feathers brushed the floor. Jasmine stood with Filo by the arch, patiently waiting to be noticed. It would be considered rude to interrupt the Metatron in prayer. The idea he could be communicating with God sent an excited tremor down Jasmine's spine.

After a few minutes, the Metatron slowly stood up and turned to face them. His hair was cut short and golden. His eyes too were golden, unlike the traditional blue of most angels. He had a handsome face, almost like that of a teenage boy, but behind it dwelt great wisdom and untold aeons of devoted service. He was very tall, at least seven foot by Jasmine's estimate, and gave off a huge air of authority and power. Jasmine bowed instinctively and noticed that Filo did the same. To be in the presence of the Metatron was an honour, but also a troubling one under the current circumstances.

"Welcome, Jasmine, I am pleased you have come so quickly. Filo, thank you for escorting our young Guardian here. You may return to your duties." The Metatron's voice was soft yet powerful. "Thank you lord," Filo replied bowing. He nodded to Jasmine before returning back through the arch to leave Jasmine alone with the Metatron. She struggled to suppress her growing unease and

Guardian Angel by David Trebus

nerves.

The Metatron seemed to notice and smiled.

"Do not be so nervous, Jasmine. I know of what has happened, and I know you tried your best. I also know your charge is fine and healthy, despite this odd occurrence. Be at ease, and let us discuss the matter."

Jasmine's nerves vanished. His voice soothed her to the very core, and she suddenly knew everything would be all right. That was his strength: total conviction, total love, that could heal any woe. However deep inside something kept on nagging at Jasmine, although now she barely perceived it.

The Metatron sat down on the floor and gestured for Jasmine to join him. He seldom used the elaborate chair, eschewing it for a more humble spot on the floor. He regarded it as a token of vanity and one he did not need. "I will sit as equal with all of the choirs" he had said "and even mortals, for we are all beloved in God's eyes." Jasmine still remembered his words and had always been inspired by the Metatron's humble attitude.

Jasmine slowly walked over and knelt opposite the Metatron, folding her wings in neatly behind her. There was no danger of them touching the floor, as they were smaller than the average span, but she wanted to look her best before the Metatron. He seemed to notice and gave her a warm smile before getting down to business.

"I do not need to tell you what has transpired on Earth, As you

Guardian Angel by David Trebus

were there with your charge when it happened, Jasmine," the Metatron paused, as she got comfortable.

"As you suspected, the incident was no act of man. We do not know exactly who was behind it, but we have our suspicions."

"However, Michael's apparent ability to see you I do not believe was in the enemy's design; in fact it, is this very thing they may have been trying to prevent from transpiring, although to what ends even we do not know." Jasmine listened intently to him. "But has this happened before? And why my charge, why Michael?" Jasmine suprised herself at the emotion in her voice. Her concern for Michael feeling well beyond that of a dutiful guardian.

"This has occurred before on rare occasions. As for why it has happened to Michael, only higher powers know. Not even I am allowed such information." The Metatron glanced up to the ceiling. "So what happens now?" Jasmine asked, following his gaze.

The Metatron grinned and looked directly at Jasmine. She couldn't help but meet his piercing gaze, pinning her in place, staring straight back at him. He looked at her for what seemed an eternity. He finally looked away and nodded, as if agreeing with himself.

"You, Jasmine, will continue to look after Michael down on Earth. In the past, such instances have been occasionally suppressed, with the human's memories removed and the guardian reassigned, but in this case, I have been instructed that you should remain by his side, and his memory be left in place."

Jasmine felt relieved at being released from the Metatron's gaze. It was not unpleasant but an intense experience that left her feeling drained. She also felt happy that she was to remain by her charge's side. She had been with Michael ever since his birth, watching over him, comforting him from afar. To lose him now would have been like losing a piece of herself.

"Thank you, High one, I can only hope I will continue to do my duties well."

The Metatron laughed loudly at Jasmine's reply and stood up. He offered Jasmine his hand to help her up. He pulled her up gently, then placed his hands on either side of her shoulders.

"You are an amusing one, Jasmine. But your devotion and respect have always earned you a special place in the symphony. Do not fear your duties, for you are easily capable of performing them. But know this. We suspect infernal involvement in what happened, so be cautious and watchful.

"You have been given an even greater responsibility. Your charge is aware of you and now has belief of things beyond his realm. Even I do not know what will happen from now, but have faith that you are where you are for a good reason, and look after Michael well," The Metatron again looked directly into Jasmine's eyes, although this time without his piercing sight.

"Thank you, I'll try my best to keep him safe," Jasmine replied, feeling her voice tremble. The thought of infernal involvement had

Guardian Angel by David Trebus

shaken her; she'd never had to face down the designs of the enemy directly before. She was having an unaccustomed bout of emotional frailty today.

"I know you will. Now go, for your charge is unsure and will need your guidance more than ever. At least you will be able to give it to him directly now. If you ever need guidance yourself, you know where I am. We are always here for you Jasmine, just as you are for him."

He guided her to the arch, where, he turned at the threshold and bowed deeply. The Metatron placed his hand on her head and smiled again, before returning to the centre of the room and watching her leave.

"Now things are truly set in motion." He whispered, looking up at the ceiling. "I only hope the two of them are ready for what awaits, them and love, faith and hope do not abandon them."

A bright light shone down upon him and a beautiful music played on the instruments encased in the pillars. Again, the Metatron smiled, nodding.

"Then I have no need to doubt. I will have faith in them."

***

Jasmine stepped out through the arch. She felt the clouds beneath her feet and all around her, other angels were busy with their

Guardian Angel by David Trebus

duties. She was having trouble controlling her emotions, with all that had occurred. She might lose her mind if she didn't find some control.

Angels had emotions like humans, so that they could feel the prime virtues of love, hope and faith. They had rejoiced, sung, loved, and prayed. However, such unadulterated emotion had led to the downfall of some, and to the wars in heaven. Some had embraced darker passions and had fallen from grace. After that, all angels learnt rigid self-control over their feelings, only expressing them in certain ways, through prayer, music or their tasks.

Jasmine took some deep breaths and mastered herself, remembering her lessons. She focused her thoughts inwards and tuned herself to the symphony all around her. She could see the notes flowing, feel the melodies in her spirit. Her calm reasserted itself as her emotions returned to their suppressed state. She smiled and opened her eyes.

"Hello, Jasmine," said an angel right in front of her. A male face with unusual green eyes and blonde hair stared at her. Jasmine almost stumbled back in suprise.

"*Jazen*. For goodness sake, don't scare me like that. I was finding my place in the symphony."

"Oh, sorry. I was just passing by and noticed you there. Are you OK?"

"Yes, fine, just running an errand," Jasmine replied

"Oh, good to hear. Your charge is well?" Jazen asked.

Guardian Angel by David Trebus

"Yes, he's fine, but why are you here?"

"Oh…well, I'm on high to be cautioned. I've violated a tenet with my charge. But I just can't help myself; I care for her much and want her to know someone is there for her in her times of need. She looks so lonely sometimes, Jasmine. It is horrible!"

Jazen's hasty explanation revealed a lot more to Jasmine than he intended. Angels seldom lied. They could obfuscate rather than lie outright, but it was generally frowned upon. Jazen was more honest than any angel Jasmine had met, and tended to talk too much.

"Violating tenets is not wise, Jazen." Jasmine said sternly. "If you truly care for her so much, you will be more careful. If you keep doing it, you may end up reassigned. You could even inadvertently harm her."

Tenets were the rules passed down to guardian angels to ensure that they operated reasonably. Rules such as no direct contact, no direct intervention, no relations and no harm. Relations between angels and humans were almost unheard of. No guardian angel ever violated the rule against harming their charge, unless they were falling. Even the most evil of humans deserved redemption. But some did break the no-direct-contact or intervention rule, and Jazen was a serial offender. Of course Jasmine would be breaking the very same rule, although with divine sanction.

"Well, anyway, I had best be going" Apparently ignoring Jasmine's warning had fallen on deaf ears . Jazen bowed and

Guardian Angel by David Trebus

hurried off before she could reply.

Jasmine sighed and waved half-heartedly at the diminishing form of Jazen. She knelt and uttered a quick and silent prayer, before preparing to return to Earth. She wanted to stop by and see some of her fellows, but she should go back sooner rather than later. She was lost and unsure of herself but, embracing the music of the symphony, her faith overcame her doubts.

She spread her wings and they began to glow. She flapped them twice to float, and below her, a ring of light formed. She slowly descended into it and started her journey back to Earth, passing through the layers of the symphony. From above, a shaft of light shone down warming her. Her doubts melted away and she knew everything would be all right.

Guardian Angel by David Trebus

Chapter 2: Getting Used to Things

Michael's dreams were disturbed. They began with pleasant memories of the home- cooked meals his mother used to make, along with a bizarre mix of winged-women cooking for him and winking suggestively. Lack of a girlfriend for over a year must have warped his mind. After a while, though, these dreams faded into something more sinister.

He was standing on a desolate plain, scorched black and devoid of life. Craters dotted the landscape. In the distance, he could see the ruins of what looked like a city, torn apart by some unknown force. The landscape was dark, and only a red glow along the horizon provided any illumination. Above, only turbulent sky of the same violent hue swirled.

Michael began to walk, then to run, anything to get away from this place. It had a feeling of wrongness, of evil. He stumbled on a stone and staggered a few paces, before landing face first in dust. He looked up at a figure that stood before him, though he couldn't make it out.

"*Soon*" it said. At that moment, Michael was pulled upwards by a bright light, taking him away from his nightmare and back into the

Guardian Angel by David Trebus

waking world.

***

Jasmine's return journey had taken longer than expected, delayed by an unknown presence causing discord in the symphony. Time flowed differently in heaven, but, had all gone smoothly, she would have been away no longer than four hours. However, the delay meant she was away for more than double that time. What was happening to her charge? Something felt wrong.

She eventually reached the Earth, curling and flapping her wings gently to slow her descent. She formed the portal and returned through the ring of light into Michael's room. He was still in bed and seemed to be asleep, but over him stood a dark figure. Danger and evil emanated from it.

Jasmine landed gently on the hospital floor, her wings folding back in and the circle of light closing above her. The figure ignored her for a moment, perhaps distracted by its labours, but must have sensed her presence eventually and turned. It was a man, clothed in a dark suit. To Jasmine, his features seemed twisted, warped into something altogether unnatural. A grin stretched all the way up to his cheekbones, and two small protrusions grew from his forehead.

Guardian Angel by David Trebus

The man was an imp. A lesser infernal creature, Jasmine remembered from her lessons. Imps were recruited from the very lowest fallen of human souls, those whom the pit saw as having true taint and potential. Hell removed them from the plains of suffering to live again in the mortal realm in exchange for their services. Imps sowed the seeds of doubt in mortals, bringing anxiety, fear and distrust in their subtle whisperings. They inspired temptation and always sought to drag mortals down, little by little, in petty ways.

Imps were not especially powerful, as their only direct ability was to influence humans in a minor manner. They could cause harm in other ways, though. There was nothing stopping them from using a gun or a knife to cause serious harm to an angel's charge, or even an angel, if they found a special form of metal.

"Hello, angel, come to interrupt my ministrations?" The imp hissed through its clenched teeth and wide grin.

"Be-gone, lesser spawn!" Jasmine said in a commanding voice. "You are not welcome here, and you will not harm my charge." She couldn't show any signs of doubt or weakness.

"Pfft, do not try to command me. I take no orders from the likes of you." The imp chuckled to itself.

Jasmine grew concerned for Michael. She had to stop whatever the imp had been doing. It was too much of a coincidence that an imp just happened to be in Michael's room so soon after the accident. She took a confident step forward, raised her hands above her head and closed her eyes to sing.

"O light on high. O song of beauty.
Shine down now, sing in purity.
Bring brightness, bring melody
Banish darkness, banish malady."

Jasmine's voice lifted up to the symphony, and a small part of its power broke off to touch the earth. As a bright light enveloped the room, the imp recoiled and shrieked. It ran out of the room, hissing in pain, not even turning to make more veiled threats or smart remarks. Jasmine ceased her song and the room returned to normal. She felt drained after her transition from heaven and use of her powers.

Michael stirred in his bed, and Jasmine went to him, nearly knocking over a small food trolley in her haste. She looked Michael over. No serious harm seemed to have come to him, and he was much as he had when she had left. Jasmine breathed a sigh of relief and relaxed.

***

When Michael opened his eyes, the first thing he saw was a

Guardian Angel by David Trebus

bright light. He blinked a few times to clear his vision, and Jasmine was standing over with a concerned look on her face. For a moment, it felt like when he had first awoken after his accident. He examined Jasmine's face and looked into her eyes. She really was quite cute. The thought brought back the more pleasant part of his dream, and he shook his head quickly to clear any impure thoughts. Thinking dirty thoughts about an angel had to be taboo.

Jasmine pulled up a chair and sat next to the bed. She decided not to tell him about the imp right away, not until he was fully recovered. There was no sense in worrying him, and whatever the imp had been doing, it had not had the chance to finish its work.

"How are you feeling?" Jasmine asked.

"Not too bad. I was having weird dreams, though. They started off nice...but then," Michael hesitated remembering what happened in them.

"Then?" Jasmine asked, leaning forward.

"Well..I was somewhere dark with ruins around and a sky of red, the whole place made me feel frightened,"

That explained what the imp was up to. It was trying to enter Michael's mind through his dreams. Visions of the pit were the first stage in dream invasion. Jasmine had arrived just in time. "Who knows what seeds it would have tried to plant in him," Jasmine thought, "or information it would have gained had I been a moment later."

"I wouldn't worry," she said. "It's probably just the trauma of the accident and the shock of all that's happened. Not every day you get to meet your own angel, especially one as cute as me." Jasmine replied ignoring all of the rules on vanity.

Michael looked at Jasmine, cocking his head slightly. He noticed little details about her that he had not seen before. Her wings seemed smaller than he would have imagined an angel's to be, now she had them tucked back. In the pictures he had seen, even when folded away, angel wings were massive. Jasmine's, however, were more like a cherubs than a majestic angel of legend.

He also noticed the details of her face. When she smiled, her eyes seemed to sparkle, like sunlight reflecting on the blue sea, while her hair framed her face perfectly. Michael blinked a few times, blushing slightly. Jasmine really was cute, but he felt far too shy to just come out and say it.

"I was hoping for cuter, you know. You look a little tomboyish." Jasmine rocked on her feet and pulled an irritated expression, leaning forward and pinching Michael hard on the arm. She seemed to puff up her cheeks when she got annoyed, which only added to her appeal.

"Ouch!" Michael pulled away, "I'm injured here, you know!"

"I'm going to blame that little comment on everything you've been through. You're clearly recovering well, as you're hiding your feelings again with sarky remarks. Don't forget, I've been looking after you for a long while Michael." Jasmine leaned back in her chair again. Oddly, her wings seemed to move themselves out of

Guardian Angel by David Trebus

the way of the backrest.

A long moment passed before Michael spoke again. He kept sneaking glances over at Jasmine, who just sat there watching him with an intent gaze. It was unnerving to think she'd probably been gazing at him for years without him knowing it.

"So…what happens now? What did they tell you? Am I going to lose my memory?"

Jasmine leaned forward again, resting her elbows on the edge of the bed. She may have been totally comfortable this close to Michael, but he sure wasn't. Before today, he had never really met her, even though she felt very familiar.

"Oh…sorry," she said sitting back, "force of habit. Well, they say that things are to be left as they are. Your memory is to stay intact and I am to continue being by your side. Isn't that great?" Jasmine giggled, making the peace sign again.

"But…I don't get it. This is all a little too much for me to take in. I'm either going crazy, or I'm going to go crazy, if this keeps on. A couple of days ago, I mean, I believed in stuff like that, but now it's right in my face, literally. What do I do?"

"Do you need another pinch on the arm? You're not going crazy, and you're not going to go crazy, so stop being a baby about it. Your life has changed, yes. But think of the gift you have been given. You know that there's someone always there for you. You *know* there's a Heaven. Not many people can claim that." Jasmine placed her hand on Michael's shoulder.

Guardian Angel by David Trebus

"But where do I go from here?" The touch comforted Michael, but he was still worried.

"You carry on. I've seen you go through so many hardships and difficulties and come out winning. You always try your best, that's what makes me proud to be by your side. So don't be scared of me, or what I represent. I'm here for you now, directly, and can help you even more. I don't know what's going to happen but I am here for you and I know you will be OK."

"Definitely cute…if a little corny and whacky," Michael thought.

He sighed, propping himself up in his bed. He knew what Jasmine was saying made perfect sense, but he still felt cast adrift on an ocean without a paddle to steer with. The future always scared Michael a bit, just like anyone, but now he was not sure what to think. Still, Jasmine's words brought some comfort, and looking into her eyes made him feel calmer.

"I guess I've no choice then, really. Don't you get bored watching me all the time? I'm going to have to go back to day to day life you know."

"Nope. Don't really get bored. Besides, I find all that you humans do fascinating. And, if I do get bored, I can always sing and do a little helping on the side, if you don't need me much. Ever wondered why people have good luck around you sometimes? That's me, sneaking in a little extra help when their own guardian isn't watching."

"Is that allowed?" The idea piqued Michael's curiousity.

Guardian Angel by David Trebus

"Of course. We angels try not to be prideful, and accept help gladly. I mean, if it helps the world become a happier place, then it's all in the greater good and makes the symphony sound all the sweeter…and I know you're going to ask about the symphony now, so let's stop. Try to get some more sleep OK? It's going to be a busy day tomorrow." Jasmine settled Michael back into his pillows gently like a caring lover.

"This time, I promise you won't have bad dreams, because I'll be here watching you."

Michael shut his eyes again feeling exhausted. Jasmine remained close, but sat back, giving him more space. She sang to herself softly, and within minutes Michael felt himself drifting off to sleep. This time, he knew there would be no nightmares.

***

When Michael awoke, bright light shone in from the window. He turned round to see Jasmine, but her chair, was empty. He looked up at a clock mounted above the door, which said nine forty-five in the morning, May twenty-ninth. He had slept almost a full day!

Michael propped himself up, rubbing his eyes and adjusting his pillow so he could sit up comfortably. He'd always complained he never got enough sleep; he seemed to be making up for it over the

Guardian Angel by David Trebus

last few days, easily. Michael felt refreshed, though, and soon even hazarded getting out of bed and taking a few tentative steps.

After so long in bed, he almost fell over, but steadied himself on the chair. He dragged it along after him and moved slowly towards the window. He put the chair in front of him, and then sat on it looking outside.

The sun was shining in a blue sky, with a few lazy clouds drifting across it. Its warmth felt good on his skin, and Michael shut his eyes for a moment, to enjoy the sensation and adjust to the light. He'd always preferred spring and summer to autumn and winter. He liked warm weather and bright sunlight. He never could understand people who liked the cold or winter.

Michael looked down out of the window into a large courtyard area. It was lined with pavement around its outer edges, but in the middle a large patch of grass, with several trees, sat like a small oasis of green amidst the grey of the hospital buildings.

A few children were playing on the green, supervised by some kind-looking nurses. Nearby, Jasmine stood with her hands raised up in the air, singing softly to herself. Michael couldn't make out the song, either Jasmine was singing very quietly, or the distance was too great.

He turned his attention to the children, who played happily with each other, laughing and trying their best to forget the troubles of the world. If he looked closely he could make out, next to each child and each of the nurses that supervised them, a guardian

Guardian Angel by David Trebus

angel. They sat, stood or hovered nearby, watching over their charges, smiling as they played or looking concerned if they fell over.

It wasn't just Jasmine he could see, but everyone else's guardian angel. That was worrying. If angels existed, and he could see them, what other, less savoury things would his new-found sight might reveal to him? He shivered despite the warm sun, and took a step back from the window. Jasmine stopped singing and looked up at him, lowering her hands and spreading her wings.

She flew up to the window ledge and perched gracefully on it. She leaned in, overbalancing as she tucked her wings back in and falling on top of Michael in a less than graceful manner. Michael looked down at Jasmine and couldn't help but blush, a sudden shyness overtaking him.

Jasmine stood up, brushing herself down and straightening out her clothing. If she noticed the expression on Michael's face, she didn't pay any attention to it, but seemed slightly embarrassed herself.

"Oops…sorry about that, I didn't mean to launch myself at you, these windowsills are thinner than they seem." Jasmine said looking a little sheepish.

"Oh.. Uhm, yeah, that's OK," Michael stammered.

Jasmine looked him up and down and smiled approvingly.

"So how are you feeling? You look much better, much more colour in your cheeks!"

Guardian Angel by David Trebus

"Better. Still, well, a bit confused by all this, but I do feel better, thanks."

"That's good. I thought you'd be feeling well by today. I put a lot of effort into my songs for you, so if you hadn't healed so quickly, I would have been very cross. I think you should be OK to leave here very soon, maybe even later today, once the doctors look over you."

"He said tomorrow. I had to use a chair to steady myself and get over to the window though." Michael felt hesitant to leave although he wasn't quite sure why.

"That's rubbish. Stand up. Here, I'll help you," Jasmine reached out her slender hand.

Was she joking? No, there was a stern and schoolma'amish look in her face, and he took her hand. She pulled him up gently but firmly and supported him as he began to wobble. She slowly led him around the room, increasing the pace as Michael's weary limbs readjusted to their natural motions.

Whenever Michael began to totter, Jasmine would lean in closer or hold out her other hand to steady him. After a while, he began to tire, and she sang softly. Michael felt his spirits rise at the song, as if it kept him moving and trying. After an hour, he was walking confidently, knowing that Jasmine was close but able manage on his own. The feeling of achievement raised Michael's confidence, as he pushed his limits further, even managing a light jog.

After an hour of effort, his body began to tire and weaken, and

Michael's legs nearly gave out under him. Jasmine steadied him, and helped Michael back to his bed. She gently rested him back on his pillow, and pulling the covers up over his legs. She smelt just like her namesake, a sweet pleasant smell that reminded him of shady trees in the sun.

"If you were going push yourself so hard, I wouldn't have bothered putting so much energy into encouraging you! You need to know when to stop, Michael. It's always been your problem. I got to say you did better than I expected though, jogging…really."

Michael was breathing too hard to reply at once, taking some time to get his breathing under control.

"Well…once I started, I just felt like I should go as far as I could. You're right, though, I could probably be out of here today."

Jasmine gave Michael a long look, but before she could reply, a light knocking on the door interrupted them. A tired but friendly-looking nurse pushed her way through with a food trolley in front of her. She looked weary and worn down, probably due to all the extra work the funding cuts had put upon her. Her angel was nowhere to be seen, and Michael, promised himself to ask Jasmine about it later.

"Hello, Mr Andrews…" The nurse paused. "Oh, I thought you had company. I heard talking."

"No no, just talking to myself, I got up and moved about a bit a little earlier, was just encouraging myself" Michael replied, resisting the urge to glance at Jasmine.

Guardian Angel by David Trebus

The nurse looked skeptical but shrugged her shoulders. "Well, that's good to hear, although I'm not sure you should be moving about on your own just yet. I've brought you some lunch anyway, in case you feel hungry." She placed a tray on the fold-out table at the foot of Michael's bed. Its contents smelled pleasant, but didn't look very appetizing, hospital food never did.

"Hey, nurse; I'm feeling much better" Michael asked hesitantly. "Do you think I could go home today?"

The nurse checked the monitors and gave a tut. The wire connected to Michael's thumb clip had stretched, as he'd been moving about. Still, she noted a few things down on a clipboard and looked into Michael's eyes.

"Well…you certainly look much better, although it really is almost miraculous. The doctor will be in later to check on you, and I'm sure he can let you know if you can leave…although, with all the budget cuts you may end up getting chucked out anyway, as we barely have any beds…but anyway sorry, that's not your problem, just focus on getting better OK!" The nurse smiled weakly, trying to stifle a yawn. Michael wondered how tired she must have been to admit something like that so openly. She pushed the tray within Michael's reach, then smiled and left the room, closing the door gently behind her without another word.

Michael felt famished and immediately dug into his meal. It was a little bland, something that might be scrambled eggs, toast and some mushrooms, but he didn't care. It filled his stomach, and that

Guardian Angel by David Trebus

was all that mattered. He gulped down some orange juice to wash it'll down and sighed. That felt better.

He caught sight of Jasmine, and realised she'd been watching him stuff his face. He smiled weakly, wiping his mouth. Could he get used to having someone there *all* the time? He was a fairly private person, and spent a lot of time on his own, except when he'd had girlfriends in the past. That reminded him of his question from earlier.

"Jasmine," He asked. "That nurse who came in, I didn't see an angel with her. The kids downstairs all had theirs, but she didn't. Why is that?"

Jasmine hesitated for a moment, shutting her eyes before replying. "It's possible that he could be up above right now, watching her from on high, or simply standing outside. I can dimly sense him now, but he's keeping his distance from her. Sometimes, Michael, I'm sad to say, our charges can reject us and push us away. Too much despair that even we can't heal it. Or if the person truly turns to a dark path. That poor nurse wasn't evil, in any way but she is under so much strain, she probably rejected her angel when she needed his help most. Still, he'll always try to watch over her from afar, even if he can't be close."

"That's terrible…it's so bad things like that can happen" Michael replied softly, sympathy evident in his voice.

Jasmine nodded. "It really is, but you should focus on yourself right now. Plenty of time to set the world to rights later. The doctor will be in soon, and I'm sure you want out of here as quickly as possible, so get some rest; I won't be far, just outside. If you need me, just close your eyes and call my name inside your mind. I'll come right back."

"OK," Michael replied. He was tired after all the exercise and his hastily eaten meal, but at the same time wired. All this was opening his eyes to a world he only ever hoped existed. It was frightening but comforting, a huge mix of emotion caused by everything that had happened.

Jasmine smiled at Michael and left via the window, this time not stumbling but gracefully leaning out. She left only an empty window frame, as Michael lay in bed pondering all that had happened. Minutes soon turned into hours, and before long the doctor re-entered the room.

His angel, a dark haired being, hung back next to the door, watching into the corridor. Michael hadn't noticed her before. Had she been waiting outside the door? Maybe they knew he could see them.

"Mr Andrews, good day!" The doctor was clearly using his bedside manner, but Michael felt nothing fake about it.

"Hey, Doc," Michael's attention was still on the doctor's guardian, even while the doctor checked on his vitals.

"How are you feeling today? The nurse tells me you were up and about earlier. If so, that's a very good sign, although I must say still almost miraculous," the doctor continued.

Guardian Angel by David Trebus

"I feel fine. Achy, a bit weak, but otherwise not bad at all" Michael replied, stopping himself from adding, "Apart from my world just being turned upside down".

"Well, I see nothing wrong with your stats. Your blood pressure is fine, even the bruising on your lower abdomen has subsided. You're one tough gentleman. If you would be so kind as to stand and move around a bit, I'd like to see your progress for myself." The doctor held out his hand to help Michael up.

Michael spent the next few minutes walking around the room, slowly at first, expecting to fall or feel weakened, but more confidently as he found his strength had returned. The doctor stood, nodding, and asking Michael to perform basic tests, like touching toes, standing on one leg, as if he were marionette. After a while, the doctor told him to stop and sit on the bed.

"Well Michael, I think we are in a position to release you now. Your health seems amazing, considering what's happened to you. Your heart rate is still a little high, but that's due to being inactive. After a few days, it should settle down to a more relaxed pace as your body readjusts.. I can see no reason at all why we can't release you today. Just make sure to take it easy for the next week. I'll sign you off work. Are you OK to get home? Would you like a cab arranged?"

Michael couldn't help but like the man. He was nothing like the GPs he was used to, rushing you in, telling you nothing was wrong or scoffing at the problems you had, then rushing you out. He

Guardian Angel by David Trebus

seemed considerate and relaxed in his job. Michael's thoughts turned to the nurse he had seen earlier. It seemed so unfair that some people had such peace in their lives while others struggled, yet that seemed the nature of life.

"I should be fine," he said. "I mean, there's a taxi rank outside right, isn't there? I can just grab one from there."

The doctor nodded. "OK then, I'll sign up your release paperwork. If you have any trouble, especially dizziness or faint spells, then go to your GP or come here as soon as possible. You'll need to see your doctor in a week or two's time anyway, for a checkup. I'll arrange the appointment for you: as I know how tough they are to sort in the Capital."

"Thank you, doctor," said Michael.

"No problems get well soon. Here's your sign-off slip. Take your time and get your things together at your own pace, and make sure to sign out at reception when you leave," the doctor handed Michael a slip of paper before turning to go.

He paused at the doorway for a moment but, instead of saying anything, stepped through beside his dark haired guardian. She smiled warmly at the doctor, and then at Michael. An image of a loving family suddenly popped into Michael's thoughts, the doctors presumably, which explained why the doctor was so happy and warm. He was loved, and it empowered his angel. Michael smiled back and got a slightly bemused look from the angel, as the doctor shut the door.

Guardian Angel by David Trebus

Michael sighed and stood up again. He figured there was no point hanging about, now he had his clean bill of health. He still couldn't quite grasp what had happened, but if he thought about it too much it would probably give him a headache, and he would end up going round in circles. He moved over to a small, pale, wooden cupboard with a small key on top. His possessions were inside, except for his t-shirt which was, presumably too damaged to salvage. He removed his undersized bed robes, which revealed a little too much, and placed them on the bed.

He pulled on his trousers, which seemed to have been washed, and his jumper, glad it was spring. He'd have had a very chilly trip home, otherwise. His light jacket was also present although slightly torn, perhaps in the accident. Amazingly, his wallet and keys were still in the pockets and even his cash was intact.

Jasmine appeared at the window, just as he finished dressing and making himself look presentable. Well, as presentable as possible, considering he'd been hit by a car, found out that angels existed, and been told he was unique in his ability to see them. She smiled at him and deftly hopped through, avoiding the ledge this time.
"Well," she said, "it seems you're ready to go."
"Yup, all checked over and ready. Even have a week off work to recover, like a holiday,"
"You know," Jasmine said, her face more serious, "even though I poured everything into helping you, you're still not superman, you have to take it easy in that week…well as easy as you can,

Guardian Angel by David Trebus

considering."

"Yeah. I'm going to get moving now, need to get a cab home. I really don't feel like walking from....whatever hospital this is." He didn't even know where he'd been taken.

Jasmine nodded and waited, as Michael gathered his things and got ready to leave. He opened the door into a quiet corridor, and walked towards what he thought was an exit but turned out to be a dead end. He finally asked a passing nurse how to get out. She pointed him to a lift at the opposite end, her guardian mirroring her actions in an odd parody.

Michael made his way to the opposite end of the corridor, cursing whoever designed the hospital. Couldn't the NHS even be bothered to put decent signs in their hospitals, these days? He got to the elevator, though, and pressed the button for ground floor.

Jasmine said nothing in the elevator, humming to herself and rocking on the balls of her feet. It irritated Michael, but he decided not to raise the issue. On the ground floor, Michael made his way to the reception desk, opposite the elevator exit. The waiting area was very quiet, with only a solitary old man sitting at the far end.

Michael walked up to the desk and pressed the bell, summoning a young male nurse. He looked exhausted, and his guardian looked down on her charge in concern.

"Can I help you?" the nurse asked.

"I was told by my doctor to inform you when I left. I'm checking out today."

Guardian Angel by David Trebus

"Name, please, sir?" The nurse asked flatly, a tired expression on his face.

"Michael Andrews."

The nurse paused for a moment, looking at his computer screen and then searching for a sheet of paper. "OK Mr Andrews, sign here and you're set to go. Take care," He pointed to where Michael had to sign the sheet of paper, and then turned back to his work without waiting for a reply. Michael didn't trouble him any further, seeing how worn out he looked. He did wonder why he looked so tired. Nothing much was happening here, but it would be a different story in A&E. Perhaps he'd already done a shift there.

Michael left the hospital with Jasmine in tow. She wasn't getting in the way much or talking to him, which was a relief in some ways. Perhaps she wouldn't be too intrusive, after all, unless something important had to be said. She could be like a good friend who was there but knew when to take a step back and give him space.

This illusion was shattered when they reached the taxi rank. He found a taxi fairly quickly and got in. Jasmine followed through the door and sat right next to Michael, almost hugging him, and her proximity made him feel strangely self-conscious Talk about invading personal space.

"Where to, guv?" the cabbie asked.

"Crouch End, near the Green Dragon, please, mate"

"Sure thing," the cabbie said, moving off from the rank.

Guardian Angel by David Trebus

Jasmine whispered into Michael's ear as they began moving on, hugging his arm slightly. "I'm so pleased you're OK!"

Michael felt even more embarrassed and tried to pull away. "Uhhh thanks!" He almost squeaked the words out.

"No need to thank me yet mate, not even got you there," the cabbie replied.

Jasmine giggled and pulled away as Michael sighed and sat back, resting his head on the seat. He hoped there wouldn't be too many embarrassing moments like that. How could he talk to Jasmine in public without people thinking he was talking to them? Unless, of course, they just thought he was just plain crazy. Another quandary he would have to address at some point.

"You don't need to talk to me in public," she said, "as long as you can hear me. Also, there's a little trick to it. If you focus on me and think the words, then I can hear your thoughts. It might be a little easier than embarrassing yourself in front of big cabbies. I mean, imagine if you were to call me pretty in public. You might end up with an admirer you could do without!"

Michael focused his thoughts to form a few word. "Pretty....yeah, right"

Jasmine pinched him hard in the arm. Clearly, insulting a guardian angel's looks had consequences. Michael rubbed his arm and grinned. At least he knew the little trick Jasmine had taught him worked.

Michael noticed the cabbie looking at him in the rear view

mirror. He hoped he wasn't thinking that he was some mental patient on the run, high, or on drugs. The cabbie increased his speed, causing Michael to give him an awkward smile.

The rest of the journey proved uneventful. It only took twenty minutes to get back close to home, and the cabbie deftly navigated the traffic, avoiding several roadworks and jams. He pulled up just outside the Green Dragon pub.

"Here we go, mate, that'll be," he paused to look at the meter "fifteen pounds fifty, please."

Michael pulled out his wallet and was relieved to find a couple of tenners in there. He'd forgotten to count how much cash he actually had. He paid the cabbie, leaving some of the change as a tip, and got out of the car.

"Cheers, mate, have a good one" the cabbie called.

"Thanks," Michael shut the door, and the cabbie pulled off with a quick wave as Michael turned to walk along the road to his home.

"You know," Jasmine remarked, "that's one of the reasons I'm pleased to be your guardian, Michael. You have such a generous nature"

"Thanks. I just try to be decent to people," Michael blushed.

It wasn't far to his house from the pub, just two minutes down the main road, and then down a side street. It would have been easier to be dropped at the other end of the high street, where he'd had the accident, but he wasn't sure he could face that yet.

He began walking, with Jasmine at his side, not really paying

Guardian Angel by David Trebus

attention to the world around him. After a while, he raised his head and took a good look around, and the sight stopped in his tracks, he took a deep breath. A strange sense of anxiety hit his guts.

All around him, life was going on, hundreds of people in the street going to work, or the shops, driving or walking about their daily business. All around him people, got on with their lives, and for every single person, Michael saw an angel.

Guardian Angel by David Trebus

Chapter 3: Life Goes On

Nothing could have prepared Michael for this. It was one thing to see Jasmine or another person's angel individually, but now he was seeing dozens, even hundreds of them all in one place. The surreal vision was almost too much for Michael; his breathing became heavy, and he was drenched in sweat. He tried to make his limbs move, but they refused. He just stood staring, as humans and their angels moved around him.

Jasmine had predicted that Michael would have to go through this moment. She had decided not to sugar coat it and to let him face it quickly rather than trying to baby-step him through it. He would have to get used to it one day, better sooner rather than later. Besides there were methods to deal with such things, or at least she hoped so. Jasmine gently placed her hand in his and hummed a song, trying to soothe Michael's mind.

Michael was awestruck; the population of the world to his eyes had just doubled. He looked up and saw still more angels flying to and fro. Was that an angel flying alongside a light aircraft as it buzzed over the busy city? He should have expected it, but still, how could he have prepared himself? He tried not to imagine what a crowd at a concert or football stadium would look like.

Guardian Angel by David Trebus

Taking deep breaths, Michael managed to slow his breathing, and relax a bit. The shock was wearing off, and he had to accept what was happening. Anxiety would not change it, and, as none of the angels were aware of him, there was no threat to him. Why was he even so worried?

"How are you doing?" Jasmine asked her voice so soft he could barely hear it.

"Better. It was just such a big thing to take in, the scale of it. Pretty embarrassing reaction though." Michael fought the impulse to blurt the words out all at once.

Jasmine smiled. "To be honest I'd say you handled it very well. I mean, everything since this started. You've managed to keep your head, but some anxiety is to be expected, with all that's happened to you in such a short time. So don't be hard on yourself."

"I don't know if I'll ever get used to this..." Michael trailed off, staring up towards the High Street.

"You will. Think of your first time in a crowd as a kid. It was scary, but you got used to it. All these things take time. Besides the angels will either get out of your way or you'll walk right through them"

"What do you mean, walk right through them?"

"Well we as guardians are only allowed to physically affect our charges and then there are strict rules even on that. We can choose to become insubstantial to everyone else. So they will never bump into us, or get interrupted in their daily lives by us. Sometimes

Guardian Angel by David Trebus

guardians break the rules but that's another matter."

"Well…" Michael wondered. "That's half a comfort and half a worry. I think it'll be even more freaky walking straight through other peoples guardians as if they were ghosts!"

Jasmine playfully punched his arm with a grin. "Stop being a baby. You'll be fine!"

"What happened to all the sympathy?" Michael teased smiling.

"Shush, let's get you home. You can have some sympathy there. I might even make you a cup of tea."

Michael nodded, a bit weary after the adrenaline burst from his earlier fear. Jasmine had been right though. Already, after only a few minutes of exposure, he was getting used to the angels. As Michael walked back home, he couldn't help but sidestep angels on instinct as they approached, trying not to bump into them. Jasmine shook her head and smiled.

They walked slowly down the high street. Michael couldn't wait to get back into his own house and slob out on the sofa watching TV for a while. Even though he'd spent days lying down in hospital, he was still tired and needed to relax. He had never been gladder he had been signed off work for a while.

Michael was about to turn into his side-road when something on the edge of his vision. A scruffy-looking man in a hoodie launched himself towards a young woman, pushing a pram just past the turning. Michael had seen this before, the man's intention was to jump the woman and probably rob her, it had almost happened to him in the past.

He was running before he knew it. His limbs ached with the effort, but he willed them to work faster. There was no way he was going to let this woman get hurt. Jasmine ran after him, shouting something he couldn't quite hear. The hooded man jumped at the woman, slamming his hands on her shoulders. The woman fell with a yelp, and her guardian, a blonde angel, immediately knelt beside her.

The hooded man grabbed the woman's purse and tried to wrest it away from her. However, in her shock though she held on tight, looking panicked. Michael shoulder-barged her attacker away, knocking him to the ground. The man rolled into a crouch and stood quickly, sneering.

"You bastard, what da fuck you think you doing." He threw a punch at Michael's face, connecting hard and knocking Michael to the ground.

The woman crawled round to her pram, where her baby had started screaming. The man got up and tried to kick Michael, who had yet to pick himself off the floor. Michael grabbed his foot and twisted, and the hoodie wearing man yelled more curses. There was a shout from somewhere and the man shook his foot free swearing. The mugger ran off without another word, trying to escape.

Michael got up and tried to run after him but Jasmine held him from behind, shaking her head. As Michael's gaze followed the

Guardian Angel by David Trebus

thief, something seemed very wrong not with the man himself, but his guardian angel, who looked warped, twisted in some way.

Chains grew out of the ground wrapping around her legs and hooking into her tattered wings. She probably had been beautiful once, but her clothing was stained black and red, and her features were distorted. She turned to regard Michael as she followed her charge. Her eyes glowed red and he could just make out two protrusions forming on her forehead. She hissed at him, before disappearing into a side street. The look on that angel's face sent a chill through Michael's body.

An elderly man was helping the woman up, while his wife approached Michael and put her hand on his shoulder. The victim clutched her baby to her chest and sobbed uncontrollably, the shock of what had happened starting to wear off. The man helped her to the ground, where she sat cross-legged rocking her baby back and forth. She looked up at Michael and mouthed the words "Thank you" through her sobs, her angel mirroring the gesture. "You did a good thing there son. Me and my husband saw it all. Are you ok?"

Michael blinked trying to shake the image of the mugger's guardian out of his mind before replying. His face ached where he had been hit but otherwise he felt ok; just shaken up, and very tired.

"I'm fine, thanks. Last thing I expected to be doing today though." Michael said, taking a deep breath to steady himself.

Guardian Angel by David Trebus

"Well you did a very good thing. You should be proud," the elderly woman said, walking over to her husband and away from him.

Michael didn't feel like hanging around, especially not for the drama of having to give a statement to the police - assuming they were even called and turned up. Mugging was routine in London. It was a sad reflection of how inner city society had developed.

He knelt beside the victim to look her over and check if she was ok before getting up and walking off. No one made any protest and the old couple said they would stay by the young woman. Michael thanked them and walked off. Jasmine supported him clutching both her slender hands to Michael's arm.

"That lady was right, you know. You did do a very good, but a bit of a stupid thing. You're not exactly on top form yet."
"I couldn't help myself, It was instinct. I hate people preying on the vulnerable" Michael yawned and rubbed his cheek absent mindedly. He was going to have a nasty bruise there by tomorrow.
"That I guess is what makes me happy to be your guardian - your stubborn good nature."
"Jasmine… I have a question…the mugger's angel…something...was..."
"Now's not the time for that. Let's just get you home, OK?"
"No, it's not OK. Tell me, what was wrong with her, I want an answer" Michael persisted feeling like he needed to know.
Jasmine sighed as they stopped outside Michael's door. She turned

Guardian Angel by David Trebus

to look straight into his eyes.

"She was…one of the fallen...or, well, not yet but she was falling. Her charge's soul was corrupt, and he was dragging her down with him, bit by bit, down into the pit where she'll become...a demon."

Michael felt his stomach lurch. It figured if there were angels, that demons would also exist, but to see an angel falling in front of his eyes was like something out of a supernatural horror movie.

"Now, let's get you inside. This isn't the time or the place to be talking about demons. No more questions, I'll tell you everything you want to know soon. I promise." Jasmine said cutting off any further complaints from Michael.

He wearily climbed up the steps, unlocking the door and made his way straight into his living room. Michael dumped himself on the sofa, and, without thinking switched on the TV; the news was on, talking about tax rises and more MP's fiddling expenses.

Jasmine sat herself down gently next to him, carefully folding her wings. She stretched them out slightly, so they rested on top of the sofa cushions perfectly. It occurred to Michael that she was probably well practiced at it, she'd been doing it ever since he had been living there. How many times had Jasmine sat next to him without him even knowing?

Michael leaned his head back on the sofa cushion and took a deep breath, sighing as he released it. The last few days had totally changed his life, but here he was sitting in front of his sofa watching telly, just like normal. Well aside from the guardian angel sitting next to him.

Jasmine leaned in closer and thrust herself up against Michael, hugging him. Michael thought to protest on instinct, very embarrassed, but the words stuck in his throat before he uttered them. He felt warm with Jasmine so close, and comfortable. As he sat by her side, his fears and worries melted away.

Michael relaxed accepting Jasmine's comforting embrace. She seemed to know exactly what he needed, even if he hadn't known it himself or was too embarrassed to admit. They sat watching the television for an hour before Michael drifted off to sleep while Jasmine hummed softly.

Being this close to Michael and comforting him directly stirred odd emotions within Jasmine, ones she was not used to feeling. Without even thinking about it, Jasmine suppressed them, but if she had had to give the feeling a name, she would have described it as affection.

***

Garamond reclined in his chair, slouching at an unnatural angle. The body he inhabited cracked and creaked in protest until it could endure no more. Garamond felt his host's pain and delighted in it, but sadly, this one had reached its limit. It could endure no more, and Garamond released it into blessed oblivion.

The Arch-Devil emerged from the host in a cloud of red mist, forming into a solid mass standing before the body he had occupied. Wings of bone sprouted from his back, with a few black feathers hanging in loose clumps. Still, he knew if he wished he could fly or descend to the pit using those long-decayed wings.

In his true form, Garamond looked much like he had before his fall. A well-muscled body, long raven hair, and piercing eyes. However now his skin had a crimson pallor, his eyes glowed red, and two large horns protruded from his temples. The changes still felt as fresh as when he'd fallen, centuries before. Just as exciting, just as tantalizingly different. He licked his lips thinking of the horror of his charge's face and her screams as he had devoured her corrupt soul, banishing it to hell forever.

She had been a murderer in life, sleeping with her lonely desperate victims, then slaying them for some kind of sick satisfaction. Garamond in his innocence had at first been repelled. However, as she continued her foul works, eventually he'd become enraptured by it, thrilled even. By the time she finally died, his horns had already grown and the chains that bound him to the pit were an inch thick. Then they had fallen and before the Beast himself, Garamond had devoured her soul, sealing his transformation into a demon.

That was four hundred years ago, in human reckoning, but to

Garamond it may as well have been yesterday. He chuckled, coming back to the present. He waved a hand dismissively at the chair, and two sultry looking women emerged from the shadows to either side. They dragged away the chair's previous occupant, pouting and grinning at Garamond. Their eyes glowed red showing the true nature of what inhabited them.

Garamond was the Arch-Devil and the Beast's scourge on Earth. He was the most powerful demon allowed to walk on the mortal plane, as ordained by cosmic law, since the birth of the universe. His job was simple: the corruption of human souls and tempting more angels to fall, swelling the forces of Hell and boosting the power of his master, the Devil.

He had not always been so powerful. Upon his fall he had been assigned to Hell's armies as a foot trooper, nothing more than a lackey. But Garamond always had other designs. He had been determined to rise in the ranks, to achieve more power. He wanted to grow stronger. Strong enough to usurp even the Devil himself one day. So he clawed his way from obscurity one depraved act at a time. Winning first the Arch-demons favour and then even Lucifer's.

Garamond's crowning achievement had been claiming the Arch-demon Hadriel's demon hammer: *Requiem.* The demoness had been tempted by Garamonds lustful advances and dropped her guard, a big mistake. He showed no mercy when he used the hammer to send Hadriel into the inferno for a few millennia to burn in torment. Hadriel had also been the previous Scourge, a title Garamond delightfully claimed from her.

Garamond sat down again now in his true form, glancing down at his throne and grinning at the memory of Hadriel's demise. The throne's arm rests were made of skulls and its back was adorned with artwork depicting two women involved in sexual acts. Lust had always been his favorite deadly sin, always the easiest way to corrupt the weak.

Garamond took his position very seriously - if he didn't he could easily be replaced by another budding Arch-Devil, and sent back screaming to the pit to pay for his lack of initiative.

So when Garamond found an opportunity, he made sure to take advantage of it as quickly as possible. The stars had aligned perfectly on the day of the accident. He had meant initially to kill the mortal, to remove a potential threat. However, at the last moment, he had decided it would be better to cripple him, leave him vulnerable for months. That would allow his minions to chip away at his resolve at their leisure, seduce him into darkness slowly. When he awoke, his angel would be in chains and his soul would be Garamond's to use.

A mortal who perceived supernatural forces was a rarity. Some could innately sense angels and demons, or managed contact them through witchcraft and sorcery. However, a mortal who could actually see them as normally as his own kind, was truly a rare occurrence. Garamond had hoped to corrupt this mortal and use him, but higher powers had interfered. His guardian angel had proved much stronger than expected, healing her charge and keeping him from slumbering too long. She had even seen off Garamond's little imp when it had tried to get close. To make things worse he also had a strong spirit and a good soul; he would be difficult to corrupt.

Still Garamond knew his opportunity had not yet passed, and he could still kill the mortal if need be. The benefit he could gain from turning him however, was too much too ignore. With a mortal who could actively influence other souls, see ones ripe to fall and help them on their way, Garamond could increase hell's army massively in a short time. With such power, he could secure his position and even return to hell leading an army strong enough to overthrow his lord and tyrant.

Garamond grinned as he reclined in his throne again, this time his inhuman body easily contorting to his unnatural slouch. His two attendants knelt by his side, scandalously clad and showing enough skin to excite even the most jaded man. Garamond smiled as they stroked and touched him, thinking of all the power he would gain once he had corrupted the mortal. Garamond just had to bide his time and find a way to bring him over to his side. It would only be a matter of time until an opportunity presented itself. Garamond laughed, a haunting sound that he sensed disturb the mortals working half a mile above his lair.

Guardian Angel by David Trebus

***

Michael awoke with a start, almost bolting upright. He could have sworn he had heard laughter. He had not been dreaming that he remembered, but just before he awoke, he heard a chilling laugh, one that made his skin crawl. He glanced around and saw that the TV had a comedy show on, with the usual canned laughter in the background. That had most likely been the source of it.

Glancing around, Michael reckoned it was late morning. He'd slept right through into the next day, and Jasmine was nowhere to be seen. For some reason, Michael felt lonely.

"I guess I am finally getting used to having her around," Michael muttered as he stretched then stood up to go in search of something to eat.

He staggered into the kitchen and made a sandwich, grabbing a can of coke as he left to wash it down. Michael remembered he had not been online since the accident, had not had the chance to check his emails. Had anyone been trying to get in touch from work?

The phone had a couple of messages from his parents and friends, asking if he was ok or home yet, but beyond that nothing. Michael had nothing better to do anyway, and, as Jasmine seemed to be away, he sat down at his computer desk.

His computer always took too long to start up, buzzing and humming as it got going. He took a couple of bites of his sandwich while he waited. Eventually the computer powered up and Michael entered his password sending him to his start up page. A tasteful picture of one of his favourite actresses greeted him, and he waved at her. He didn't really know why he did it, he just always had.

As expected the fifty new emails were almost all newsletters. However, a couple were get-well messages from distant friends, and one was from a work colleague called Claire.

Claire was roughly equal to him in seniority, but worked in the publishing firm's other department overseeing printing and corporate duties, rather than the magazine and book side of things that Michael oversaw. They had exchanged pleasantries, and even been out to lunch once when neither had anything better to do. Beyond that, Michael couldn't really say he was close to her or that they had much in common. She had always seemed a bit guarded and Michael hated to say it, odd.

Michael opened the email curious as to what Claire had to say. He expected a message with the usual "Hope you're OK" spiel. As he had thought, the first part of the email, wished him a speedy recovery and explained how she had heard about the accident.

It took Michael a moment to realise; the email was dated the day before the accident. If it wasn't a mistake, it was creepy.

Guardian Angel by David Trebus

"I know it's kinda strange Michael, but I saw you in my, dreams last night. I saw your accident. I had been worried but somehow I also knew you would be ok, I saw a blonde woman with wings standing over you, taking care of you."

"Please don't stop reading or think me some kind of freak, but as soon as you're better I would like to meet up to discuss all this with you."

The rest of the email sank back into vague pleasantries, providing a contact number and signing off.

Was this some kind of wind up or cruel joke? Then again, the blonde woman could easily have been Jasmine. But Claire? She had always seemed like such a straight arrow, she was strong-minded, factual and sometimes even cold.

He was finding it hard to believe she paid close attention to her dreams and even harder, that she would discuss the matter with a co-worker. Surely that meant she was on the level and that at some point it might be a good idea meeting her. It would also be worth mentioning it to Jasmine as hopefully she could shed some light on Claire's behaviour.

Right on cue, a small circle of light formed on Michael's ceiling. It expanded, slowly growing until it encompassed the light fitting. Were his lights going to be sucked up through it? Two small feet emerged, followed by slender legs and finally Jasmine's torso and head. Her wings were the last to emerge. They glowed bright, each

Guardian Angel by David Trebus

feather emanating light, and were cast up above her, their tips holding the edge of the portal open until she was fully through, shutting it off as they folded down to tuck behind her back. His light fitting was still in one piece. that shouldn't have been disappointing, but it was.

Michael noticed Jasmine smile, as he swung his computer chair round to face her. He felt much healthier upon seeing her return. The sight of her, brought faint memories of Jasmine singing to him again. Had she sung to him while he slept again?

"How are you feeling?"

"Fine…actually, I hadn't even noticed. Amazing what a bit of TV and sleep can do."

"And a little song or two."

Michael cocked his head a bit confused "I guess so…Where have you been?"

"Did you miss me?" There was a mischievous glint in her eyes.

"Well uh, I was just expecting you to be about" Michael could tell he was blushing from the smile on Jasmine's face.

Her charge had always been hesitant showing affection or admitting feelings, it was cute in a way to her. She decided not to tease him and walked over to stand by the computer facing Michael as the glow of transition faded from her wings. She leaned against the wall, her wingtips brushing the wallpaper and casting odd shadows as the sun shone in through the window.

"I went on high again to check on a friend, and to see if I could

Guardian Angel by David Trebus

find out anything more about our…pretty unique situation."

Jasmine sighed.

"And...any news?"

***

Jasmine recalled her attendance at Jazen's choir. The choir was an angelic court, although dissimilar from the human version. The senior angels would hear Jazen sing and read his intentions, his thoughts and his past actions. They would then judge him and hand down appropriate punishment.

He had once again gone too far in contacting his charge, spurred on by Jasmine and Michael's situation. Jasmine regretted even mentioning it to him the last time they spoke. It was bound to encourage him in trying to contact his charge. Again, Jazen had appeared before Claire during one of her occult rituals. He again had broken one of the oldest rules of being a guardian.

During his song, Jazen had mentioned Jasmine in one of the more sorrowful refrains, pleading for permission to speak to his charge openly as Jasmine could to Michael, but his pleas had been ignored. The rules were there for a good reason. They were first ordained on high when guardians first stood by Adam and Eve the day they were cast out of heaven. Even in his wrath, the almighty refused to leave man completely alone in the world.

Jazen was denied his pleas. He had been found wanting and given his final warning. A chorus of voices half sang, half spoke the verdict. "No direct contact or you will be reassigned; a young cherub will stand by Claire. Further direct contact risks her memory being altered, a confusing process for any human. This is the Choir's verdict, so it is said"

After the Choir, Jazen gave several of the Seraphim an acidic look. She was surprised to see such raw emotion on his face and even more surprised that the emotion was anger. Jazen really was treading a dangerous path, even coming close to falling, all over his unrestrained emotions and desire to be noticed by his mortal charge. Jasmine felt a shudder remembering her own emotions towards Michael. Loving one's charge as you would love a child was part of the job, but even that feeling had to be measured and contained. Falling for your charge was a completely different thing and altogether more precarious.

Jasmine decided not to speak to Jazen as he left, not wishing to agitate the situation, merely giving him a soft smile and wave as he rushed past. He looked at her briefly, the sorrow in his eyes shining through, but then walked away rapidly, opening his wings to return to Earth. Jasmine had sung for him in the sunlight corridors outside the choir chambers, praying for a positive outcome.

Afterwards, Jasmine walked the white corridors staring up at the blazing sun. Its light reflected off the gold and bronze archways that overhung the walkways of the angels' sanctum. Beams of light bounced off the pillars and arches casting golden echoes of the sun's glory all around, creating a haze of light. It all soothed Jasmine's mind as she strolled along.

She eventually came to the Metatron's chambers again, where only a day previously she had stood hearing her orders for the future. He wasn't there most likely conversing on a higher level. But outside a small scroll, floated in the air on a pair of comically small wings. As she approached, it fluttered towards her and landed in her hands. The message was meant for her and its sender had known she would pass by this route.

Metatron had always said, "There is no coincidence, only certainty in action". The message would be another of his ways of proving that fact. That he had known she would walk past this point, just as a human knows the sun will rise the next day. She sighed and smiled at the small scroll, as its wings settled and folded in on themselves. She opened it tentatively and began reading.

"Dear Jasmine

I hope you and your charge are well. I know your situation is difficult, but I have faith in your ability and you will adapt and change.

Everything happens for a reason. Michael will soon ask to help in the wider world. Do not discourage him, merely stand by him and keep him safe, for the darker forces seek to influence him.

In addition, keep an eye on Jazen. His charge is close to your own which will allow you to mind your friend and watch him for signs of the fall. He is a passionate angel and it would sadden us all to lose him. Do not let him directly contact her anymore; he has been warned. Also, keep in mind the lesson that Jazen represents to us all.

Remember Jasmine "There is no coincidence, only certainty in action". These events occurred due to the actions of others, on High and in the Pit and in the universe at large. You will always have the power to influence the world around you.

I have faith in you

Metatron."

The scroll shut and fluttered off, its contents erased now it had been read. Jasmine felt a little flustered after reading it. She had felt hot, her cheeks turning red from the line about the lesson Jazen represented. Jasmine shut her eyes and took a deep breath her emotional suppression kicking in to relieve her troubles. She opened them again and felt better, the worry now pushed to the back of her mind for contemplation on a calmer level.

Guardian Angel by David Trebus

After reading the scroll, Jasmine decided to return to earth. She had spent more than enough time away from her charge. It was part of a Guardian's make up to miss their charges, but this was something more. Again, she ignored her feelings, remembering the scrolls words. She opened up her wings and returned through the circle of light, manifesting herself back onto the mortal plane to find Michael sitting by his computer looking up at her in wonder as she emerged.

***

"And…any news?" Michael asked again as Jasmine stared at him for a long moment. She shook her head slightly, as if a cobweb had been caught on her face, before smiling. She seemed a little ditzy and absent for an angel.

"No nothing new really. My friend is ok. As for our situation no change, or new information," Michael got the impression Jasmine was not saying everything.

"Oh…well, that's good I guess. They say no news is good news."

Jasmine flexed her wings, letting the feathers unfold like a bird preparing for flight, before gently tucking them back. It reminded Michael of a small cockatiel he had when he was a child, who used to stretch her wings constantly, loosening her feathers and shaking

Guardian Angel by David Trebus

off any excess dust.

"So Michael, any news for you? Anything interesting going on the internet?" Jasmine asked settling down on the couch. The sunlight caught her hair and the outline of her wings giving her a beautiful glow, just as Michael had always pictured an angel to have. Although this time purely through earthly means.

"As it goes, yeah. A work colleague called Claire emailed me. She said she had a dream about what happened to me, but knew I was going to be ok. She even loosely described you. The whole thing seemed a little weird, but what with everything that has gone on, I can believe maybe she did see something. She also said she wanted to meet up to talk about it. Do you think I should?"

"I think you should. It is possible she has some kind of connection to you or a special gift. Either way it would be worth looking into."

"Somehow I thought you would say that." Michael stood up and picked up a pen and paper from a small table. He noted down Claire's phone number from the email before turning off the computer.

"You know, Jasmine I've been thinking…since I saw that mugger's angel. I cannot stand seeing things like that. People suffering and stuff you know. I mean I've always felt a bit powerless, like I couldn't help. Now I have a gift, something special. Maybe that means I can do something to help those around me. Maybe I can save a few people. After all the rules that prevent you from interfering don't apply to me" Michael paused feeling

Guardian Angel by David Trebus

embarrassed "I don't know. I'm rambling."

Jasmine smiled widely again thinking back to Metatron's letter. Then Metatron's words pushed their way back into her mind. "There is no coincidence, only certainty in action". She felt another emotion push up inside her with such force she could barely contain it. She felt pride in her charge. She had felt pride when he had taken his first steps, when he had won his first sports game, but never anything as strong as this. Without thinking, she kissed him on the cheek and hugged him.

"I am so glad I was chosen to become your guardian Michael," she whispered into his ear.

Michael stood frozen, embarrassed and started squirming. Why did he feel this way? He had been hugged and kissed by plenty of girls. However, with Jasmine, it felt different. He coughed to clear his throat and pulled back a little, not wanting to break the embrace but at the same time too uncomfortable to maintain it.

Michael noticed Jasmine pull back a little, a single tear in her eye. He saw a brief flash pass over her face as she seemed to struggle with something, and then her expression returned to its normal warm but controlled smile. Jasmine avoided direct eye contact with him though and Michael wondered what had happened.

"I think it's a good idea. You weren't rambling…well a little bit maybe, but your goals are good ones. I don't see any reason why you can't do a little good with your ability. I mean you have it for a reason, and I will be right there with you to help you out."

Michael smiled feeling stronger and more confident."I think I know just where to start. Let me find the phone..." Michael said grabbing the piece of paper with Claire's phone number on it.

Chapter 4: Claire and Jazen

Claire had taken a few days off work to concentrate on her meditation. Ever since she dreamt about her co-worker's accident, she hadn't been sleeping properly. She kept seeing visions of the event, replayed over and over. Claire always took notice of her dreams; it was part of her beliefs that they were important windows to the past, truths in the present and events in the future.

Breathing deeply, Claire tried to relax. She closed her bright green eyes and removed an irritating strand of long dark brown hair from her forehead. She placed her hands in her lap and tried to calm her mind, replaying the dream she'd had the previous evening. It still disturbed her, no matter how much she meditated.

At the same time, she felt thrilled by the dream. It had such force, that whenever she went to sleep, it truly felt she had achieved a real connection with the other side. Outside influences were trying to tell her something; she just had to work out what it was. She had already spoken to her co-worker Michael and asked to meet. Hopefully he would be able to shed some light on what was going on.

During her meditations, usually after about ten minutes, she felt a presence near her. It always spoke to her, but she couldn't make out the words, slightly too quiet to be heard. However, the presence always made Claire feel safe and comfortable. She imagined it was her guardian angel watching over her.

While at work and during the day, Claire went through the routine she required to put food on her table and a roof over her head. She worked with Michael at the publishing firm and, even though the work could be boring, sometimes it did bring a small sense of satisfaction. She wore smart clothing, short skirts (but not indecently so) and blended in with the crowd.

In the evenings or in her free time, though, Claire practiced altogether more esoteric arts. She was a modern-day Witch. Some people had tried to class her as a "Wiccan" or "Goth" on various forums and occult chat sites, but that had just made Claire laugh. She didn't believe in female empowerment, wearing black clothing or rituals in graveyards. In fact, she wore a t shirt and jeans during her occult dabbling, and often practiced alone at home.

Claire practiced spiritualism and attempted magic to enrich her life. She believed it would help find a connection with the universe at large and escape the mundane of a normal life. Deep down, Claire's choices stemmed from years of loneliness and difficulties.

Realising her focus had drifted, Claire began a low murmur and tried to bring her meditation back on track. The dream she was trying to replay eluded her, shifting like a snake, just out of reach. Claire became more and more irritated; she did not like being out

Guardian Angel by David Trebus

of control or unable to order her thoughts. Her meditation slipped away further as her frustrations grew.

Her heart quickened again as her feelings rose to the surface, her breathing becoming fast and shallow. Claire began to sweat, but she was shivering at the same time. She knew what was coming but tried her best to push it aside. She was in no mood for her body to throw a temper tantrum.

"Ohh…no not again, not now…" Claire pleaded.

She kept her eyes tightly shut as her heart raced as she shook. Panicked thoughts raced through her mind. What if her practice caused something to go wrong? What if she accidentally stepped into the path of a car in the busy London roads?

She knew the thoughts were irrelevant and unlikely to happen, but they still would not abate, forcing their way into her mind. She had pushed herself too hard. The meditation was to calm her and relax her not bring on a panic attack. In fact her doctor claimed it was the need to be in control constantly that contributed to her episodes.

Claire's breathing came in ragged gasps as she fought the panic attack that gripped her, until calm came over her, soothing the fears away. She finally succumbed to the temptation to open her eyes, and for a moment she thought she saw a nimbus of light around her, a faint caress on her cheek as her panic melted away. Strength spent, Claire lay down on her bed and tried to relax. She would be meeting Michael tomorrow and knew she badly needed

Guardian Angel by David Trebus

to get some rest.

"I guess I'll just have to rely on you, then, my guardian," Claire said to the ceiling as she fell asleep.

***

Jazen hated to see Claire push herself too hard. A lot of the time she could cope and she was fine, but sometimes when things got on top of her, her anxiety would return. Jazen had watched Claire since she was a little girl growing up, observing the trials she had endured and finally seeing the cold sometimes distant young woman she had grown into. Jazen knew that was just a façade, a shield to protect her from the world.

He had watched as she meditated, trying again to force the dream she kept having to the surface of her mind. She always had to be in control, she always had to confront bad things in her life, it was just her way.

During one of Claire's spell-castings, an imp had been summoned. It was ironic that one of Claire's greatest fears had come to pass yet she had not even been aware of it. It had been when Jazen was back on high, summoned to be chastised for his direct interventions in his charges life. However Jazen knew the pain Claire had been through, he couldn't just stand by while he

Guardian Angel by David Trebus

had the power to help the one he cared for.

The Imp had implanted the dream of Michael's accident in Claire's mind in order to feed on the terror it elicited. Jazen had luckily interrupted the Imp before it could complete the dream. Had he been any later it would have entered her mind to corrupt her soul directly. He had banished it with a brief song of purity but by then the dream had already been deeply rooted in Claire's soul. Knowing her, she would focus on it, thinking it had some deeper meaning.

Did the dream have some hidden purpose?. The Imp had manifested due to some infernal design rather than Claire's spell-casting, but he could not be certain of the intention behind it. Whatever the case, he had to watch her even more intently now and take care of her all the more. The choir would not stop him from keeping her safe, even if he had to break their mandates. Claire seemed to sense him on some level, know he was there...maybe even share his feelings, if only on a subconscious level. There was no way he would ever let himself be parted from her.

Claire's meditations weren't going well. The dark dream played havoc with her mind and disrupted her calm. She was having a panic attack, she was suffering. Jazen did the only thing he could; he manifested his wings and wrapped them around her humming a soothing song. One of the wingtips accidentally brushed Claire's cheek while Jazen sang and she opened her eyes. For a moment,

Guardian Angel by David Trebus

Claire's dazzling green eyes seemed to meet Jazen's, and he gasped thinking. Could she see him?

Then she gave a weary smile and lay back down, murmuring before she fell asleep, "I guess I'll just have to rely on you then my guardian."

Jazen sat down by her bed to watch her. She had only faintly perceived him, rather than truly seeing him, but despite this he was happy.

"You can always rely on me my love" Jazen whispered.

***

Michael had arranged to meet Claire at Liverpool Street station, an idea he now regretted. They were both off work so it made things a little more convenient than trying to fit the meeting in after. They agreed to meet around midday under the large board that displayed the train arrival and departure times but usually just showed "delayed" or "cancelled".

Liverpool Street was a huge station hub in the heart of the London. It was constantly packed with people, mostly due to the transport links it provided. It was also coincidentally smack bang in between where Claire and Michael lived, as Claire commuted from the suburbs. It was always busy, full of commuters, tourists, staff and people meeting up to go on their various travels. Michael was regretting his choice to meet at this location.

The moment he stepped off the bus outside the station and looked inside a wave of nausea hit him. The place was packed, mostly either parents and kids or tourists. Michael hadn't realised, but it must have been half term holidays. Thinking about it, he had seen kids on his way to the station, it just hadn't clicked in his mind.

The sheer amount of people with their guardians was overwhelming. It made the station seem claustrophobic and small with the press of people and angels, despite its large size. Jasmine noticed Michael's discomfort and took his hand gently, squeezing it for reassurance; she hummed softly, smiling at him.

Michael shut his eyes and focused on Jasmine's voice, the sound of her humming and the warmth of her touch. His nausea melted away as he took a deep breath. He opened his eyes again nodding to Jasmine in thanks. Michael entered the station and headed for the board to look for Claire,. He had arrived a little early but still hoped she might be there already.

Michael walked through the station with Jasmine still holding his hand; it was comfortable and relaxing. It was a little embarrassing holding hands in public, and it made Michael feel bashful. Also the fact, if people could see Jasmine the thought of him holding her hand would be the last thing on their minds, the halo and wings would probably be somewhat more perturbing to them.

Guardian Angel by David Trebus

As they walked, Michael scanned the people in the station, noting the condition of their Guardians. No one near him had a guardian who looked chained or dark. The majority of people's souls probably weren't dark even if they went through troubles; they were just trying to get on with their lives.

Children's guardian angels were a suprise ,childlike versions of an angel, with a smaller halo, and tiny wings that stayed manifest and seemed to always be moving. He even noticed a baby's guardian, a small cherub with a cheeky face, floating over the baby's pram giggling.

"Do angels grow up like people do?" Michael asked Jasmine, curiousity getting the better of him. "There's loads of angel kids around here?" Some people gave him an odd look, but most probably assumed he was just talking on a hands-free mobile rather than to himself.

"Not really. Why do you ask?" Jasmine replied looking a little confused.

"I've just noticed, the kid's guardian angels, they look like kids. Does that mean you looked like that when I was little too?"

"Ohhh!" Jasmine exclaimed, giving a look like she had never even considered it before.

"We take on the appearance of children for our charge's sake. Even though they can't see us, on a subconscious level and in human's dreams you can perceive us, so it makes things easier on you. We try to grow up in appearance at the same rate you do. We

Guardian Angel by David Trebus

do however change to adult form in special circumstances, like with those children at the hospital; those angels were trying very hard to help their charges recover." Jasmine explained waving her hand towards a few examples around them.

   Claire was nowhere to be seen when they reached the notice board. Feeling curious about the origin and nature of guardian angels, especially his own. Michael leaned against a pillar and let go of Jasmine's hand, turning to face her.

"Does that mean you looked as cute as those other little angel's when I was a little boy?" Michael asked, thinking he might try and tease Jasmine.

 Jasmine blushed in response, simply nodding.

"So then" Michael paused, remembering when he asked his dad about the birds and the bees.

"How are angels created? Are you born? Do two angels get together and...well...you know?"

Jasmine pulled an odd face before replying. It looked to Michael like the sarcastic look his mother used to pull when he asked a daft question.

 "We aren't born in the tradition sense...and no, two angels don't get together and get busy. Although we can procreate with humans, but that is forbidden and not something we need to go into right now. We are created by the Almighty. Whenever a human soul is born into the world, an angel is born from the creator to watch over that human and add his or her voice to the Divine Symphony."

Guardian Angel by David Trebus

Jasmine looked at Michael and he nodded to show he understood. "It wasn't always that way. Before the great battle in heaven, where Lucifer fell, there were a set number of angels. A perfect symphony they called it: not too many voices, not too few. But after the great battle, when the Almighty in his infinite wisdom gave life to humanity, he decided that more voices were needed, on high and on Earth. So now for every human there exists an angel…or, when a human's soul has fallen a dark angel or demon."

This clearly wasn't the whole story, but from the look in Jasmine's eye Michael decided not to push for more information. She had already told him everything she was prepared to and there was no point in upsetting her. He nodded and managed a small smile.

"I see, well that all makes sense I guess."

Breaking the tension, Claire had finally arrived. A sullen-looking male angel hovered close beside her shoulder. She was wearing a short red skirt and a form fitting sleeveless top, a far cry from her usual business like appearance at work but still highly attractive. Michael stared and got pinched for his trouble by Jasmine. He thanked Claire's timely arrival and stood up straight to meet her. He felt a little underdressed in just jeans and a long sleeved blue top.

Claire spotted Michael instantly and walked over wearing a half grin. He could tell it was just something she wore on the surface, she probably felt a lot different, and she looked a little tired. Her guardian by contrast didn't just look tired, but positively depressive. He wore a dark look on his face that Michael had only previously seen on sulky teenagers.

"That angel there with Claire, his name's Jazen." Jasmine whispered.

"He may look a little off but you will never meet a more devoted guardian. He's just a little…too devoted. Try not to do anything to get him started, like stare at his charge's cleavage" Jasmine whispered.

Michael felt a little confused "I was no…" He trailed off, lowering his voice.

"I was not staring at her cleavage ok? But point taken. Jeese I never knew you were the jealous type." Michael tried twice as hard to keep his eye level above Claire's shoulders, and Jasmine laughed.

Claire waved to Michael as she approached.

"Sorry, have I kept you long? My train was a little delayed as usual!" Claire said sighed.

"Nah it's ok I haven't been waiting too long. Besides, watching all the people go by has kept me entertained. How are you? How's work been?" Michael fell in beside Claire as they started to walk away from the board.

"It should be me asking you that! I mean, with the accident and all. You look fine though, I mean it's almost miraculous," There was excitement in Claire's voice.

Guardian Angel by David Trebus

"Well I guess I was just lucky all my injuries were minor or easy to treat. Still signed off work for another week or two while I rest up a bit more." Michael glanced behind him. Where had Jasmine gone?

Jasmine and Jazen had formed up behind Michael and Claire, and seemed to be deep in a conversation of their own. Jazen kept glancing up nervously at Claire, as well as giving Michael wary looks. Could he be jealous? Jasmine had mentioned that angels kept a tight rein on their emotions, Jazen clearly wasn't very good at it.

"That's good to hear." Claire reply brought Michael back to his own conversation.

"So what would you like to do?" They were just walking around aimlessly. Go for a walk down the Thames, get the tube somewhere, and hang out?"

"Well… I just came here to talk. I can't say I'm too interested in seeing the sights today if that's ok by you. Let's just grab a drink and go sit by the river. I really want to talk to you about everything that's been going on." Claire paused "And about what happened to you," she finished, her voice trailing off.

Michael nodded and managed a weak smile. He led Claire to a small café inside the station, and ordered them a couple of drinks. He kept hearing the angel's chattering behind him but couldn't quite make out what they were saying. It made him feel uncomfortable, and he had to resist the urge to turn round to check constantly.

After paying they left the station and took the short walk down to the Thames. It only took them about ten minutes to reach the waterfront, although as usual all the benches were occupied by businessmen on their laptops, tourists or old couples eating cheese sandwiches. The conversation between Michael and Claire was a bit stilted, with minor pleasantries and Claire talking a little about work. Jazen and Jasmine, however, continued to chat away. The conversation between the angels seemed to become a bit heated, as Michael heard Jasmine raise her voice to Jazen a few times.

Michael couldn't help but wonder what they were talking about, but again felt reluctant to listen in or interrupt them. Claire would probably think he was insane if he turned around talking to thin air or just stopped randomly. Better not to bother trying, than make up excuses like "thought I heard something" or "just the wind," which probably wouldn't wash with a serious person like Claire. Jasmine would likely tell him later anyway if it was something concerning him.

As they walked along the riverfront looking for a bench, Michael couldn't help but notice how neglected the area looked. They had only been walking for a few minutes, yet in patches signs of depravation were obvious. The recession had really taken its toll. A couple of homeless people rummaged around in bins for food. Another homeless woman was sleeping rough outside a small maintenance shed, probably turfed out of the city in the clean-up and left with nowhere else to go.

The two people rummaging in bins had guardians watching over them; both looked concerned and sang softly to their charges in barely audible melody. The guardians did not look damaged in any way, and Michael sighed in relief; at least they still had protection, even if they were on the streets. The sleeping woman, however, was a different story. Her guardian looked worn; the feathers in his wings had turned black and were falling like a bird in full moult, leaving skeletal wings permanently exposed. They looked like trees in winter, with only a few leaves desperately hanging on.

Michael stopped walking. Claire took a few steps ahead before turning around.

"You ok Michael? We aren't walking too fast are we?"

"I'm fine. Just give me a moment if that's ok? I want to give that woman a little spare change." Michael gave Jasmine a look, hoping she would pick up on his intentions.

"You shouldn't give them anything Michael" Claire's voice was cold. "Some of these people are dangerous. She could be a druggie. I feel sorry for them but we can't change the world."

"Maybe not, but I can help this one person a little. Just wait here a moment, I won't be long." Michael walked off the path towards the woman. Claire was right, though he wasn't even sure what he was going to do to help her. What could he possibly even do to change her situation in any meaningful way.

Michael stopped just beside where she was sleeping. Her

Guardian Angel by David Trebus

guardians eyes glowed a faint red, his face just showed bitter sorrow, rather than rage. He didn't even have chains binding him to the ground yet. Michael smiled weakly at the guardian before crouching down. The woman couldn't have been older than her late twenties. She would have been beautiful, had it none been for the grime coating her long dark hair and face.

Jasmine crouched down beside Michael, putting her hand on his shoulder to reassure him. "Is there anything you can do for them?" Michael asked her.

"Leave usss be….." the red eyed guardian whispered before she could reply.

"I...I don't know. I can sing songs to heal, to help but it's really only something I can do for you. The corruption that hurts her and her angel comes from within her. She's given up hope; she feels she has nothing to live for any more."

"Try anyway; sing for her, for him…please?" Michael pretended to get change out of his pocket to keep Claire from getting impatient and coming over.

Jasmine shut her eyes and stood up slowly. She tilted her head to the heavens. Her small wings manifested and spread out behind her, bathing Michael in light no other human could see and she sang softly.

"When all hope is lost, when love is gone
Sing with me, raise your voice

Guardian Angel by David Trebus

When all is sad, when you're alone
Be healed, rejoice, For hope is never lost."

The only effect was the woman's guardian starting to cry and singing the same song softly himself. The woman didn't stir, the guardian didn't heal. Michael looked at Jasmine desperately, and she repeated the song again, seeming to feel the same sorrow he felt.

Michael hummed the song out loud, oblivious to Claire as she walked towards them. He murmured the words, repeating what Jasmine was saying in a kind of duet. He even raised his head up to the sky, somehow imploring the powers on high to help this woman.

A single sunbeam shone on them from the sky. A cloud had passed over the sun and through a small gap, one lone ray of light shone down directly onto the woman. It was like something from a movie, just as corny, but just as moving.

The woman stirred in her sleep. Her guardians wings began to glow, and his feathers returned to a lustrous white, although only a few new ones grew, leaving his wings still bare. The red faded from his eyes, replaced by a soft blue, and he looked up at Michael in amazement, tears streaming down his face.

The woman awoke and rubbed her eyes. She looked at Michael in an odd way but didn't recoil at the stranger sitting right next to her. She even smiled slightly.

Guardian Angel by David Trebus

"I saw you in my dreams…," she murmured, half asleep.

Michael almost burst out laughing in joy, but contained himself. "Sorry to wake you up...Here, I just had some spare change for you." Michael stood back up to give the woman some space.

"Thank you," she replied, her guardian mirroring the words as she spoke them.

Jasmine, Jazen and Claire all stared at Michael in wonderment. The Angels had seen what had just happened in all its glory, the restoration of a blighted soul. Claire also had seen the sunbeam and dimly perceived something special had happened. Michael tried to focus on Claire, knowing if he started speaking to Jasmine it would look like a crazy person.

"Uh...sorry to keep you, just got talking," he managed weakly.

"What did you do?" Claire's eyes narrowed.

"What do you mean? I just gave her some spare change."

"No, not that. Something's changed. What about that sunbeam? Don't tell me nothing happened I even heard you humming, sounded almost like a spell."

"Don't be ridiculous. I was just talking to the girl." Michael tried to flannel Claire and get away from the topic. In reality he wasn't even sure what he had done; he was just happy it had worked.

Michael breathed a sigh of relief when Claire seemed to let the matter drop. He knew she suspected him, with the sun beam, her instincts, the spell or song, the girls comment and reaction. But he wasn't going to tell her willingly and pressing him would be pointless.

   Michael gestured for Claire to carry on; they still had not found a bench or even had their drinks which were probably bordering on cold by now. She walked back to the path and they resumed their search. Jasmine and Jazen again fell into step behind them although, while Michael and Claire walked in an awkward silence Jasmine and Jazen were talking.

"What happened back there?" Jazen demanded. "I don't think I have ever seen a human do that before, use an angel's song."

"I don't know...He just sang with me and I could see and feel the woman's hope returning. It's like he managed to shine a tiny light into her soul and bring her back from the brink. I mean...thinking about it, is that strange? Humans console each other all the time, use inspiring words, and comfort each other. That can have the same effect."

"Oh come on we both know it was nothing like that. The woman wasn't even awake, and the effect was almost instant. Also, don't tell me that wasn't the divine light shining down in response to your song. The symphony heard and leant its strength to your...his pleas." Michael overheard Jazen argue.

"I really don't know, Jazen; this is as surprising to me as it is to you. But...he can see us, he's different to a normal human. Perhaps this is just part of that. He really is special you know, such a kind, loving soul." Emotion crept into Jasmine's voice.

"Now you're starting to sound like me..." Jazen replied causing

Jasmine to hesitate for a moment. What did he mean by that?

***

The Symphony heard the human's song. His gentle voice lifted up borne on his Angel's wings and joined the great chorus. Metatron heard the change instantly and smiled, a small luxury he allowed himself on occasion. Jasmine and Michael really had been destined for each other since Michael had been born. There was to be another angel assigned to the new born but Metatron had been told to intercede and assign Jasmine for reasons at the time even he didn't fathom.

Those reasons now became clear to him, hearing for the first time in decades a human's voice born aloft to join the angels and seeing how strong it could be. A song that could bring hope, and could heal, probably the most powerful gift anyone on Earth had. It was worth more than fame, than riches, more than career. The simple gift to change people's souls for the better.

Metatron knew, however, that the gift would attract the attentions of others; the infernal too, would have noticed what just happened. Michael had been of interest to them before, especially to Garamond, the Beast's hand on Earth. Now he would be a threat to them. When Metatron had asked this question on high and asked

Guardian Angel by David Trebus

what he should do, the reply has been two words.
"Have Faith."

***

"This human is more powerful than we had imagined. We must turn him to our cause." A dark voice spoke from a pool of utter darkness suspended on a wall. The chamber was dimly lit with gothic-style sconces whose flames burned a dull purple. Even this light however could not permeate the dark rippling pool where the voice had come from.

"I have put things into motion that will corrupt the mortal my lord; we will have him join us." Garamond despised kneeling to anyone. To this being, however he had no choice.

"See that he is. Failure on this issue will make me most displeased, Garamond. If you cannot turn him, then you must dispose of him. A mere human cannot be allowed to disrupt the flow of my legions." The dark voice boomed with malevolent force causing Garamond to wince.

"Yes my lord," Cowed by the sheer power of his master, Garamond even felt a thrill of fear run through him, shaking his tattered wings. He relished the sensation for a moment letting it fuel his malice and determination to grow in power.

Guardian Angel by David Trebus

The dark pool faded, ripples vanishing to leave a mirror. Garamond looked up at his reflection, standing slowly from his prostrate position. His reflection stared back at him with fierce red eyes. He shifted his featherless wings hearing their bones creaking. He stood up straight and walked towards his own Earthly throne room, he hesitated at the doorway still enraptured by his demonic reflection. His legs ended in large, obsidian hooves, which stamped as he moved.

Garamond looked upon himself and smiled- he was a Prince of Hell. He had gained dominion over the Pit's works on Earth so long ago in mortal terms, yet to him it felt like yesterday. He still remembered his fall from grace, his corruption by mortal soul, but in truth before that he had always wished he had joined the rebellion in heaven. One day soon he would rebel again; it was in his very nature. Why would anyone settle for prince, when they could be King?

The mortal, Michael, presented a golden opportunity to realise that ambition. With his abilities, the souls of weak mortals would be his for the taking, along with their angelic guardians. The army he could build would be enough to besiege the gates of Hell itself before moving on to destroy the heavens.

Garamond was lost in thought staring at his reflection and imagining all the possibilities that lay in front of him. All he had to do was gain sway over one small mortal. The thought amused him, even with the tiny amount of power they had, one single mortal

Guardian Angel by David Trebus

could still make all the difference.

He stretched out large dark wings and stood to his full height. He continued to revel in the possibilities of future glories and his ascension to the infernal throne. He could picture himself sitting on that throne of dark iron surrounded by lava, succubi at his feet performing base acts for his pleasure.

"Soon!" Garamond hissed.

***

Michael and Claire finally found somewhere to sit; they had ended up drinking their coffee and eating their snacks on route to avoid them growing cold. They sat on a graffiti covered bench by the old British Warship HMS Belfast, a London tourist attraction. The sight of the ship brought back memories of his trips into London as a child with his father. Michael couldn't help but smile looking at it.

Michael remembered being so excited about setting foot on the ship, seeing the big guns, being on the water. He also remembered getting very scared when his father took him into the lower decks of the ship. He had cried and wanted to go back up, scared to be so deep in such a confined space. He had felt soothed after seeing a young girl. He wondered if it had been Jasmine? The souvenir shop and an ice cream back on top had cured him of any remaining fear.

Claire looked the old ship up and down, seeming to Michael like she wanted to say something, but was hesitating. Jazen and Jasmine stood by the grass verge a few metres away paying little interest to the ship, it being just another monument to humanity's desire to cause harm. They continued to talk softly just out of Michael's earshot.

"It's a nice view isn't it? My father brought me here as a kid" Michael followed Claire's gaze.

"I suppose. I can't say I ever visited it. Big guns and grey metal never really did it for me, I was more of a Barbie girl as a kid." Claire spoke coolly, brushing a strand of blonde hair from her face.

"I loved all that stuff, which I suppose is kind of normal, being a bloke and all. I always wanted to join the RAF, become a hero. Never thought I would turn out working in some publishing firm and seeing…" Michael stopped himself short and swore at himself in his mind for almost letting something slip. He was so used to discussing the issue with Jasmine, now he saw it as normal conversation.

"Seeing what?" Claire asked her eyes narrowing into accusing slits.

"Uh... Seeing sights like this instead of working on them," Michael managed awkwardly.

"Uhhmm…ok then" Claire shrugged, looking at the grass.

Guardian Angel by David Trebus

The awkwardness broken a little Claire leaned forward. She shifted in her seat, biting her lip and feeling the nerves creep up on her. She pushed them down with sheer willpower, refusing to allow any anxiety to take hold. In reality, the fear that she'd lose control was what made Claire seem so cold to others.

"About my dream Michael... I know people think I'm a little weird, it's just the way I am..." Claire hesitated.

"But I honestly had a dream about your accident, Michael; it's not just coincidence or me being odd. I saw you getting hit by that car and some...force, something else behind it guiding the car that hit you. But I also saw a woman with wings standing over you, and I knew you would be ok. I know we aren't exactly close, but I was still really worried about you." They sat in silence. "Blah I'm rambling," Claire said after a while.

"First, ok, I admit you do come off a bit strange sometimes Claire." Michael strained to think of a way to respond.

"But you're a cool person, and I have always enjoyed working with you. As for your dream, well, I don't know what to say other than I believe you."

"Really? Even the blonde woman with wings bit? I mean, most people don't believe in angels and all that. Everyone these days seems to at least be poser atheist."

"Even that bit. The accident...well, it kind of changed my perspective on a lot of things, including angels. So don't worry, I believe you. The last few days have been a bit of an eye-opener for me, just hope things calm down a bit." Michael hazarded a glance at Jasmine, who grinned broadly and waved like a Japanese tourist.

Claire narrowed her eyes. What had Michael had meant by "change of perspective." Something about the way he had said it meant more than simply being involved in a bad accident and gaining a new lease on life. When Claire had first met him he'd seemed fairly mundane. Slightly above-average looks, fair sense of humour but just...normal. Now that perception of him was being blown out the water. The guy was surrounded by mystery.

***

Jazen sat next to Jasmine on the grass. Just like Claire, he narrowed his eyes at Michael, and Jasmine could tell it was because of Claire's growing interest in him. She put her hand on his shoulder to reassure him.

"You know, it's just because she's interested in all the mystery around him, Jazen, so don't get worked up." Jasmine suppressed a tiny pang of her own feelings as she watched Michael and Claire talk.

"Anyway even if she decided to date someone it's not your business to interfere." Jasmine went on looking directly at Jazen. "You're her guardian and not her lover; you could even end up hurting her. That's why there's so many strict rules for us, that's why we always have to keep most of our feelings suppressed."

"I know Jasmine!" Jazen raised his voice.

"I had the lecture from the Choir, thank you...I just can't help it, I really…am devoted to my duties. I will try to abide by the Choir's wishes, but I will always stick by her side, Jasmine. And my feelings help me help her not hinder, if only those on high realised it."

"I think they do, but we are also here to help them, not to follow our own selfish needs. We are angels, we don't enjoy the same freedoms humans do. It's not the purpose for which we were made. We are here to serve and protect. Our love comes from the lord and the great symphony." Jasmine felt her conviction wane slightly as she talked. In some ways she was starting to feel like Jazen; she was just better at hiding it.

"Whatever, Jasmine. I doubt we will ever agree on this one. Don't you ever feel jealous when your charge is with other women?"

The question caught Jasmine off guard. In the past, she would have replied with a very quick denial. Jasmine had watched over Michael while he'd been with girlfriends, although she'd always left the room during intimacy. It was only decent, after all. But now, when she thought of the prospect, she wasn't so sure she would feel the same.

"No," Jasmine replied, after a pause.

"Fair enough," he replied. Jasmine saw that Jazen knew he had hit a raw nerve, from her reaction.

Jasmine tried again to suppress her emotions. She felt no jealousy about Claire. She knew Michael's type well enough and Claire definitely was not it. But Jazen had tapped a part of her she had not even known had existed until today. It might not have even been there until recently. The thought of Michael with someone else troubled her now and being troubled by it, disturbed Jasmine even more.

Jasmine sighed and thought of Metatron again; his letter, his advice that she should take note of the lesson that Jazen represented. Maybe somehow he knew what was happening, what was going to happen with her and Michael. She stood up and stretched. Things would be ok as long as she had faith in herself and her charge. She should just focus on being there for him and everything else would fall into place. She watched Michael from where she stood, Jazen still sitting on the ground next to her. He seemed to be awkward.

***

"So." Claire decided to cut through the treacle. "Would you like to meet up again sometime to talk more as I have to be leaving soon, perhaps for dinner?"

Guardian Angel by David Trebus

"Uh…uh yeah, I suppose so. I mean I'm still off work for another couple of weeks, so I should have plenty of free time. When were you thinking?"

Claire put on mock-pouting expression. "You suppose? Charming."

"I didn't mean it like that." Michael stammered out quickly. "you just caught me by surprise with that one."

Claire laughed "That's more the Michael I know. I was thinking Friday this week. Unlike you, I only have today off. Some of us have work."

"Yeah, should be fine. I don't have anything planned. What time and where?"

"How about round mine? I'll email you my address and directions. It isn't a long walk from the station and I could meet you there if you like. At around seven?" Claire replied shifting her position. She was exposing her cleavage again, it might be deliberate but he couldn't be sure. She was so calculating.

"Ok then, sounds fine." It occurred to Michael that it had been ages since he had last got a train. "Uh...do you know when the last train is?"

"Not a problem. If you end up round mine until late, you can just sleep on the sofa and get back in the morning," Jazen's ears pricked up from behind and he pulled a sulky expression.

Was Claire really coming onto him? Or was it just his imagination?. He had that sense from women before and been way

Guardian Angel by David Trebus

off, though. Perhaps she was just trying to pry. While he found Claire physically attractive, for some reason the thought of intimacy with her wasn't quite as exciting as he imagined. Everytime he thought about it, like any young healthy male, he couldn't help but wonder how Jasmine would react. It was an odd feeling.

"Anything wrong?" Claire asked

"Oh no, nothing, that's fine. It might make life easier, if I end up missing the train. A cab back from outside of London would probably cost a fortune." Michael stood up to stretch his legs and to change his view from Claire's assets.

"Then it's settled, keep an eye on your inbox. Well it's been lovely but I had best be heading off home now, chores to do, cats to feed, spells to cast…" After a pause Claire added "That last part is a joke by the way."

"Coming back to the station with me, or would you like to stay here for a while?" Claire asked.

"Do you mind?" Michael felt a little rude, not realising feelings were so easy to read.

"Nah, it's only a short walk and it's still early yet. Besides I think I'm old enough to take care of myself now, Claire winked.

"Ok well take care and safe trip home," Michael said exchanging an awkward half hug with Claire, trying to keep his mind on the big metal ship in front of him and off other big things in his field of view.

Guardian Angel by David Trebus

"You too. See you on Friday," Claire replied as she began walking off. Jazen said a hasty goodbye to Jasmine, glared at Michael and hurried to catch up with Claire. Michael just sighed and sat back down on the bench, feeling very drained.

Jasmine sat down on the bench next to him. She manifested her wings to give them a quick stretch and shake before folding them neatly back behind her again. She looked a little like a parakeet or finch stretching their wings before takeoff, except it was even cuter on an angel.

"Interesting conversation?" Jasmine asked, an edge to her voice.

"A little too interesting." Michael replied slouching on the bench and leaning his head back to look at the sky.

"Claire is a pretty intense and perceptive person. She's invited me for dinner on Friday." Michael replied slouching on the bench and leaning his head back to look at the sky.

"Well that should be nice, I would watch out for Jazen though. He was glaring daggers at you."

"Well it's your job to keep him entertained while I'm there. Besides I don't really intend to do anything apart from have dinner and spend time talking with her," Michael thought about Jasmine's feelings," Besides I don't really see her in that way…"

Why had he felt the need to add that last bit? It instantly seemed to make Jasmine more relaxed, and the edge he was sensing from her disappeared.

"That's good; I will do my best to keep the guy off your back. He really is a good and devoted Guardian, he just…"

"Loves her to much?" Michael finished

"Yes…although he really shouldn't. It's not our place to love our charges in that way, only to look after them."

"I wonder why it has to be that way?" Michael asked the sky as he leant back staring.

Jasmine joined him looking up, letting Michael lean his head on her shoulder.

Guardian Angel by David Trebus

Chapter 5: Unwelcome Developments

It was time to head home. An hour had already passed by without Michael noticing. Again the day had been full of interesting events, although they seemed relaxed compared to the previous day. Was he starting to adapt to all the strange things occurring in his life? After finding out angels were real, anything else seemed a bit tame.

It was so comfortable leaning on Jasmine's wing, Michael didnt really want to move, but it was late afternoon, and getting a little chilly. Did people think it was strange, him sitting with his head leaning on thin air? A child stopped to look for a moment, but no one else had paid him any attention; there were tons of weirdos in London.

Yawning, Michael shifted and got himself to his feet. Jasmine didnt move from the bench, staring up at the sky. Michael couldn't help but grin at the bright warming smile she wore. A strange thrill ran down his spine as he thought about her, butterflies swarming in his stomach.

Jasmine turned to face Michael, an expression on her face that mirrored his own. Her sparkling eyes lingered on him for a moment, before she held out her hand. Taking the cue, Michael

Guardian Angel by David Trebus

helped her up. Jasmine made a little bounce as she stood, and also de-manifested her wings. She had mentioned to Michael that keeping them released for too long was tiring.

The walk back to Liverpool Street station was filled with an odd silence, a mix of awkwardness and anticipation. Michael tried to start a conversation a few times, but every time the words eluded him and faded on his lips. Jasmine remained deep in thought and didn't speak.

Jazen's accusation of jealousy hung in her mind. Such an emotion was not befitting of an angel. In truth, it was this kind of dark feeling that caused the Great War in heaven so long ago.

They arrived at the station just as dusk was starting to settle. Light shone through the huge glass ceiling, casting strange shadows and reflecting off surfaces to form in hazy orange pools.

Michael pushed his way through the throng of commuters finishing off their day, eager to return home for dinner and television. He tried not to pay too much attention to their Guardians. With such a crowd, it would be difficult to single out anyone in need of help and even harder to actually assist without drawing unwelcome attention. He was very tired and weary. It was tempting just to get a cab home again but, with the way things were going in the world, saving the fare was the sensible thing to do.

Jasmine surprised Michael by grabbing his hand. She wore a guilty expression, and Michael could tell something was troubling

Guardian Angel by David Trebus

her. The sudden physical contact surprised him; it felt different from when they had held hands before. This time, it sent an electric jolt up his arm, causing him to snap his head round. The feeling was energizing, and from the expression on Jasmine's face, she had the same sensation.

Michael made his way out of the station. The bus stop had the usual line for the rush hour. He'd walk down to the next stop, where there would likely be a fewer people and less wait to get onto the bus. He was weary but somehow, with Jasmine holding his hand, he felt just that little bit better.

The next stop along the road was no less busy and had a huge line too, but this time of shoppers carrying bags brimming with clothing, DVDs and all sorts. There were even a few tourists sporting geeky union jack baseball caps and carrying souvenirs; Michael had almost totally forgotten there had been a royal wedding recently.

Bored of the repeated bus lines, Michael was tired enough to spend the money on a cab home. He doubled back on himself with Jasmine in tow, cutting through a side street and alley to get to the nearest taxi rank. He avoided returning to the station though. He'd have about as much chance grabbing a cab there as winning the lottery with a baseball card.

The side street was quiet with just a few people packing up storefronts and emptying bins, but the alley was deserted. Jasmine resisted as they walked down it, pulling back on him a little. She

Guardian Angel by David Trebus

leaned closer to whisper to him.

"I have a very bad sense down here, Michael. We should turn back and find another route,"

"It'd take another ten minutes. Come on, we're almost to the end. Besides I've got you to protect me." Michael felt uneasy. But he felt too tired to give it any thought.

Jasmine sensed evil as they continued to walk, but guessed as they were halfway through anyway it would be pointless to turn around. She muttered a silent hymn under her breath and stretched her wings one at a time, preparing just in case something happened, but hoping it wouldn't.

A few metres from the end, a figure blocked their path. It had no clear form, and was only visible as a shimmering humanoid shape of darkness against the light cast into the alley. It made no aggressive moves as they approached, but stood directly in their path, blocking the way. Michael stopped as he felt a sudden coldness. The figure blocking their path was most definitely supernatural.

"What the heck is that?" Michael whispered.

"That's a spectre, it's another type of lesser demon. They are born of man's petty desires. It's probably why it's being spiteful and blocking us." Jasmine tugged Michael to turn around.

"I think it's time we started heading back. We can go the long way round."

Michael stepped backwards slowly, keeping his eyes on the

shimmering form of darkness before him. It made no move to advance, merely blocking their exit.

Michael continued to back up, but a scream from Jasmine sent him stumbling in surprise, and he lost his footing. Michael fell over and scrambled to stand up. He tried to find something to fetch up against, and quickly glanced at the spectre to check if it had attacked. The creature had not moved. Michael turned to see Jasmine cowering on ground, hands over her head. Behind them stood a man in a dark blue suit and sunglasses.

A sense of danger came from the man, but why? He looked fairly normal apart from wearing sunglasses at dusk. The man was tall, with very pale skin and a strong build. He wore a superior grin that irritated Michael.

"Hello there, are you ok?" The grin never left the man's face.

Michael glanced towards Jasmine, who stood up but still seemed shaky. She was clearly terrified. This man had to be bad news, neither the specter or the imp had affected her so badly. Michael faced the man defiantly, and for the first time noticed the red aura that seemed to surround him.

"Fine, thanks, just a bit startled. We took a wrong turn and need to go back," Michael answered. An ordinary person wouldn't be able to see Jasmine. Michael wondered if he would react to the word, "We?"

"Oh, well, don't mind me. I'm just passing through." The man pushed past Michael, walking towards the spectre.

Guardian Angel by David Trebus

"You take care of yourself, Michael. Don't let the spectre bother you. He's just there to keep an eye on things. You had better talk to your angel before she pees herself. We will be seeing you very, very soon." He disappeared round the corner.

Michael would at that moment have breathed a sigh of relief, but the stranger's last words were like daggers in his mind. The man knew his name, he knew Jasmine was there and he knew about the spectre. Michael's felt his face drain of colour and his hands go tingly. The stranger could only have been a demon…the "We will be seeing you soon," what could it have meant? What did this man have planned for him?

***

Around the corner, Garamond stopped and laughed silently. It was funny how the world worked. The very person he'd been watching so intently had walked right above his lair. He'd sensed Michael and couldn't resist the chance to play with him. He had used one of his nearby lackeys to possess. Perhaps he could play with him a little longer. It was not time to put his plans into action yet, but that didn't mean no fun could be had. He turned to the spectre and raised his right arm, palm flat and facing it.

"*Infernus,*" Garamond whispered the trigger spell. "Attack them, but *do not* severely wound either of them." The spectre shimmered more violently in reply.

He felt like enjoying a night of excess in his possessed body. The brief, but amusing encounter had left him in the mood for some drinking, sex and random petty destruction. He left the Spectre to its fate, content to sense how things played out from a distance.

***

Jasmine recovered her senses just in time to see Michael rushed by the Spectre. Within the dark shimmering mass, two angry red glows sat roughly where its eyes should have been. She knocked Michael to the ground just before the creature rushed over, leaving an ice cold wind in it's wake. Small puddles of water froze in the alley around them and Michael's breath misted in the air.

It was the second time now she had nearly failed her charge by focusing on her own emotions. She was not supposed to feel fear like that, but what simple guardian could stand against one of the infernal scourges? It had to be Garamond or one of his most powerful minions. She kicked herself mentally, and promised to return on high. She needed to find a way to overcome how she had been feeling. She needed to regain her focus.

"Who the hell was that guy, and why is that thing attacking us now? I thought it wasn't dangerous unless hungry?"

"*That guy* we can talk about later. The spectre has been commanded to attack us, and we need to get into some light." Jasmine helped Michael to his feet and urged him into a run.

The Spectre had turned and was making ready for another pass, Jasmine felt angry red eyes boring into her as she ran. They reached the end of the alley as it rushed at them. Jasmine pulled Michael down at the last moment, but the Spectre grazed him, and ice formed over his right shoulder. Michael grimaced in pain.

The sun was low on the horizon now, the street lights had come on. The side street they had emerged on was almost deserted, with only a couple of store holders packing up inside their shops.

The Spectre was lining up for another attack. Jasmine pushed Michael under a street light and stood directly in front of him. She still held onto his hand tightly.

It moved towards them more slowly this time. It surrounded the patch of light cast by the street lamp, enveloping Jasmine in darkness. Multiple angry red eyes bored into them from all sides as she stood defiantly with Michael up against the street lamp. Jasmine shut her eyes and looked up directly into the overhead light as she recited:

Guardian Angel by David Trebus

"Darkness of spirit
Darkness born of desire
Go now diminish
Burn in purest fire. "

    The Spectre faded slightly, but came back stronger. The darkness reformed and pushed up against the light cast by the street lamp. The lamp flickered, Was the bulb about to burn out? Jasmine repeated the verse with similar temporary effect. Michael, to Jasmine's suprise, took her other hand, and began repeating her words, whispering it as she sang.

"Darkness of spirit
Darkness born of desire
Go now, diminish
Burn in Heaven's purest fire. "

    The extra word came naturally and without prompting. Having Michael recite the verse with her had made her add it without even thinking. The result was miraculous, a blinding flash of light as the bulb burnt out and exploded. Thousands of tiny, incandescent sparks showered over the darkness surrounding them. Each spark ignited on the Spectre and burst into a tiny flame. The small flames joined into a pyre, banishing the Spectre into the pit.

    Jasmine breathed a sigh of relief, there was nothing around them

Guardian Angel by David Trebus

but paving stones and a few lazy pigeons. No one seemed to have noticed, or the store holders were ignoring them thinking they were lunatics.

Jasmine turned to Michael and before she could think her lips met his. Her whole body felt hot and her emotions became a confused mess making Jasmine feel dizzy. It all happened so fast, she barely had time to realise what she had done. She quickly pulled away looking shocked at herself.

"Uh...can we forget that happened?"

Michael simply nodded in reply. Jasmine knew he wouldn't forget it, but hoped he would at least not bring it up with her.

Jasmine praised the Symphony that she had been chosen to be Michael's Guardian. He was special, and not just in the way all humans were. There was something about him no other mortal could claim. Somehow, he could sing with her and boost her abilities. Who knew what he might be capable of in the future? It wasn't all roses however; Garamond seemed to be showing an interest and, the Spectres attack only suggested more danger in the future. Jasmine decided she would have to return on high as soon as she could for guidance.

"Let's get home." Michael said disturbing Jasmine's chain of thought. "It's getting late and, after this day, I could really use a strong drink and a good night's sleep."

"Sure let's get out of here!" They headed off to find a taxi home.

Guardian Angel by David Trebus

***

Garamond had sensed the Spectre's demise even from the early-opening gentlemen's club, where two women sat indulging him with drink and something a bit more adult. The lesser demon's destruction had been inevitable, but to sense the mortal's power in action had been positively delicious. He would be a very strong asset when turned.

"Almost time, Michael my friend. Just wait a little longer."

"Sorry hun?" One of the women leaned up.

"Shut up and carry on, I wasn't talking to you."

Garamond said through his possessed body's voice, enhancing its depth and strength. The woman shrugged and got back to her business. Garamond ignored how she dipped her fingers into his wallet and lifted some money in response.

Garamond shut his eyes and leaned back, starting an atonal hum through his borrowed body's voice box. The two women around him both winced as the sound shot straight through their brains. They jerked upright in an instant, faces masks of fear and began shaking violently.

Bat-like wings sprouted from the two serving girl's backs, elegantly curved horns pushing through the skin of their foreheads. A baleful glow lit up blue eyes even as a whipcord thin tail emerged just above an elegantly formed behind. One of the girls saw Garamond's half-nakedness and plunged down to resume her previous business. The other crept towards him, purring like a cat and grinning widely to show a mouth full of serrated teeth.

"Hello succubi. I'm glad see you,"

"Garamonnnd, it feels like years since we saw you." The purring woman said pouting lips the colour of blood.

"You always summon our sisters and never us. We were feeling neglected."

"It's because you two are very special to me. I could never use you in the way I use your sisters." Garamond felt a trickle of blood run from below; the other sister had finished her ministrations. Hopefully she hadn't damaged his host too badly. The security guard was useful and very discreet...and utterly corrupt of soul.

"You sureeee know how to flatter us, Garamond" The succubus on the ground said. "Buttt we're sure you didn't summon us for a little possessed foreplay." Her sister continued. "What is your desire, O mighty scourge of Earth?" The second sister's voice was exactly the same as the first but with a mocking tone.

Garamond ignored her tone; like most other demons, succubi were notoriously flirtatious, rude and condescending. They were the corrupted souls of Guardians, but these had fallen due to their charges' overwhelming lust and sins of the flesh. The most common form of succubus was born from the rapists and serial cheaters of humanity. But these two sisters were special, created from the massed orgies of Roman times. All that carnal lust, murder and decadence had culminated around the Emperor Hephastus and his family members to create these two beautiful but deadly demons: the Lilith Sisters.

"Indeed. I have summoned you here for something very important, something I can't trust to mere imps and spectres. I need your…finesse," Garamond exited his host, to allow it to recover and spoke through his own voice.

"Ohh…do tell," they purred in unison, creeping towards the now totally human individual, lying unconscious on the sofa. Garamond slapped one of the sisters hand as it crept towards the human. He needed the man alive and wasn't prepared to let the sisters get their claws on him. She yelped and crept back with catlike movements, grinning all the while.

"There is a mortal on this little green ball I wish to corrupt, and I need your help to do it. I need you to influence the mortal's passions, bring his emotions to the fore. Then, afterwards, I need you to create a little….accident, a lethal one for him."

"Why can't you do it yourself?" One sister begun before her sister mocked, "*mighty one.*"

"Because I cannot be seen to be involved. Other infernal powers must carry out this act, and I know you're perfectly suited to the task. Here are the details. I trust your human hosts will allow you to move around more easily, although don't hesitate to discard them if you need to."

Guardian Angel by David Trebus

Garamond handed the women a slip of paper each. They would get jealous if only one received it, as had occurred in the past. It had cost him a very important victory. The note contained the details of Michael's dinner date with Claire, including the train times, and her address. Infernal spies really did find dirt easily; they likely worked for tabloid newspapers when they had been mortal.

In reality, the accident Garamond had created had been intended to Kill Michael. But the plan's failure had created an even better opportunity. He was going about it all wrong and had already planned an excellent way of corrupting the mortal.

"Oooo, this sounds like lots of fun." Both succubi said at once. "Thank you for bringing us in on this one. It'll be delicious," The sisters coo'd in excitement.

"See that you don't fail."

"Weee won't." Their reply was in a child's mocking tone.

"Now go. Replenish yourselves. You're going to need plenty of power on this plane and I'm sure you'll have fun getting it."

The sisters bowed in unison, their demonic forms melding and finally disappearing into their human hosts. They looked like the two serving girls they had possessed, with the exception of deep purple eyes. They left the bar, swinging their hips sensuously with every movement. Garamond stood up, leaving his previous host a wedge of money to pay for his excesses. Garamond summoned deep red infernal flames around him, returning to his throne

Guardian Angel by David Trebus

beneath London to await the next phase of his plan.

***

It was half past eight in the evening when Michael and Jasmine got home. What Michael thought would be a short trip to see a work friend had turned into another long and eventful day. It didn't help that, as usual, they got stuck in traffic on the way home.

During the trip home, the taxi driver had kept talking, banging on about the latest celeb gossip or football scores. However, eventually he stopped trying when Michael's polite replies turned into short murmurs as Michael struggled to focus his thoughts. The cabbie eventually gave up.

Of all the things to be focusing on, after the long day filled with miraculous songs, strange dark men and demonic attacks, Michael found himself fixating on that short but electric kiss from Jasmine. She had told him that kind of thing was a taboo, that guardian angels didn't do that kind of thing, yet she had still kissed him. Had it simply been born of the moment? Or a platonic kiss? If so, it seemed to mean more. Then again, maybe he was just indulging in wishful thinking.

The ideas churned away as he pondered the consequences and imagined all kinds of possible futures. What if the kiss did mean more? What if they wanted to take things further? What if they wanted to get married?

The last thought had Michael struggling to stifle his laughter. All they had shared was a brief kiss after a dangerous situation, and here was his mind creating outrageous scenarios. He had a tendency to go off on tangents and imagine things to all kinds of extremes; it was that he often felt nervous in romantic situations.

He looked over at Jasmine a few times during the journey, but she stared out of the window with a thoughtful expression on her face, never turning round, even though Michael was sure she knew he was glancing at her.

***

Jasmine was too focused on what had happened. Like her charge, the thoughts of the kiss played in her mind. She forced them away, to consider things far more important; the Spectre's attack and the dark man who could only have been an Infernal, one of the strongest types of demon. He could have been a true fallen, one of the Beast's chosen. It could have been Garamond himself, for all Jasmine knew.

Things were getting dangerous, and far quicker than Jasmine had imagined. If that creature had intended true harm to Michael, it could have killed him in seconds while she cowered on the floor. That thought was what kept Jasmine from looking Michael in the eye; the idea she had failed him, been unable to help. It was something she had never experienced before, feeling powerless.

The cab journey ended, and Michael paid the driver his fee, politely thanked him and got out. Jasmine followed, hopping daintily onto the pavement just before Michael shut the door and the cab drove off. All the levity and happiness she used to feel was fading from her. Jasmine used to feel so light and was kind of ditzy, but her focus had become sharper now, and her soul deeper, more determined. Was this a gift or a burden?

They walked over to the door in silence, Jasmine focused on her thoughts and worries. Michael had just opened it up when Jasmine felt the urge to grab his arm. He immediately tensed up his tired body, looking like he was getting ready for danger.

"Michael…." Jasmine's voice was barely above a whisper.

"What's wrong?" Michael replied shaking slightly. He looked worried about something. Was he expecting something to be waiting for them at home?

"I'm sorry," Jasmine looked up with tearful eyes.

"Huh?" was all Michael could manage, looking confused more than scared now.

"I let you down in the alley." Jasmine said at length fighting her tears down.

"My job is to protect you, not cower when real danger comes. I just couldn't carry on without apologising to you. I promise to never let you down like that again. No matter what happens, I will keep you safe."

Michael was stunned; As far as he was concerned, she had done nothing wrong. What was she even talking about? She had protected him from the Spectre, although with his help. She had been nothing but a source of strength since before he even realised she was there. His first thought was to tell her not to worry, and that she had done everything right. Maybe the tiredness was addling his reason, or maybe it was just empathy, but Michael hugged Jasmine tightly.

He'd never put more feeling into an embrace in his entire life. He held Jasmine with all the love, caring and forgiveness he could muster. She tensed up in his arms, even manifesting her wings in surprise. The feathers tickled Michael's arm, but he wasn't going to let go. Jasmine stared past him with wide eyes before slowly shutting them and hugging him back.
"Thank you," she whispered into his ear.

That night Michael and Jasmine needed no more words. Jasmine sat in silence for a while before Michael went to bed. She followed, lying next to him, on a bed that seldom kept more than one. She stared into his eyes for a long while before Michael finally gave into his tiredness and fell asleep. Jasmine had never felt more like Jazen and his inappropriate feelings, but for some

Guardian Angel by David Trebus

reason it didn't feel wrong anymore. She lay behind Michael and covered him gently with her wings, draping her arm over his side.

She lightly kissed the back of Michael's neck and ignored the voice of reason telling her this was against all the rules. She allowed her feelings to flow free for a few precious moments as she hummed softly to Michael while he slept.

"I will keep you safe, Michael, I promise," Jasmine whispered. She sang through the night to ward off any nightmares and ensure Michael's dreams were pleasant.

Guardian Angel by David Trebus

Chapter 6: Difficult Choices

Sunbeams shone brightly every day in the heavens. On this day, however dark grey clouds loomed on the horizon. Such an omen was never a good one; the darkness usually meant infernal activities. The symphony though sung even more strongly than usual, the rising voices and heavy notes resonating with a powerful passion that only rarely manifested.

Metatron stared at the dark horizon and shuffled his wings to loosen his feathers. He had been aware the moment Jasmine had broken the rules with her charge. The emotions, the closeness, had influenced the symphony in a subtle way, at first, but later had formed the rising notes he now heard. There was a risk of them growing closer, of course, but he'd been told not to interfere, to "have faith." But now a doubt niggled at the back of his mind.

For a moment, Metatron found himself questioning the rules. Why couldn't a Guardian develop feelings for their charge? Such things had occurred in the past, on a fairly regular basis, leading to the birth of the half-angel Grigori. The Grigori had, for the most part, only added to the heavenly Symphony and been an asset to Heaven's hosts. Some fell, though, corrupted through their human halves.

He leaned on the balcony, staring deep into the storm clouds, and shook his head in frustration. Questioning divine mandate was wrong. He should not be allowing himself such latitude, not in his position; second only to Gabriel in the choirs and the direct voice of the Almighty.

He should ask for guidance again, if only to clarify whether Jasmine should be reprimanded for her behaviour. Metatron left the balcony and returned to his chambers. He knelt within the centre of the room, carefully folding back his wings so as not to sit on them. He raised his head up in prayer and pressed his palms together.

The instruments suspended around him began playing in unison, connected to the heavenly music, A few discordant notes had crept in, but Metatron ignored them, focusing on the task at hand. His wings glowed, and a shaft of light enveloped him. He closed his eyes, enjoying the moment of contact; the sensation of warmth and love never failed to move him.

"Lord, I pray for an answer, regarding Jasmine and her human charge, Michael. Do we interfere to help them? Do I punish Jasmine for breaking the laws of our Guardian Angels?" Metatron half spoke, half sang into the light. It wasn't necessary to say it out loud, but he preferred to, anyway.

The reply was instant, sounding within his mind; a voice so powerful it could shake the very foundation of the Earth, yet so gentle it would not disturb the slumber of a child.

"Jasmine is not to be punished, only watched. Her charge is facing

Guardian Angel by David Trebus

a time of trials, but he has the tools and strengths he needs. Have faith"

The beam of light vanished as abruptly as it had appeared, ascending into the ceiling. Metatron climbed to his feet, pondering the words. The Lord's replies were always cryptic but always true. In this case, however, they confused Metatron. Jasmine had grown too close to her charge, and yet she was not to be punished, where Jazen had been reprimanded for exactly the same thing.

Perhaps Michael being aware of Jasmine made them a special case, but surely a word of caution would have led Jasmine down a safer path. The whole situation created a dangerous conflict of interests.

But the words "Have faith," spoken again, rang like a gong in Metatron's soul. He knew there was a plan for the pair, he just had to believe in them, in the Almighty, and as always in himself.

"Have faith" Metatron whispered the words, as he left his chambers to go about his daily duties.

***

Thursday morning came down on Earth with a bright ray of sunlight through Michael's window. He opened his eyes, blinking against the penetrating light, and raised an arm over his head to

Guardian Angel by David Trebus

shield his eyes. He turned to stare directly into both the most beautiful and frightening sight for any man, first thing in the morning: the face of a woman lying next to him.

Jasmine's eyes were shut, and she breathed softly onto Michael's skin. Her breath smelt of her namesake, sweet and refreshing. She looked serene, lying there asleep. Michael was suprised Guardians even needed sleep, but it seemed the last few days had taken their toll on Jasmine as much as him.

Memories of the previous night flooded back to him, how they had lain there staring at each other, not speaking any words but saying more than an entire conversation. A pang of nerves made his stomach spasm uncomfortably. Would Jasmine get in trouble for being so intimate with him? Would she end up getting reprimanded like Jazen?

What worried Michael more was his own feelings. He had grown very attached to Jasmine in such a short time, and now those feelings seemed to be growing stronger. He pictured the whole relationship in a few moments, running through all the possible futures in his mind. All the joy, all the private moments, the way she looked na....

He shook his head violently, breaking his chain of thought. That kind of thinking really wasn't the best right now. They couldn't be together. She was his Guardian, he was her charge; it was a friendship at best, and a business relationship at worst. Michael looked again at Jasmine as she slept, and watched her. She sighed

Guardian Angel by David Trebus

softly in some dream.

He decided to get up, swaying slightly as his tired limbs protested at the movement. He stretched a little and tip toed to the kitchen to prepare some food. He looked back a couple of times to make sure Jasmine had not woken up. But she lay there silently, her eyes closed.

Michael checked his answer phone for any new messages. The light flashed a couple of times to indicate no, but then changed and showed a single unlistened-to message. He shrugged and played it. The message played, but some words seemed distorted and hard to hear.

"Hello Michael, my name is Lil***. I am phoning you on behalf of Gar****d. Please listen carefully to my w**ds. *Lustful, inflammar, passionate*. Tha** you for your time." The message was somewhat confusing and garbled in parts. Whoever the caller was must have used a mobile or had a bad line.

Was it just a sales call? It may have been, but listening to it made Michael feel a little strange. Images of Jasmine, and even Claire, kept flashing into his mind, some a little X- rated.

He shook his head but couldn't stop the images flashing into his mind; he almost took a step back to the bedroom on instinct, before he caught himself.

"What on Earth has got into me?" Michael decided to skip breakfast and go straight in for a cold shower.

Guardian Angel by David Trebus

***

Outside, near a payphone, two women stood staring up at the apartment. The woman who had made the call grinned widely, while the other, standing near her, kept getting distracted by every man who walked past. She winked seductively at them, pouted, even went so far as to bend down and show some cleavage. One man stared so much he ended up bumping into a lamp post.

"Eldith, focus. You had your fun last night. We have a job to do."
"Oh come on, Lilith, just a few more. I don't feel satisfied yet, and it's not as if we haven't got time to kill until tomorrow. Your lustful enchantments aren't going to work on them; I can feel the resistance from here." Eldith stretched so that her chest thrust out for all to see.

"It'll do for now" Lilith pouted. "It doesn't have to get them jumping into the sack, just fan the flame they've already started. Lust and love are so similar, it's just that lust is much more fun. Eh, Eldith?"

Eldith grinned, her eyes trailing a group of older teens passing by. The boys stared at them both, while the girls looked increasingly jealous. She pulled herself closer to her sister, running her hands through Lilith's long, blonde hair. She kissed her passionately.

Guardian Angel by David Trebus

Lilith leaned in, stroking her sister's back and watching as the teenagers jaws dropped. The men stared with barely contained lust, while the girls' faces turned red. They tugged their boyfriends or suitors away, clearly jealous of the attention being paid to the other women.

Eldith broke the kiss and laughed as the group passed them by, performing a mock bow to incite further staring. Lilith grinned widely and sighed at her sister.

"Well, I guess a little more fun couldn't hurt; the spell did drain some of my power." Lilith said whispering seductively into Eldith's ear.

"We still need to set things up for tomorrow, though. Garamond won't be happy with us if we mess this up. This could be our big chance to gain more power."

"YAY!" Eldith squealed. "You're so nice to me, Sis. Let's go find us some footballers to corrupt; they're always quick'n'easy! And then maybe someone more satisfying. A rugby player, or fencer, or athlete would do"

"You're so single minded, Eldith." Lilith shrugged, before taking her sister's hand and skipping off down the road.

***

Guardian Angel by David Trebus

The shower helped to cool Michael's head a little, decreasing the risqué images a little bit but not stopping them entirely. He took the opportunity to shave and wash, no point in looking sloppy.

As he stepped out of the bathroom, Michael smelled something coming from the kitchen. Jasmine must have woken up and decided to make herself some breakfast. Did Guardians actually need to eat? He'd find out soon.

He shut the bathroom door behind him and ambled over to the kitchen to find the source of the delicious smell. He walked through to the living room, tripping over a small box he had left out. In the kitchen, Michael was met with a surreal sight.

Jasmine stood near the table, wearing a green apron over her usual regalia of white robes. It had been a gift from Michael's mother but, not being one for housework, he had never bothered to wear it. The table had been set neatly, laid out with cutlery and a glass of orange juice next to a plate.

"Morning. I thought I would fix you some breakfast while you were in the shower," Jasmine's usual chirpy voice tinged with nerves.

"Uh...thanks. Aren't you making yourself some?" Michael asked as he sat down.

"Don't be silly, we don't need to eat. Well not unless we want to," Jasmine had made him a traditional English breakfast, placing it in front of him with an expectant look.

The sight of it made Michael salivate, he hadn't been cooked for

Guardian Angel by David Trebus

since he lived at home. He hungrily shoveled the food down. The toast was fine, lightly buttered and tasty, but when Michael got to the cooked foods, the taste was something akin to charred rat.

Jasmine beamed at him from across the table, watching him eat and clearly waiting for an opinion of her cooking skills. Michael's first thought had been *"Don't give up your day job,"* but he couldn't find the cruelty to say such a thing. Instead, he forced down his mouthful of food, and tried not to pull a face.

"How is it?" Jasmine asked, leaning forward.

"Yeah… it's great... Really tasty," Michael managed, finishing off the toast and staring at the rest of the meal, while worrying about how he could avoid eating it.

"Oh great!" Jasmine squealed enthusiastically. "I'm so happy you like it. I made sure to use loads of Earth spices in it. Tons of pepper, salt, cinnamon, garlic and sugar! I haven't really cooked before, but I knew I could do it."

Michael smiled and nodded, he would probably have to eat more of the offensive mishmash to avoid hurting Jasmine's feelings. He managed another bite, this time of bacon, trying to stifle a retch from the flavour. He pushed the plate away slightly and rubbed his stomach, drinking deeply of his orange juice. Thankfully Jasmine had not decided to spice his drink up any.

"Finished already?" Jasmine asked.

"Yeah, I'm not very hungry just yet. Perhaps I could cook us something later, or we could go out to eat!" Michael tried to be

Guardian Angel by David Trebus

subtle but was aware of sounding a little strained.

"Oh, ok. Well, I guess that's understandable after everything. Hope you enjoyed it!"

"It was definitely unique, Jasmine. Excuse me a moment, I just need to go to the loo," Michael muttered as his stomach clenched from all the pepper. He jumped up and left the table. He had to teach Jasmine a little about human cooking, or at least keep her away from the kitchen.

***

After he had gone, Jasmine pulled Michael's plate over with a puzzled look on her face. She sniffed it, then took a cautious bite of some egg with a little bacon. Her face twisted into a mirror image of Michael's when he had first tasted the food. She managed to swallow her creation but took a sip of the remaining orange juice to wash the taste away.

"Humans really do have some strange tastes," Jasmine commented, oblivious to her culinary failure.

***

Guardian Angel by David Trebus

Following Jasmine's dodgy breakfast, Michael got dressed and decided to pop out for a walk. Right on cue, just as he was about to leave, his mother called to check up on him. With not much to say beyond "I'm fine." and the usual "How are you?" the conversation didn't keep him too long. He wanted to discuss his recent special situation but felt it best not to. His mum would probably think he was crazy.

Michael had no work and wasn't meeting Claire until the next day. He felt at a loose end with not much to do, and so, like every time he felt that way he went out. Naturally, Jasmine went along as well, after having disposed of her breakfast feast into the bin. She almost forgot to take off the green apron. Would people see the apron floating around on its own? . She took it off, though, and left it in the house before Michael could ask.

As they walked along the road, Michael noticed a kind of tension between them. Jasmine would have previously grabbed and held Michael's hand. This time, she seemed to pointedly avoid even brushing up against him, though he felt somehow she wanted to. Michael thought of making the move himself, but a pang of nerves struck him every time he thought about it. He felt like a teenage boy trying to ask out a girl he liked.

It didn't help either that the x-rated images kept flashing into his mind. He couldn't work out where they were coming from; he certainly didn't remember having such vivid thoughts before about any girl, even those he fancied like crazy. It felt as if he and Jasmine had grown much closer but had somehow hit a wall, or pushed past the comfortable friendship zone and into something deeper.

Michael decided to head down to the High Street. He couldn't be bothered travelling further afield and certainly didn't fancy the idea of getting onto a crowded bus or train. It wasn't that far and he was looking forward to the mundane routine of browsing through some shops for goodies like dvd's or food. A taste of normality was just what he needed.

Many of the guardians around people looked normal, hovering close with a look of care or concern on their faces. However, Michael also noticed a large proportion of angels who seemed haggard or worried. This made him feel a little on edge himself. Their charges looked normal however, none of them seemed particularly aggressive, angry or evil, but then the old adage "*Looks can be deceiving*," sprang into his mind.

As they walked, more and more guardians appeared distressed. On instinct, he checked Jasmine was okay. Aside from the strangeness between them, she looked fine. However, the worry didn't diminish. Something strange was definitely going on, he could sense it.

Michael hurried along the street, feeling he should run but having nowhere to escape to. He bumped into someone at the edge of the road, stopping him in his tracks. He made a quick apology and took a deep breath to calm himself down. "Panicking won't do me any good, there's nothing going on, just relax." He muttered under his breath.

Something was familiar about this place. He was standing only a few feet away from where the accident happened. The accident that had changed his world completely, that had allowed him to meet Jasmine for the first time. All around him, worn-out angels moved with their charges. The sense of worry exploded into full-blown anxiety as his instincts took over. Something was very wrong here.

Michael began to shake and had to shut his eyes and clench his fists to keep control. He must be having a panic attack brought on by the overwhelming sense of wrongness around him. The thought that the accident must have had an ulterior motive behind it, beyond just himself, made him sick.

***

Jasmine saw her charge suffering and hesitated for a moment, remembering how she felt whenever she touched him now. She had already broken so many rules as well as letting Michael down so many times. Instead of spurring her forward, it kept her from comforting him. She swallowed hard, not sure what was troubling

Guardian Angel by David Trebus

Michael, but hearing a discordant note in the heavenly symphony which seemed to spring from the site of the accident.

Jasmine fought with herself, trying to gain control. She felt confused and, for the first time, truly lost. She reached out again but hesitated, her hand pulling back at the last moment, and only fuelled her guilt and despair. Desire built within her, unholy desire for her charge adding itself into the maelstrom of her feelings.

Then a clear note sounded in the symphony, a single note played from on high by Metatron on his harp. It pierced through the frenzy in Jasmine's mind, and she felt better. A passage Metatron had quoted sprung into her mind *"There is no greater gift one can give another than love."*

Jasmine's head cleared and she reached out, grasping Michael's hand. She pulled close, hugging him tightly and whispering a soothing song into his ear. She couldn't believe she had left the most precious person suffering because she was scared of her own feelings.

"Im so sorry, Michael, I promise I will always protect and….love you," Jasmine whispered with newfound conviction and certainty into Michael's ear.

Tears streamed down Jasmine's cheeks as all her barriers finally fell. All the walls of discipline, all the control developed during decades of service. Her hold over the emotions inside gone in an instant. She finally understood Jazen's situation and, for the first time, doubted the divine wisdom behind the restrictions on a

Guardian Angel by David Trebus

guardians feelings. She felt stronger where previously she had been paralyzed. Jasmine's love for her charge gave her strength and determination. What was wrong with that?

Jasmine could see Michael relaxing. He seemed calmer, less stressed. He shakily raised his hands and embraced Jasmine back.

Before Jasmine could react, he kissed her their lips meeting with what felt like an electric charge. Jasmine didn't pull away; instead she tightened her embrace, pouring all her love through the physical contact they shared. She stood there , locked in a lovers embrace while the world seemed to slow to a crawl around her.

Eventually Michael broke the kiss and took a step back with his hands on Jasmine's shoulders, looking into her eyes. He smiled at Jasmine nervously, even as she mirrored it back.

"I love you too," Michael whispered in a gentle voice only Jasmine could hear.

"I promise to always keep you safe, Michael. Not just as your guardian, but as someone who truly loves you."

"I know. Somehow even, though I've only known you for a few weeks, it feels like I've known you for years, it feels like this was meant to be."

"Well you have known me for years in a way, silly, but I think this really was meant to be."

"Oh, I... uh, well you know what I meant."

Jasmine smiled and took Michael's hand. "Come on, didn't you want to get some shopping done?"

Guardian Angel by David Trebus

***

A palpable aura of light developed around the couple , invisible to human eyes but to every Guardian around blinding in its intensity. The angels close by turned to look at Jasmine and Michael. The aura spread in all directions soothing every Guardian it touched, banishing the weariness from them and leaving them feeling refreshed. The discordant note in the symphony however continued to chime, unrelenting even in the face of newborn love.

***

Garamond reclined in his throne, free of a possessed body. His wings always felt massively constrained when inhabiting a human, even though the sensation was purely in his mind. Possession was a spiritual act, and as such physical attributes didn't really matter. But still it always felt as if he was cramped.

He took a sip of blood-red wine from a golden goblet at his side, enjoying the taste as he swallowed the spiced liquid. Choosing the Lilith Sisters had been a good move. So far, they had done an excellent job of inflaming passions in Michael and his Guardian, as well as preparing for the next part of his plan. The one thing Garamond couldn't understand was why Heaven had not intervened; that thought vexed him no end.

Also, the purifying light emitted by the newly formed couple had been unexpected. The accident site was supposed to be an unstoppable taint, the location of a spell years in planning, corrupting everything nearby; yet for a time the pair had nullified its effects, reversing some of the damage done to the humans and their Guardians. However, the discord in the symphony remained, so he'd let the matter lie for now. In the end, it wouldn't matter. It should be the last time Michael and Jasmine got to perform such a feat.

Garamond grinned, relishing the corruption and carnage that was yet to come. He would soon have all the pieces in place, and everything was moving steadily towards the culmination of his plans. In the end, he would have the mortal's special power, several new high-powered demons and, after that, the whole world in his sway.

Garamond laughed, his booming voice shaking the room. Every demon in Garamond's lair felt their lord's joy and took up his laugh themselves, knowing that the time for corruption, sin, unfettered decadence and war was near.

Guardian Angel by David Trebus

***

The shopping trip Michael turned out to be a fairly brief one. they spent some time browsing through CDs, video games, movies and even some models. Michael initially felt embarrassed, taking a girl into what many regarded as a nerdy shop. Then again, Jasmine had been with him in such places all his life, and he had nothing to hide.

They strolled down the High Street, popping in and out, but Michael grew tired pretty quickly. Anyway, as nice it was doing something normal, it just didn't hold the same appeal anymore. After an hour or so, he'd finished browsing and bought some food and a movie before suggesting they head home.

To add fuel to Michael's desire to cut the trip short, grey clouds, threatening rain were building. Were those rumbles of thunder in the distance? The change in weather seemed quite sudden, but this was England after all.

Jasmine looked at the clouds thoughtfully, before turning to face Michael.

"You know, there may be consequences for what I've done. I used to think Jaden was such a fool, until I experienced the same with you."

"Do you think the clouds are a sign that someone's angry at us?" Weren't there Bible stories about that kind of thing?

Guardian Angel by David Trebus

Jasmine pulled a face and shook her head.

"Don't be so silly. You've been watching too many movies. The clouds up there are the clouds up there. They do what they do because of moisture building and weather systems. If something truly biblical were to happen, or I had transgressed massively, there would be a much stronger sign of it."

"Oh… ok." Michael looked back at the clouds as a few spots of rain began to fall.

"It makes me wonder, though. I should have received a summons for what I did earlier, or have felt some kind of disturbance at least. I broke one of the biggest rules we have, and…well, nothing's happened."

"Maybe they are making an exception for us; I mean, our situation is far from normal."

"Maybe... I hope so! But I'm not so sure. There's a lot going on here behind the scenes we don't know about," Jasmine smiled warmly. "I guess all we can do is keep having faith that things will work out, and keep trying our best."

"Sounds like good advice to me."

He had forgotten where they were standing, just outside a shop on a side street. Not many people were about, but some had noticed him talking as if to himself. A young couple laughed as they walked past, while a woman with children gave him a wide birth. She must have thought that he was some kind of lunatic.

Flustered and embarrassed, Michael leaned in closer to Jasmine

Guardian Angel by David Trebus

to whisper.

"Definitely think it's time we were going home. If I stand here much longer talking to you in the open, someone's going to get me locked up in a looney bin."

Jasmine laughed and took Michael's hand. "Let's get out of here, before the heavens open. Pardon the joke."

"Pretty lame." Michael commented, and Jasmine playfully punched his arm.

They made it back to Michael's house in record time. The rain had started as a drizzle but soon built up into a thundery downpour, catching Michael and Jasmine mid-journey. They ran through the rain, but Michael still couldn't avoid getting wet. Jasmine, however, avoided getting wet entirely.

The rain fell around her, the drops bending their trajectory to miss touching her. It created an odd image: raindrops falling vertically, then suddenly changing direction away from Jasmine. Michael envied her ability, the rain showing him no such mercy. By the time they reached his doorway, he was soaking wet, water dripping from his hair and clothing in large, heavy drops.

"You'll have to teach me how to do that one day. The rain thing I mean," Michael said as he searched for his keys.

"Sorry, it's an angelic secret." Jasmine replied playfully "Angels only!"

"Fine, then. Best make sure I take an umbrella next time, or hide under your dress." Michael opened the door.

Guardian Angel by David Trebus

"You definitely won't be doing that, young man. Stop making jokes and get inside before you end up ill. I don't fancy having to nurse your snotty nose again, like I had to last year. I never knew a man could produce so much goo!" Jasmine gestured for Michael to go first.

"Blimey, I had forgotten all about that. I remember my nose drying up suddenly one night, so I could actually get to sleep. Was that you?"

"Yup. I couldn't watch you suffer any longer, so I sang a short soothing song to help you." "Well, thank you. That night's sleep was the only thing that got me through work the next day."

Michael took off his dripping coat and hung it over the radiator. His shoes were soaked through, like all good trainer brands, they seemed to act like sponges, and he left them by the door to dry out. Jasmine went off to the bathroom, returning quickly with a towel which she threw over to Michael. He nodded in thanks and tried and dry himself off as best he could, shivering all the while.

"I think it's time for a warm shower. I won't be long; will you be ok waiting?"

Jasmine laughed. "Don't be silly. I've waited so many times before, I won't start minding now. Stop being so formal with me. Nothing's changed between us, other than we know how each other feels. Let's just take everything else as it comes and try to act normal, okay?"

Michael nodded feeling sheepish. "Ok, sorry. I just go into a different mode with this kind of thing. I'll try to keep it normal."

"Don't try, silly, just do it. Now go have your shower," Jasmine pushed Michael towards the bathroom and shut the door behind him.

***

Once she heard the shower start up, Jasmine knelt on the living room floor and shut her eyes. The thought that she hadn't been summoned troubled her. She had definitely transgressed, and under normal circumstances she would at least be called to account for what she had done.

She released her wings, letting them spread out in a glow of golden light. She connected herself to the Symphony and listened to the music. The same slightly discordant note played in the background, but nothing seemed amiss. No messages or songs came asking for her to return on high.

Jasmine listened for a good twenty minutes, probing and even adding a short song of her own in the hope of a response. All she got in return was the standard *everything is normal, continue as you are* reply. Eventually, sensing Michael would be done soon, she folded her wings back inwards and stood shaking her head in confusion.

Guardian Angel by David Trebus

She didn't want to risk a trip on high and leave Michael unattended, with everything that had been happening. If the Heavens had chosen not to take action, then there was nothing wrong at least for now. Any consequences could be dealt with later. She uttered a silent prayer on high, then sat down on the sofa to wait for Michael to finish his shower.

He emerged from the bathroom with his hair dripping and a towel wrapped around his waist. Jasmine couldn't help but blush at the sight. This was confusing, as she had seen a lot more of Michael's body and had experienced no reaction or emotion. Things had changed, though. Rather than just seeing him as a human to be protected, she now saw Michael as a partner, a lover to be cherished. Unaccustomed feelings again pushed past Jasmine's emotional barriers, and she looked down at her feet, her face bright red.

Michael stammered "Oh shit." He seemed to realise the state he had come out in. He retreated out of Jasmine's sight, and returned a few minutes later in jeans and a t-shirt looking a little embarrassed. "Sorry Jasmine, force of habit, you know. Let me cook us up some dinner to make up for it."

She raised her eyes slowly, trying to purge the image of her half-naked charge from her mind. An unfamiliar lust had crept over her when she had seen him, both exciting and deeply troubling. Love and emotion were treacherous things, Jasmine thought. She could see how it could easily lead from innocent intentions into sin.

Guardian Angel by David Trebus

"That would be great. Do you need any help?"

"Uh, no, it's ok. You just relax." Michael replied quickly, before going into the kitchen.

They didn't talk while Michael prepared the meal, Jasmine in her own thoughts. He made a simple pasta dish with tomato sauce, ham and cheese, and quickly set the table.

The silence continued as the pair ate, Jasmine savouring the tastes and textures of the meal. She caught herself making "*mmm*" noises on a couple of occasions and smiled when Michael noticed. She had not indulged much in human food, not needing it for sustenance. But she was capable of eating and enjoyed the tastes regardless.

"Thank you, that was lovely!" Jasmine leaned back in her chair and patted her belly playfully.

"Ahh it was nothing. I didn't realise how hungry I was until I started eating." Michael cleared up the plates and bunged them in the dishwasher, leaving the rest of the mess. Jasmine assumed he couldn't be bothered and would do it later.

"Well, thank you anyway, I still enjoyed it. I don't eat human food much and it was a nice change."

"You're welcome, then. I had forgotten you don't eat; I did it on instinct. I always try to cook for girlfr...... friends!" Michael trailed off. Why he couldn't say the dreaded G word?

Jasmine blushed again, feeling like a schoolkid. She decided enough was enough and suppressed her emotions again. She couldn't afford to get giddy and awkward during every conversation. She was a Guardian, and despite how she felt, her first duty was to protect her charge.

"Michael, you know things are only going to get more dangerous from now on. Everything that has been happening will only get worse. You need to be careful from now on, even tomorrow." Jasmine spoke in a harsher tone than she meant. It was frustrating, being unable to control her feelings.

The sudden change caught Michael off guard. Jasmine seemed to turn from a normal girl to a cold Guardian at the touch of a button. Then again, she was a girl, in the end; after all, changing moods and minds was a "lady's prerogative". The hot and cold treatment put him on edge, as he could not work out how to behave around her. Were they growing closer? Or still in the limbo of an undecided path.

"I understand." Michael replied. He looked annoyed but Jasmine ignored it.

"That's good, then." Jasmine felt her charge's mood change, but tried to maintain her formal manner. Her previous behaviour the blushing, the stammering was so inappropriate. She had admitted her feelings to Michael and meant it, but her job came first. Getting all lovey-dovey was as bad as being distant; both were distractions that could get her charge hurt.

The contradictions and the warring thoughts and feelings inside Jasmine threatened to emerge in laughter. Here she was in love

Guardian Angel by David Trebus

with her charge, wanting nothing more than to embrace him; the biggest taboo, one she had already broken many times. And now she was rejecting those very feelings to retain her focus, and because she was…afraid of them.

The conversation stalled after that. Michael finished and went to catch up on his emails. Jasmine, meanwhile, decided to go and sit on the tree outside Michael's home. She had spent a lot of time there since he moved in, watching Michael, watching the world and staring at the heavens.

Michael waited up, sitting on the computer, watching T.V. and even cleaning. By midnight, he looked and turned off the computer. Jasmine saw him look out of the window a few times hoping to catch her eye, but she ignored him.

Michael got straight into bed without bothering to change his clothing. He missed the feeling of the previous night, with Jasmine lying next to him. He shut his eyes slowly, sleep came quickly, and before he knew it, Michael was dreaming again, as Jasmine sat in the cool night air watching the heavens.

Chapter 7: Beginning of the End

Friday morning came with a dark, cloud-filled sky. Small spots of light rain pattered against Michael's bedroom window, running down in slim transparent lines. The tree where Jasmine sat the previous night was now empty, rustling in the wind. Jasmine had come in a few hours after Michael went to bed.

She'd waited on purpose until he was asleep, giving her time to think. No matter how hard she tried though, she could not make up her mind what to do. The rational side of her mind warred with her newly awakened emotions. She loved Michael, she couldn't deny it, but she was also his Guardian and, more importantly, an Angel. She had to be above such things.

Jasmine's thoughts had turned to the Grigori and their interactions with humans. They had taken lovers, grown close to humanity, but in the end it led to disaster. From what Jasmine had read, though, it created a lot of good for both the mortal realm and the Heavens. The results of the Grigori's close relationship with humanity could have ended very differently.

Eventually, Jasmine just gave up. She was unable to decide what to do, and sitting outside wouldn't do her any good. There were even more reasons now, than before to stay close to Michael, but she also needed to retain her focus. Her love for hm could be a big benefit but, in a bad situation, could also get him seriously hurt.

Jasmine crawled in through the window and sat by Michael's side, singing softly to him as he slept, trying to calm herself as much as her charge. Looking at him sleeping serenely made her feel warm inside, until he farted in his sleep and she had to poke him hard as punishment.

As false dawn came, Jasmine left Michael and went into the living room, where she sat down on the sofa and watched the sun rise. While the lazy glow of dawn came, casting a red haze, a bank of ominous dark clouds rolled in from the west. Jasmine watched the weather change with a growing sense of unease and concern.

Weather changed suddenly in England often, but the deep dark of these clouds seemed unnatural. They were an omen, a sign of bad things to come. Jasmine shut her eyes and muttered a silent prayer. Friday was going to be a dark day.

***

Michael awoke with a start to the sound of rain splattering against his window. Faint light filtered through the thin curtains as he blinked sleep from his eyes. Looking over at the clock out of habit, he saw that it was already past midday. He had slept through the entire morning.

What had he been dreaming about? All he could remember was the sound of singing and images of the previous day's events. Everything since his accident seemed to be happening at an amazingly fast pace. One moment he had been a normal guy going to work, the next he was in a world of supernatural beings and biblical events. Thinking about it so soon after waking up made him dizzy.

After a few moments, Michael pushed the covers off and stood up. He stretched his muscles and yawned deeply, glancing out of the window at the dark sky, and the tree where Jasmine had sat; but she was no longer there.

Staggering into the bathroom and cleaning himself up before getting dressed, he made his way into the living room to be met by the sight of Jasmine lying asleep on the sofa. She lay curled up with her wings behind her head like a cushion. Michael had thought that guardians didn't sleep, but before him lay evidence to the contrary.

He couldn't help but stare for a few moments at the cute image. "If only I had a camera." Though all the picture would show was an empty sofa

Michael made his way quietly into the kitchen, trying not to awaken the sleeping angel. He poured himself some juice, grabbed a slice of bread and sat down opposite the sofa on a small chair, watching Jasmine sleeping. He ate his breakfast, unable to take his

Guardian Angel by David Trebus

eyes off her.

In sleep, she looked even more beautiful than awake. All of the worry and discipline had fallen away from her face, leaving her looking younger and carefree. She was serene and comfortable, her eyes shut and her mouth slightly open as she breathed softly. Her wings rustled slightly as she slept.

After an hour or so, Jasmine sat bolt upright with a yelp. She startled Michael who had after a while moved over to his computer. "Are you ok?" Michael asked.

Jasmine stared at him for a moment, a confused look on her face. She stretched her wings cautiously checking them, before leaning back and relaxing.

"I think so. Was I…sleeping?"

"Uhh, yeah, you were. It's something most people do when they get tired."

"I am not a person, Michael, I am an angel. We don't need to take naps." Jasmine used a voice that might have been reserved for ignorant children.

"Oh, well, perhaps you're just going native, too much time spent on Earth. That or you're ill. Do angels get unwell?"

"Maybe. I mean, it does happen occasionally that we need to go dormant under a lot of pressure, or after expending a lot of energy. I suppose it could have been that. It feels bizarre, though. It has never happened to me before." Jasmine looked thoughtfully out of the window.

Guardian Angel by David Trebus

"Did you dream?" Michael asked.

Jasmine hesitated for long moments while Michael sat awkwardly. Was she hiding something? Did she have a nightmare? Jasmine shuddered and whispered something under her breath, before finally replying.

"No, we don't dream, even when dormant. The closest we come is during meditations on High. We get visions from the Almighty, or prophesies conveyed through imagery."

"Oh, that must suck a bit," Michael replied. Jasmine's expression seemed so severe, he felt he had to do something to lighten to the mood.

"I like dreaming; even the bad ones can sometimes be interesting. But I suppose being an angel has other advantages, the flying for one."

"I don't think it's something I would enjoy," said Jasmine.

Michael nodded, feeling awkward. He stood up and went to the kitchen to make himself a proper breakfast, now Jasmine was awake. As he busied himself breaking eggs, preparing cutlery and frying bacon, Jasmine remained sitting on the edge of the sofa, staring out of the window with a grim look on her face.

Michael again found himself confused and unsure what to do. They had grown so close so quickly, and he could tell something was wrong. However, Jasmine had pulled away from him, either from fear or concern. Trying to work it through in his mind, threatened to bring on a headache . The best thing for now was to just try and act normally, hoping things would sort themselves out in time.

"Do you want some?" Michael asked before thinking.

Jasmine cocked her head to one side quizzically before replying. "Uhh, yeah, why not? No meat, though." She stood up.

"For a moment, I thought you were going to pull a face and say Angels don't eat."

"We don't need to, but we can eat when we want. Right now, I feel like I could use the energy." Jasmine glided over and took a seat at the table.

***

A thought struck Jasmine. The symphony sounded quieter than usual. angels didn't need to eat or sleep, they gained all their energy from on High, through the Eternal Symphony. But, ever since she had heard that discordant note, the Symphony had seemed distant and less potent than before. She remembered the other guardians she had seen at the site of Michael's accident. They had seemed worn and tired, until she and Michael had banished their fatigue, at least temporarily.

From the look on Michael's face, he was thinking along similar lines, but had decided, like her, not to voice those thoughts out

Guardian Angel by David Trebus

loud. Instead, he served Jasmine a simple breakfast of toast, mushrooms, tomatoes and hash browns. All the making of an unhealthy English breakfast, minus the meat. That part Michael reserved for himself: eggs, bacon and sausage.

They ate in silence, both lost in their respective thoughts. Jasmine nibbled tentatively at her meal but, before she knew it, was taking large bites. The food tasted good, better than the ambrosia-covered fruit she had eaten on High, better even than Metatron's famous spiced bread. The food banished her tiredness, and slowly Jasmine felt a little more energized. She cleaned her plate before Michael had even half finished.

Michael looked up and grinned, making Jasmine blush in embarrassment. She hid it by taking a long swig from her orange juice before settling down to watch her charge eat. Pangs of emotion welled up again, threatening to overwhelm her judgment. Gratitude and love seeped into her being unbidden; all she felt like doing was embracing her charge. Jasmine shoved the feelings down, suppressing them with all her will and training. Now was not the time to be acting like a love-struck teenager. Something big was happening, and keeping Michael safe had to come first.

She reached a decision. Jasmine did not want to leave Michael's side, but she needed guidance desperately. When Michael left to see Claire, she would go on high and seek some answers. She would find the Metatron and request an audience with the Almighty.

Guardian Angel by David Trebus

The thought struck her as impertinent. As a rule, no angel simply barged in and asked to talk to God; they spoke to him through the Metatron or, in rare cases, were summoned by the Almighty. Jasmine had to know what to do though, as well as why no action had been taken against her.

Jasmine had broken countless rules in the last few days, and yet there had been no summons, no warnings, nothing but the usual song of the symphony. Again she wondered about that discordant note that kept playing again and again, disrupting the perfect balance of the heavenly choir. She had to find out the reason for that.

Jasmine found it difficult to leave Michael alone even for a moment, but things couldn't continue as they were. She rationalized by remembering that she could return to Earth at a moment's notice be by her charge's side. In any case, Jazen would be there to protect him when Michael arrived at Claire's. She couldn't escape the fact though, that the decision was partly selfish. Jasmine needed to know what to do; she could not stand being unsure of the path in front of her.

Michael finished his meal, while Jasmine pondered and stared at him. He had always been a slow eater; rushing his food tended to lead to stomach aches. She could see that it made him feel uncomfortable, but was too engrossed in her thoughts to care.

After a while, Michael got up to do the dishes. He picked up the plates and cutlery, rinsed them off and placed them in the dishwasher. Jasmine's musings were finally broken by the clang and clatter of pots and pans and she looked up.

"Michael… when you go to visit Claire, I am going to return on High." Jasmine's tone was a little guilty.

"Oh, ok." Michael replied, looking disappointed. "Didn't you want to check on Jazen while we were there? It's a shame you're not coming."

"I'm sure he's doing fine. He is impulsive and very attached to Claire, but he seemed to take my warning seriously." Jasmine replied feeling a bit hypocritical.

"Ok, how come you're returning? Has something happened? I've noticed you've been looking and acting a bit…distracted since last night."

Returning to the table, he sat down and reached out his hand in a gesture of comfort, but Jasmine stood up and walked over to the window. Michael withdrew his hand quickly, looking a little awkward. Jasmine stood with her back to him watching the rain, a pained look on her face. It was because of their recently intimacy. She had told Michael angels suppressed their feelings and weren't supposed to grow close to their charges.

After a pause, Jasmine answered Michael's question. "I need to get some answers about what's happened and get some information. I also need to check that I'm….following the right path."

Michael sighed deeply and leaned back in his chair. "Well you gotta do what you gotta do."

Guardian Angel by David Trebus

"Thank you, Michael. I promise I will be back as soon as I can." At that moment all Jasmine wanted to do was reach out for her charge, but she suppressed the urge with one strong push of will. "If it's OK with you, I would like to spend some time in meditation before I leave. Can I use your room? Do you need me for anything?"

"No, there's nothing I need in there, so feel free to use it. I won't disturb you." Michael replied shifting awkwardly. He looked like he wanted to say no, make up an excuse for her to stay, but Jasmine had made up her mind.

Jasmine stood up and walked over to his bedroom door, hesitating at the threshold. She looked back at her charge and was again overwhelmed by a surge of feelings, some of them less savoury than mere affection. She violently quelled the aberrant emotions, bunching up her fists and shutting her eyes tightly. The mere thought of lust at a time like this made Jasmine feel disgusted at herself.

She pushed through the bedroom door and slammed it shut behind her. Jasmine took a deep breath to master herself, then sat cross legged on Michael's bed. The cool sheets felt good against her skin as she shut her eyes and began humming softly. A light breeze blew in through the window bringing a faint smell of rain.

Jasmine imagined the breeze cooling the raging fires in her soul, the rain putting out the flames as it pattered outside and against the partially open window. Her thoughts kept turning back to her

Guardian Angel by David Trebus

charge, but little by little Jasmine regained her composure and detachment. She listened to the symphony, ignoring the bizarre note that kept playing in discord to the whole. The sound soothed her further, and her breathing steadied to a slow rhythm.

Jasmine remained in a meditative state all morning and most of the afternoon. She was dimly aware of Michael's activities outside. He watched some television, took a couple of phone calls from his parents and confirmed his visit to Claire later on that day. A pang threatened to disrupt Jasmine's cool when Michael was speaking to Claire, but it was easy to suppress in her relaxed state.

Eventually, she heard Michael go to take a shower and decided that she was ready to leave. Jasmine had originally intended to say goodbye and let Michael know she was leaving, but when the time came, she couldn't face leaving the room. The comfort of being as she used to, without confusion, was too much to disturb and , even though it was an unangelic act of selfishness, Jasmine decided to just leave without a word. She could always apologise later when she returned.

Jasmine shifted her position until she was kneeling and pressed her palms together. She raised her head to the heavens, letting her hair fall about her slender shoulders. She shut her eyes and let her wings slowly spread out behind her. Her wingtips stretched and lightly brushed the ceiling. Jasmine sang softly, touching her feathers together and slowly opening the portal to the heavens. She stood up, hesitating at the last moment.

Guardian Angel by David Trebus

"Goodbye, Michael, I promise I'll be back soon," she murmured, unable to go without saying something, even if it was just to the rain outside. She beat her wings once, propelling her into the portal. The ring of light shut just as a knock came on the door.

***

Outside the window, two women leaned against the tree Jasmine had sat on the previous night. The rain fell all around, but not a drop touched them; the Lilith Sisters never did like to get their makeup smudged. They smiled up at Michael's apartment as Jasmine departed, satisfied with the results so far. They walked away slowly, rain falling around them, to prepare the finale for their master.

***

Michael felt awful by the time he was making ready to leave for Claire's. Jasmine had left without even a single word of goodbye, just like all those times a girl he had been dating changed her mind or found someone else, leaving him in the lurch.

Guardian Angel by David Trebus

Even knowing that wasn't the case here, couldn't stop him being hurt and very confused by Jasmine's recent behaviour. She had been with him all his life, and caring for him. Being able to see her had only strengthened their bond, forming into a friendship and even something more.

Over the last day or two, though, Jasmine's actions had become erratic: one moment deeply affectionate, the next cold and distant. Obviously the situation between them was anything but normal, but still the way she acted was giving him headaches. A little consistency would have been nice.

The days since his accident had been a rollercoaster of new discoveries, experiences and emotions, a very confusing and scary rollercoaster, with big highs and deep lows. Somehow, Michael couldn't imagine his life the way it used to be, mundane and boring. Just going to work, coming home, going to the pub and watching telly seemed pointless. w Even with all the confusion and fear in his life now, he didn't want to return to how it had been, and he didn't want to let go of Jasmine and his feelings for her, either.

Taking a deep breath, Michael stood up straight and looked himself over in the mirror. "Things will work out, I just know they will," he said to himself. "I can get through anything if I try." The words had become a kind of mantra whenever he faced difficult times. Even when he was back in school he had said those words and drawn strength from them.

Guardian Angel by David Trebus

For all his sometimes sullen and apathetic nature, deep down Michael cared a lot about the world around him, and he didn't have it in him to give up, no matter what happened. It was a part of him that served as a double edged sword. A few times in the past, when trying to raise extra money, or help a friend, he had pushed himself too hard. It was a part of himself he was proud of, and was sure would help him through now.

His mantra spoken and his appearance taken care of (the look in the mirror serving a double purpose) Michael decided he might as well leave for Claire's. It was still a little early, but waiting for Jasmine to return seemed like a forlorn hope.

Michael hesitated at the doorway, hoping that Jasmine might return, even though he knew it wasn't going to happen; he sighed after a couple of minutes and shut the door. As he left the house, Michael looked up at the tree by his window. He remembered the morning when his life changed, the day of the accident. It had been bright and sunny, nothing like this grey, rainy day. Hunching his shoulders and pulling his coat tight around him, Michael hurried down the road to the bus-stop, hoping to catch a bus before the rain got any worse.

His luck was not holding that day. The rain turned into a heavy downpour as he made his way down the street. Large drops hammered into the pavement, making small splashes on the paving stones. The world rushed past as Michael ran for the bus-stop. He paid no heed to the various people hurrying around or past him. He

Guardian Angel by David Trebus

didn't even notice their guardians, too focused on getting himself out of the rain. He got a vague sense of unease as he ran, catching brief glimpses of the angels around him. He thought he heard someone shout his name, but he ignored it thinking the person wanted someone else's attention.

Eventually, Michael made it to the stop. Despite running, the journey actually took slightly longer than usual due to the heavy rain. His jacket was soaked, dripping water under the shallow shelter of the bus-stop. A sultry looking woman was the only other person waiting. She wore a revealing, low-cut top and ultra-short skirt, presumably to go out for a night on the town. He tried not to stare but found himself stealing guilty glances at the woman. There was no guardian around her. Had her angel abandoned her too? Was she just like him?

After a few minutes, the bus turned up. Michael got on board, paying his fare. The driver gave him a dirty look for dripping water into the bus but Michael ignored it. If anything, the few drops from his coat would clean the dank and dirty interior of the London bus, not add to it. As he found his seat, Michael cast a glance outside. The woman had not moved from her position leaning against the shelter.

As he looked at her, she bent down low to reveal her cleavage and winked at him with a huge grin. Michael felt himself blushing and turned away on nervous instinct. He thought guiltily about Jasmine, but still couldn't help but cast a second glance as the bus

Guardian Angel by David Trebus

pulled off. Who was that woman, and why was no guardian was with her? It occurred to him she could have been in a similar situation to him.

***

Back at the bus stop the Eldith straightened, grinning. She had taken great care with her makeup and appearance before setting out to wait for Michael. Her sister had only told her to wait at the bus stop until he arrived, but Eldith liked any excuse to get dressed up and bring a little lust into boring mortals lives.

She had even taken a short break when a moderately attractive man had shown an interest in her. Taking him to a quiet alley, she had satisfied his desires twice before consuming his soul and leaving his spent husk to wither on the ground. His guardian had been powerless, watching helplessly as the man was consumed by his own lusts. The man had not been truly corrupt, though, just a little stupid and lonely and his angel too pure. A pity, Eldith would have loved to add another succubus to the infernal ranks.

When Michael arrived, she was careful to subdue her demonic nature. The spell was a difficult one, but one her sister had drummed it into her over the centuries. She found the mortal curious. He was average looking, skinny and dressed normally, yet

Guardian Angel by David Trebus

something about him aroused her interest and, when he looked at her, a slight shiver passed through her. If Garamond did succeed in turning him to their side, she would spare some time to find out just how he could perform.

Best of all, his angel was absent. What was her name again? Jasmine? It didn't really matter to Eldith anyway. Their plan had obviously worked even better than expected. The spell they had infested Jasmine with through Michael must have worked like a charm, sowing confusion between them and kindling doubt, and a tiny spark of darkness within Jasmine. Eldith smiled and pulled out her mobile, dialing her sister's number.

"Hello, Eldith dear." Lilith's voice chimed through the small phone, "Why are you phoning me when you could just contact me through your mind? Silly girl."

"I thought I would surprise you, dear sister. Besides, why have this marvelous looking little device if I can't even use it a little bit?"

"Awww, Eldith, your fixation on humans and their toys will get you in trouble one day. Anyway, what's up? I felt the tremor of you having fun from here." Lillith sounded a little annoyed.

"I couldn't help myself. I got bored, and a lovely man came along to keep me company. But anyway… Michael arrived as expected; he is on his way to the station now. And you'll love this. His guardian was not with him. We won't even have to separate them now!" Beaming with pride, Eldith noticed a man staring at her, and so leaned over exposing her rear to him. The old man stared,

Guardian Angel by David Trebus

ignoring his wife until she pulled him violently along.

"Excellent work, sister. Now come and join me. I've set things up this end, and I'll make sure everything goes to plan. By this time tomorrow, Hell's legions will have two new allies, and the world will be set to burn." Lilith broke into a giggle as she hung up.

Eldith felt elated and hailed a cab. She couldn't wait until the party started and she would have millions of souls to sate her lusts. But for now she was only looking forward to having one special little soul she could enjoy for eternity.

"Take me to Liverpool Street gorgeous, make it quick" Eldith said as she got into the cab. She would have to hurry if she was going to make Michael's train before it left.

***

The bus journey was uneventful. Michael spent most of it staring out of the window into the pouring rain and thinking about Jasmine. Was she OK? Had she found the answers she was looking for? Her behaviour had become more and more confusing over the last few days, but Michael had just put it down to the odd situation they had been placed in. How many times had he tried to understand and failed miserably?

As the rain beat down against the window and people hurried past outside, Michael's thoughts turned to the woman at the bus stop. She'd had no guardian, but hadn't seemed in any way evil or bizarre, just flirty and very forward. Her guardian must have been hard pressed to keep her safe, considering the way she behaved - assuming she had one.

People filed on and off the bus at the various stops along its route, and Michael continued staring out of the window. Lost in his thoughts, he almost missed his stop. Leaping up, he ran down the aisle and squeezed through the doors as they shut, ignoring the dodgy looks he got.

Without waiting, he ran straight into the station. It was half-past four on Friday and close to the rush hour, the place was heaving with tourists and day trippers returning from seeing the sights of London, shoppers laden with bags after a spell of retail therapy, and workers eager to get home after a long day in the office.

Pushing his way through the throng was a huge task, and Michael quickly found himself tired and irritated. After five minutes of pushing, and being pushed, a determined effort got him to the automated ticket machines. Most as usual were out of order, adding to the lines.

After a further ten minutes and a lot of messing about with convoluted menus and correct change, Michael managed to purchase his ticket. His train was scheduled to depart at 6:20, but he'd believe that when it actually started moving. He still had twenty minutes, but perhaps he should check the timetable

Guardian Angel by David Trebus

anyway.

Braving the press of people, he pushed his way through towards the information board. He had to stop several times as people barged and shoved. At one point, a little girl was knocked over by a passing businessman. Michael instinctively stopped to help her and received a grateful look from her mother, who had been separated from the child. The little girl's guardian also looked grateful, and nodded to Michael. This guardian obviously hadn't heard about Michael's ability and looked stunned when he nodded back and smiled.

As he looked up at the board, the sight took his breath away. Flying above the throng of people was an equally large mass of guardians. With no space down below, most of the angels in the station had taken to the air above where a huge group of them flew around. Michael was awestruck. Hundreds, even thousands of angels, all in one place, all dutifully watching their charges from above. Michael felt a pang of loneliness at that moment, knowing Jasmine was not among them.

Tearing his eyes away from the angels, Michael turned his attention to the board. He was right to doubt the train timetable; his train had been moved forward, due to a previous cancellation, and was scheduled to leave ten minutes early. Looking at his watch, he started running for the platform and pushed through the press in the hopes of not missing his train.

To his surprise, many people cleared from his path, leaving a

Guardian Angel by David Trebus

route all the way to his platform. At the far end, near the entry gates, Michael swore he caught a flash of red, but it must have been blinking light. Above him, the angels stopped moving and all looked towards that platform. Michael dimly heard a few cries of alarm but didn't pay any attention, catching the train was the only thing on his mind.

For once, the barriers didn't hold Michael up, and he managed to jump on the train in the nick of time. The door-closing chime had just finished as Michael squeezed his way onto the last carriage on the train. Trying to catch his breath, Michael couldn't help but grin. "Seems like my luck is finally turning," he whispered to himself.

***

At the other end of the train, two women watched Michael board before stepping back through the doors. "That was a big risk Lilith," Eldith hissed to her sister. "With all those angels up there, we could have been mincemeat."

"It was that or have the whole plan go down the pan because of a stupid train company and a few pesky mortals. It worked out in the end. The spell held, and the guardians couldn't tell who did it."

"Well, it doesn't matter. He's here now. Is everything set up?"

"Yes, dear sister." Lilith Licked her lips. "The driver was nicely

Guardian Angel by David Trebus

distracted while I modified, the brakes, and I trust you saw to the other part of our plan."

"Uhh, you hussy! I wanted the driver, he was cute." Eldith pouted. "But yeah, everything else is set up, it's all sorted."

"Good. Let's stay on here till the stop before, just in case someone screws things up." Lilith brushed a stray strand of hair from her eyes. "The accident has to occur on schedule and look natural, or won't work."

"Oooo, can I have some fun while we wait?" Eldith licked her lips, and eyed a pair of business-men in the next carriage.

"You're so single minded. But sure, go have some fun, just be ready to get off in time. We don't want these bodies getting damaged. We might miss all the fun." Lilith sighed.

Eldith squealed with glee, and skipped off to sit by the business men, leaning forward provocatively as she sat down to expose as much cleavage as possible. Lilith grinned at her sister and, shrugging, walked over to join her. "May as well recharge my batteries, too, while we wait for the show to get started."

***

Jasmine arrived on high later than she expected, her usual ascent turbulent and unsteady. The symphony played in the background, but the discordant note ringing in every verse refused to disappear. It was becoming so annoying, if she could find its source she planned to stop it in a most un-angelic manner.

The clouds on the lower levels had grown as dark and menacing as the earthly clouds. The initial stages of ascension took an angel up into the sky through the portal of light. Jasmine was used to passing dark rain clouds, having been stationed in England ever since Michael was born, but to see dark clouds on the upper plane, was considered a bad omen and a sign of dark things afoot. In fact, the last time Jasmine had seen such clouds had been just before the terror attacks in America.

Eventually, Jasmine left behind the banks of roiling, dark clouds and ascended to calmer planes. She landed softly and let her wings settle against her back as she pushed thoughts of her ascension aside. She also had to fight thoughts of her charge and stay focused on finding some information.

Without a moment's pause, Jasmine headed straight for the Metatron's chambers. She passed groups of angels talking quietly to each other. Most ignored her, but some gave her strange looks of concern. Jasmine pushed on. No time to worry about their expressions.

Up this high, the discordant note was barely noticeable. If she focused on the primary harmonies and sounds she could ignore it entirely. The holy song calmed her as nothing else could and, for the first time in days, she felt as relaxed as before things got

Guardian Angel by David Trebus

complicated. There had been times since Michael's accident that she had almost questioned divine wisdom, why this had to happen to her and her charge. Now, hearing the beautiful song of order, she knew everything was fine.

Jasmine strolled briskly through the cloud-lined promenades and up the golden stairs leading to the Metatron's chambers. She took the stairs two at a time but was stopped short when she reached the top. Outside stood a group of angels in ornate golden armour, all with swords buckled to their waists. The swords glowed with faint, red light, but Jasmine knew, if they were ever drawn, that light would erupt into violent crimson flame.

At their head stood an angel a full head above his subordinates. Above his head a golden halo sat, pulsing with light to show the power of the being it sat upon. His hair was blond and curled, falling to his neck, while piercing blue eyes shone from beneath it. Gabriel, the messenger and sword of retribution.

Gabriel faced Jasmine as she slowed her pace. She couldn't help but bow as his piercing eyes bored into her, examining the very core of her being. The sensation was uncomfortable, and it was as if something were squirming inside her like a snake, writhing and wriggling to stay out of sight.

"What are you doing here, Jasmine of Seraph?" Gabriel demanded, his tone strong and commanding. It had been a long time since Jasmine had been addressed formally, adding her choir to her title. That was usually only done at formal ceremonies. Taken aback,

Guardian Angel by David Trebus

she hesitated a moment but decided to reply in kind.

"Gabriel of Ascendant, I have come to petition the Metatron for answers. I need knowledge to better protect my charge from the harms that assail him." Had that sounded confident enough?

"You do not tell the whole truth, Jasmine of Seraph. You are here as much for your own benefit as your charge's. It is your duty to be concerned solely about him. It is him you should be with, in this time of trials." There was a hint of chastisement in Gabriel's voice.

"I...I...I didn't know what to do, my lord. I needed guidance to find the path to follow," Jasmine stammered. Gabriel had seen right through her intentions. Although what she was doing was not against any rule, she felt scorn from him.

"Regardless, it seems your coming here was not entirely of your own design. It was also foreseen - although a little too late." Ignoring Jasmine's reply, Gabriel casting a sidelong glance at one of his companions, in the robes of one of the Throne choir. Thrones were seers, and closest to the material plane. They were regarded as Heaven's scouts, reading the symphony, observing Earth and the Pit from just outside the physical plane. The angel shifted uncomfortably.

What did Gabriel mean by: "Not entirely of your own design?" Before she could reply the doors to the Metatron's chambers opened. The Metatron stood at the threshold, leaning against one of the doors and looking tired. He glanced first to Gabriel and then to Jasmine, his face full of concern.

Guardian Angel by David Trebus

"It is time, Jasmine of Seraph" Said Gabriel. "Join me in speaking with the Metatron ascendant, and you will gain the knowledge you sought" He held his hand out to gesture Jasmine forward.

She suppressed a surge of anxiety, awed by Gabriel's command, and strode into the Metatron's chambers with as much dignity and poise as she could manage, feeling inside like a frightened human child. Behind her, Gabriel entered with the Throne angel and shut the doors. Metatron stood in the centre of the room.

Once the door had been shut and only Jasmine, Metatron and the Throne were able to hear, Gabriel turned to Jasmine. "First things first. Let us remove that filth from inside of you."

He drew his sword. The blade leapt into flames, filling the chamber with red light. Gabriel pointed it directly at Jasmine and took a step forward, so that the blade hovered mere inches away from Jasmine's head. As sweat poured down her face, Jasmine looked desperately from Metatron, to the Throne and to Gabriel. Metatron's face remained impassive, while Gabriel's was full of righteous fury. Was this her punishment for abandoning her charge? She shut her eyes and prepared for the worst.

Gabriel held the sword there for what seemed hours. He grunted in effort as if wrestling with something powerful.

"This is strong" Gabriel muttered to Metatron. "No wonder she found it so difficult to contain. This child should be commended."

"Can you deal with it? Do you need my assistance?"

"No, I should be quite sufficient to this task," Gabriel replied

Guardian Angel by David Trebus

through gritted teeth.

He raised the burning blade above his head, as if preparing to strike at Jasmine. He held it there poised, closing his eyes and whispering a quiet prayer.

"Taint of darkness, scourge of light
No longer are you welcome
Remove your evil, fade into night
No longer are you welcome
BEGONE"

Gabriel yelled the final word out loud and swept his sword down towards Jasmine. She shut her eyes as a burning heat washed over her, but the blade passed right through her. One moment she felt searing fire, the next cool air. She felt like a burden had been lifted. Her mind was clearer and more focused, as she stood up and faced Gabriel.

Impaled upon his sword, a small, worm-like creature wriggled and writhed. Its mouth was a gaping orifice with sharp teeth, and it screeched and squealed as the burning blade destroyed it. Gabriel scowled at it with barely contained disdain before throwing it to the floor and smashing it.

"Do you mind, Gabriel?" Said Metatron. "These are my private chambers, and I don't really like spell-spawn remains soiling them."

Guardian Angel by David Trebus

Gabriel snorted in reply before allowing himself a small laugh. Both he and Metatron seemed relieved, Metatron's joke breaking the tension.

"What…what was that?" Jasmine managed, confused by what had happened and the Archangels' levity.

"That, Jasmine of Seraph, was a spell-spawn." Gabriel's tone was once again stern. "You were bewitched by a demon's curse. Such things are unusual; it takes a strong demon to place such a spell upon an angel." He glared at Jasmine and was clearly cross about something. Unless of course, Gabriel always seemed that way.

"Jasmine," Metatron said at length, his expression as grave as Gabriel's, "your return here was expected, especially in light of the spell you were subjected to. We need you to return to Michael as soon as possible, as it is probable he is in danger. First, though, Gabriel and I, feel it is time you knew a little more about your charge and the situation in general."

Jasmine steeled herself, and stood up straight facing Metatron. With the spell lifted, her emotional control returned in full force. She suppressed her anxieties, fears, concerns, but one emotion she couldn't entirely push down. Her love for Michael remained, although now in the background rather than screaming in her mind. She nodded to Metatron in assent, anticipating to hear what he had to say.

"You must have noticed by now that your charge is not ordinary, Jasmine." Metatron moved to stand beside Gabriel. "His ability to perceive you and other angels, for example."

"I have. The accident seemed to give him a great deal of perception. I've never heard of anything like it before, and then there were the songs."

"The songs," Gabriel cut in. "A simple accident and a bump on the head could not give a human the ability to sing like an angel and tap into the eternal symphony. We were aware of Michael's ability, even though you neglected to report that aspect to us. Just as we have been aware of your…involvement with your charge, even before the demon spell." There was a note of chastisement in his voice. Jasmine shifted her feet, feeling ashamed of her conduct and weakness. How could she have been so stupid?

"Did you not find it strange" Metatron said, ignoring Gabriel's interruption, "that at certain times Michael has had the ability to help people? A spoken verse here, a dropped hint there, and someone's life would improve."

Jasmine paused for a moment in thought. She did recall odd events as Michael was growing up. Little things that, in isolation, could have been coincidence but, when put together, formed a pattern. Michael's failed relationships had always led to the other party moving on to success and happiness. When he sung a tune that meant something to him, a kind of aura would develop around him. One incident, when Michael was eight, sprang to her mind. He was playing with friends when a girl had an allergic reaction. While her guardian sang desperately for her, Michael ran over crying and held her hand. He hummed softly, apparently without knowing, in time to the angel's song.

Jasmine leant over his shoulder adding her own song when, miraculously, the girl's breathing eased and a steady, golden glow surrounded her. She opened her eyes and smiled up at Michael as he held her hand. At the time, Jasmine and the girl's guardian had looked at each other in relief and dismissed the event, but now Jasmine realised it had been Michael's song that had helped heal the girl.

"I do remember some events. In the past, I paid no real attention to them, but I suppose, they were a lot like what Michael is capable of now, only intermittent."

"Those events occurred because Michael has Grigori blood in his veins." Gabriel stated abruptly.

"Grigori…"

"It is the truth. Michael is descended from the offspring of an angel and a human. We believe it occurred somewhere in the Eighteenth Century. His great-great grandmother bore the child of a Grigori, who escaped our notice until it was too late. The renegade angel fell from grace, leaving the mother to fend for herself. The child showed no aberrant traits and so was left to live and exist as a human. The Almighty himself decreed the child to be assigned a Guardian and left in peace." Metatron paused to take a sip of spiced water.

"It seems," he continued, "that those dormant traits have now

Guardian Angel by David Trebus

awakened several generations down the line in Michael. He, like an angel, has the ability to access the symphony and sing angelic songs to affect the world around him. The accident, it seems made him consciously aware of his abilities, rather than accessing them on a subconscious level. His seeing you, Jasmine, was merely a side effect of that awakening."

"But…surely his abilities must have been noticed on high before now. Also, why was I not told about this when I was assigned to be his guardian?" Gabriel grunted. He must have considered her rude for shouting.

"It was hoped that," Metatron explained, "as his abilities lay dormant, Michael could live a normal human life. Our Lord wants nothing more than for each and every being to live as peaceful an existence as possible. He may not be able to control the actions of other humans, but he can control us and ask us to leave an innocent soul be. The only other option would have been to induct him as a lesser angel; or, worse, bring him on high like the other Grigori offspring before their time."

"You were not informed, Jasmine of Seraph, because you had no need to know." Gabriel's stern tone was at odds with Metatron's reasoned and kind voice. "Your duty was simply to keep him safe, not to interfere with divine mandate."

Jasmine blanched at Gabriel's voice but, with the spell gone and her control restored, she restrained herself and instead bowed low, asking pardon. Her mind was spinning with the revelations, but her instincts were telling her something was wrong. She was missing something obvious about recent events but couldn't put her finger on what.

"Michael is the first human in centuries to be able to sing angelic song and tap into the symphony." Jasmine pulled her attention back as Metatron continued. "He is singular as an individual on Earth. There are many perceptive humans, and probably more Grigori offspring out there also, but Michael, despite his normal appearance, is very special. This is why we believe the Scourge Garamond has taken such an interest in him."

"Garamond....!" Gabriel snorted. "That filth should have been destroyed long ago, by my blade no less, but he cowers and hides, playing through agents."

"Indeed. However, he is still a powerful demon, and his interest in Michael is disturbing. We believe his interest is not Michael's sight, as we first thought, but rather his ability to sing." Metatron paused, letting Jasmine and Gabriel take in the information before he continued. Gabriel stood with his arms folded, glaring at the instruments suspended in the room, while Jasmine tried to wrestle the thought she was missing.

"Imagine the damage Garamond could do to the heavenly hosts if he were able to access the symphony again. When an angel falls, he is cut off from that divine music, that guidance, and is forever bound to the Pit. Never in our history has a fallen angel been redeemed. If Garamond could corrupt Michael, turn his abilities against the heavens, he could attack us through Michael and lay heaven low in one fell swoop."

"Such a thing could never be allowed to happen!" Gabriel shouted, his arrogant composure gone. "I cannot stand the harming of innocent mortals but this Michael must be kept safe. He cannot be allowed to roam free on Earth any longer when he poses such a threat."

"It is divine will that he remains free," Metatron countered. "He is a human, unlike us, and has already done so much good down on the mortal plane. Imagine the further good he could do, if he were allowed to continue."

The two Archangels' voices seem to fade into the distance as Jasmine pondered all that had been said.. Then one word boomed out in her mind, a single word, spoken as if shouted, "Alone."

"Alone," Jasmine murmured as the argument continued. The two Archangels' turned to her, despite her quite voice.

"Jasmine?" Metatron asked.

"I have been such a fool. The attacks on Earth: they weren't meant for Michael, they were meant for me. The only incident that Garamond intended to harm towards Michael was the original road accident, to force the awakening of his abilities. Ever since then, they have been trying to separate me from him. The imp, the attack in the alley, the spell, it was all meant to get me away from him. Oh lord...no...they succeeded. I am such a fool." Everything suddenly made sense to Jasmine.

Guardian Angel by David Trebus

She stood up to her full height and opened her wings. It was forbidden to open portals to Earth in the Metatron's chamber, but she didn't care. There was no time to lose. She flapped her wings once, then opened the glowing ring of light that would allow her to descend into the mortal plane. She sensed Michael down there, but something already felt very wrong. She passed through the portal and rushed down, her wings cast behind her like a swooping hawk.

***

"Putting aside the affront that guardian just perpetrated in front of our eyes, do you think she was right?" Gabriel asked, turning to Metatron.

"Yes, Gabriel, I believe she was." Metatron sighed. "However I also sense it may already be too late."

Gabriel stood beside him, looking out through a small portal in Metatron's chambers. The dark clouds still loomed and a rumble of thunder could be heard in the distance. Gabriel instinctively reached for his sword hilt, and gripped it tightly.

"What does the voice of God command?" Gabriel asked.

"What it always commands: Have Faith," Metatron turned his face to look up.

Guardian Angel by David Trebus

Chapter 8: The Fall

The train ride was as boring as usual for Michael. He hated trains. They always made him feel uncomfortable, mostly due to the odd smells and unreliable nature. The train kept juddering too, which only added to his nerves. Michael found himself staring out the window for things to distract himself and thinking about Jasmine.

Teenagers kept running up and down the train, shouting and swearing, yanking Michael away from his thoughts. "Bet they end up sitting across from me," Michael muttered. To his suprise they congregated at the opposite end of the carriage; it soon became clear why.

"Ticket please," a train guard asked. Michael rummaged through his pockets to find the ticket, and handed it to him. The guard looked it over in great detail before thanking him and walking off into the next carriage. He pointedly ignored the teenagers, obviously looking for easier targets to give fines to.

A woman somehow managed to bump into Michael, interrupting him for a third time and nearly causing him to lose his temper. The woman looked like the girl he had seen at the bus stop, but with longer hair and a more slender figure. She smiled, apologised and went on her way, casting a couple of glances back at him. Why did she make him feel so uneasy? He just couldn't put his finger on it. Michael put it down to feeling guilty for looking at other women when his feelings for Jasmine were so strong.

He glanced around at the people in the carriage. A father sat with his son in the seats directly to his side. In front of him, an elderly couple talked loudly about the failings in society and the public transport system, and a young man stood by the doors with a bike, propping it up between his legs as he read a book. All of these people had their guardians watching over them, unlike him. That was why the woman made him feel uneasy, just like the woman at the bus stop, she had no guardian.

A sense of danger and a pang of anxiety built within his gut. Feeling very exposed without Jasmine, he looked to see if he was nearing his stop. No, he still had three more stops to go, which would be good ten minutes. He stood up just as a juddering tremor ran through the train, followed by the screech of failing brakes.

The screeching stopped for a split second. Then came a huge bang and a tearing sound, louder than anything Michael had ever heard. He was thrown to the ground and thrown forward. The tearing sound continued. All around him, there was nothing but a chaotic frenzy of noises, the smell of smoke and darkness.

A second, louder bang came from behind, and the train trembled with the impact. The carriage behind them gave way and was replaced with nothing but wreckage before Michaels eyes. He was

Guardian Angel by David Trebus

thrown back like a rag doll, slamming into another set of seats and coughing blood.

A deathly silence descended, only broken by the sound of burning flames and the occasional sob or cry. Michael blinked tears of pain out of his eyes and tried to look around, even turning his head was a momentous, and painful effort. Through the fire-lit and smoke-filled carriage, he made out the little boy and his father lying on the floor, the father wrapped around his son to protect him. He could hear the old lady crying from somewhere, and her husband trying to comfort her. The man on the bike lay nearby unconscious but uninjured, as far as Michael could see.

Next to each of those people Michael could see their guardians leaning over them, with desperately worried looks on their faces. A young dark-haired angel sang over the boy and his father, while a brown haired angel had released her wings and held them around them both.

The young man's angel stood over him, glowing brightly as she sang a song of healing, and the elderly couple's angels sat next to them, hands of comfort placed on them.

Looking around made Michael feel Jasmine's even more keenly than before. He steeled himself as best he could, feeling truly alone for the first time in his life. He tried to move, but his leg was twisted and trapped beneath a piece of large metal jutting from the seat. Michael felt cold and, placing his hand over his chest, he felt warm wetness against his skin. He looked down to see a piece of metal protruding from his abdomen.

The sight of it yanked him out shock, the merciful numbing sensation disappearing. The pain flared up all at once, and he had to grit his teeth so he didn't cry out. He stopped trying to move, realising it would only make his injuries worse and desperately called out to Jasmine. Hours seemed to pass as he lay, waiting and hoping, before he finally lost consciousness.

***

Lilith watched the trains collide with a sense of satisfaction. The plan they had created had gone perfectly on schedule. They had arranged for a car to be driven onto the tracks in advance, Eldith using her unique seductive charms to get the man to part with his prized four-by-four vehicle, and had then tampered with the brakes while Lilith distracted the driver. She had checked to make sure Michael was still on board, before finalising everything.

The easiest part had been separating Michael from his guardian, as without that, the rest of the plan would have failed before it even started. She'd succumbed to their spell so easily and fled back to the heavens, just as they had suspected she would.

The final part of the plan, had been to arrange a second collision from behind, but that had been the hardest part. Lilith had to teleport herself onto that train in demon form and kill the driver before he had any chance to react, then back into her body. She left a random man she'd previously drained in the bathroom holding the murder weapon.

"Oooooo destruction always makes me so horny!" Eldith squealed, "Lilith, I just need release now!" She rubbed up against her sister, barely able to contain herself as they watched the burning wreckage. Both of had shed their human hosts the moment the collision occurred and now stood on a hill in full demonic garb, relishing the feeling of walking the earth unfettered.

"So single minded,although I must admit it has made me feel a bit....naughty." Lilith reached over and gently stroked her sister's shoulder.

The accident had been truly horrific . The train had ploughed into the parked four-by- four at full speed, partially derailing it. Even while the passengers were reeling from the initial impact, the second train had smashed into the rear and sealed the fate of those inside. They didn't care about the passengers on the train. All that mattered was Michael and that he was injured. Lilith extended her senses to look for him; he was unconscious, which made it easier for her to track.

"He's still alive, " she reported. "Although he's hurt worse than we anticipated. Garamond better hurry if he's gonna pull this off. Where is that damn she-angel, too? Doesn't she even care about that tasty little morsel in there?"

Guardian Angel by David Trebus

"Can I go into his dreams, sis?" Eldith pleaded. "Can I go and play with him? I'm sure it'll keep him motivated to live, annddd it will give me some release too!"

"No, Eldith, we'd best make ourselves scarce for now. We've done what we were ordered. If we were spotted here, it could make Garamond's job harder. Let's go find ourselves some new bodies and enjoy some more pleasures of the flesh for a while. You can go dream-invade some men and steal their souls later!"

"*OOO,* goodie! There's a little bar I know down in Soho. The barmaids there are just the cutest, and the men who go in there are the most corrupt!"

Eldith stood with her sister for a moment longer, as long, pure-white horns jutted from raven hair that caught the red light of the train-wreck before them. Burning eyes set in perfectly formed faces regarded the wreck with cruel smiles as they released their wings of bat-like leather and muttered an infernal song. A pillar of flame emerged from the ground beneath them both, enveloping the sisters, leaving nothing but a black scorch-mark on the grass.

***

Jasmine rushed down through the planes in a hawks plunge. She tried with all her spirit to speed her descent but couldn't have gone

Guardian Angel by David Trebus

any faster if the hordes of Hell were behind her. She could feel something had happened to her charge, she could sense his pain, but nothing she could do could speed her descent.

Time and space rushed past her, the many layers of the heavens a blur. She plunged past the domains of the Throne, heavens seers busily tending to their gardens. She raced past the Cherubim, who tended to the symphony's instruments. She plunged past the cloud covered layer of the Grigori, who watched Earth from the lower levels; forbidden to return there, only to watch in penance. Then, finally, she passed through to the mortal plane.

Jasmine was focused on reaching her charge, the only thing in the universe that mattered to her. She was so stupid falling for one of the oldest tricks in the book. The demons never played fair, that was their nature. They had obviously foreseen some tragic event in Michael's life and made sure that she wouldn't be there. That way, they could get their filthy claws on him.

Even with her emotional barriers re-established, Jasmine was overwhelmed with feelings of guilt and a less savoury sensation of anger. The Archangels knew the touch of righteous fury, but this felt a lot more like rage than acting as the divine sword of vengeance. Her affection for Michael only made the emotions even worse, magnifying them to a point she couldn't control.

Her thoughts focused on the task at hand as she hurtled down through the sky. There were dark storm-clouds over the whole South of England, a huge, roiling mass of darkness, illuminated by the occasional flash of lightning. She passed into those clouds and felt the malign intent behind them. Something stirred this veil of blackness, something evil. The wind seemed to whisper taunts in her ears as it whistled past "You'll never make it. He's already dead."

She paid it no attention, finally reaching her destination. The train wreck was a vision of true disaster. Debris was scattered everywhere: bits of seats, twisted metal, bodies. People tried desperately to clamber out, but the emergency services were nowhere to be seen. Jasmine zeroed in on Michael, it was clear that the tormenting wind might have been telling her the truth after all. His life force felt so weak. The thought of having to ferry his soul up to the heavens so early in his life made her heart clench in her chest painfully. The thought she would be reassigned to another human, never to see him again was almost enough to make her collapse and crash.

The portal of light came into view, her gateway into the mortal plane. She beat her wings several times, attempting to slow her mad descent . She almost crashed through the portal anyway, such was her speed. Jasmine landed hard on the floor inside the train, beating her wings twice more to gain her balance, and finding herself in the midst of true horror.

The carriage was dark and filled with smoke from fire, which cast strange shadows as it flickered weakly from the other side of the carriage. People lay strewn in various positions all around her:

Guardian Angel by David Trebus

some still alive and being tended to by their guardians, and some already departed for the Heavens or pulled down to the pit by the talon of Hell.

Michael lay passed out on the decking in front of her, a large piece of steelwork jutting from his abdomen. Jasmine sensed he was still alive, but his life force felt so weak; she could only just feel it pulsing from his body as blood pooled around him. Jasmine was horrified, stifling a gasp. She knelt beside him, placing her hands gently on his chest.

She sang all the healing songs she could think of, going through the hymns of regeneration all the way through to the psalms of Catherine, (which healed minor illnesses), but Michael's injury was too great. He needed medical attention desperately, but even then….

Jasmine, with a strong effort of will, pushed the thought from her mind. Tears were running down her cheeks as she gazed at her charge, frustrated by her impotence, and mouthed the words "I'm sorry" over and over. She looked around desperately. Why hadn't the emergency services turned up? Where were the ambulances? Where were the fire engines to cut people out of the wreckage? No, on Earth, only a few minutes had passed since the accident. They'd be on their way, rushing towards the accident in the hopes of saving people.

She looked down at Michael again as his breathing became more laboured. She felt so helpless. Soon his soul would lift from his

Guardian Angel by David Trebus

body, to be either washed clean of its sins and pass into the Heavens, or pulled down to the fiery pits of Hell. No! Jasmine had been Michael's guardian all his life, and she couldn't believe he'd be going anywhere except the Heavens. She should be feeling joy, since death was just another stage of things, but Michael would lose a lot of his memories; all his pain would be washed away.

Jasmine knew she was unlikely to ever see him again, but it was the thought that she had not been there in his time of greatest need that galled her to the core. The final thought that pained her so much was the love that had formed between them would forever be out of reach, the forbidden love of an Angel and her Charge. Her hands shook as her wings grew, unbidden in her grief. Jasmine cried out, a wordless shout of pain as a tremor passed through her body.

The fire at the other end of the carriage seemed to burn brighter and a deeper red glow that filled the whole carriage, cast a single shadow on the ceiling. The other guardians shouted in surprise or hissed quiet warnings to each other, spreading their wings over their charges to keep them safe from the malign presence that had entered the train.

Jasmine felt the evil force behind her and risked a glance away from Michael to confirm her suspicions. All her anger bubbled to the surface, surging into a tide of barely controllable rage. She stood up slowly, her eyes glowing so bright they cast green light around her. She regarded Garamond, the scourge of the Pit, the

Guardian Angel by David Trebus

darkness manifest on Earth.

All her fear of facing such a powerful demon melted away. She stood her ground as he casually walked down the carriage, leaving small burning footprints in the decking. He had taken on the slim elegance he once had as an angel, but with glowing red eyes, large horns and dark black-feathered wings. Jasmine steeled herself and uttered through gritted teeth a hymn of battle, a rare song, meant for the righteous in times of need:

"As I walk through the Valley of Death
I shall fear no Evil
Bless me now
So that I can stand for those in need."

Armour formed over Jasmine's white tunic. A breastplate of polished silver, gauntlets and shoulder-guards of gold and a mailed skirt of silver rings. A burning short sword formed in Jasmine's hand as she stood before Garamond, eyes fixed on his. As an angel, Jasmine could summon a burning blade and divine armour, but she wasn't one of Heavens soldiers, and her chances of beating Garamond were slim. Nevertheless, she stood her ground in front of Michael with fury burning in her soul. There was no way she was going to let Garamond take her charge for his vile purpose.

"Get back, foul spawn of the Pit. Your plans will not succeed here. You will not take Michael. You can go back to that *shit-heap* you

Guardian Angel by David Trebus

call a home and rot there."

Garamond continued his slow advance. His only reply a small smirk, until he was just outside of Jasmine's reach. He glanced around the carriage with an expression of mock concern before his eyes alighted on Michael's prone form. Jasmine tensed herself to take a swing, spreading her legs wide for balance and her sword drawn, when Garamond finally spoke.

"What a tragedy this truly is. His voice seeped out like a pit of slivering vipers. "And I had such grand plans for him."

"I suppose your plans included the spell on me, the attack in the alley and this train wreck," Jasmine replied, trying to keep her anger in check.

"The attack? That was just a co-incidence, I couldn't let such a special guest go by without at least saying hello. As for the spell, I don't know what you mean; there are many demons and magic users on this little ball. I can't be expected to keep tabs on them all." Garamond casually ran his fingers over the feathers of a nearby angel. The guardian recoiled as if struck and fell slumped over her charge.

He was lying, of course. Garamond was a fallen angel: a demon. Almost every word they uttered was a lie; it was their nature. "So what about this...this atrocity," Jasmine demanded. She maintained her poise, ready for any sudden moves from the demon. "Direct action such as this could bring war with heaven, Garamond. Even for your schemes, this has pushed things too far."

Guardian Angel by David Trebus

"I really don't know what you mean. This terrible event was a simple accident. the usual human incompetence and greed caused this, and, as usual, your divine master saw fit to let it happen without lifting a finger. Truly terrible!" Garamond's voice was now a chorus of whispers, all straining to be heard at once.

Michael coughed on the ground and moaned in semi-consciousness, a small puddle of blood seeping onto the ground from his mouth. He didn't have long, his soul starting to drift from his body. She was only grateful that he was unconscious; the pain would have been terrible had he been awake.

Jasmine wanted nothing more than to kneel at his side and sing songs of soothing and healing, to say sorry for not being here, to confess how she felt. It still wasn't impossible that the paramedics might help him, save him so she her life with Michael wouldn't end. But Garamond stood in the way, stopping her tending her Charge. The devil grinned at her as if sensing her desperation.

Enough! Tensing for a moment, she lunged at Garamond with a mid-level swing. The devil seemed to be caught off guard and took a surprised step back. Jasmine pressed into the opening she had created, chopping down and reversing the strike upwards. The blade caught a feather on Garamond's left wing, burning it away instantly in the heat of her righteous fire.

So this was what the Cherubim and Archangels felt when they took on the burning blade. God's wrath manifest, dealing out divine judgment in his name, was a powerful calling. As she

Guardian Angel by David Trebus

attacked the devil, not through song or spell but with a bare blade in her hand, she almost forgot what she was fighting for.

Pressing her attack, Jasmine lunged again, but with a quick motion Garamond grabbed her wrist and lifted her above the ground. He stood for a moment, glaring at her. With lightning speed, he plunged a black-armoured fist into Jasmine's stomach, crumpling her armour into pieces before twisting the sword from her grip to send it clattering to the floor. He held her up before him and leaned in so that Jasmine was looking directly into his eyes. He leered, then glanced at Michael again.

"Now little girl." Garamound sneered, "you cost me a feather, no easy feat. So now I'm in no mood for games. Listen closely. I didn't cause this little accident, but I offer you an opportunity now to save this pathetic mortal's life. Will you listen, or will you resist what you know you cannot defeat?"

Jasmine couldn't form a reply, coughing as she tried to speak. She nodded instead, trying to keep Garamond talking to buy time for the paramedics to arrive or heaven to send messengers. No, they wouldn't come, Heaven relied on its guardians and, unlike the demons, only interceded in truly exceptional circumstances.

Garamond dropped Jasmine to the floor next to Michael. He seemed to relish the pain he was causing. He was about to speak when another guardian found her courage and struck out at him from behind. This time, a burning dagger sliced into the small of Garamond's back. He had manifested no armour, and the tiny blade

Guardian Angel by David Trebus

bit in an inch, burning his flesh and he swung around in surprise. Catching the guardian by the throat, he flung her against the far wall, and advanced on her to stamp on her chest.

She yelped in pain, dropping her dagger. Garamond gave her no time. Grabbing both her wings, he tore them away from her body and left her slumped on the ground. Jasmine looked on in horror as the guardian lost her armour, stains spreading across her robes as she crawled to lie over her charge before collapsing. The guardian had lost her wings. She would either return to God's side or wander lost as a human, seeking redemption for her failure.

Jasmine heard sirens in the distance now. She could feel Michael's life force ebbing, and prayed for them to hurry but deep down she knew they'd be too late. Tears of frustration ran down her face as she struggled to her feet and faced Garamond again. He turned back to her, casually picking gore and feathers off his hands.

"So, as I was saying before I was rudely interrupted, I can save your little Charge's life. I didn't cause this accident, but I can help you fix the consequences of it."

"What do you say?" Garamond grinned, exposing serrated teeth. "Angel girl?

"You just killed a guardian before my eyes. Her name was Eila, she was one of the most devoted guardians I've ever known, and now you expect me to treat with you?"

Jasmine's anger built as she wheezed out the words. She'd been created into the Seraph choir. one of the highest. Chosen to be a guardian as part of her training. In the future, she could have become an Archangel and served as one of Heavens commanders. Now, her choir's legacy burned within her as she stood before Garamond, the untapped power awakening.

Jasmine felt new strength rush through her body. Her wings shone with blinding white light. Her armour mended itself, even as a new burning blade formed in her hand. Jasmine flew at Garamond with a quick beat of her wings. She swung her blade at his throat, ready to strike him down for Eila, for Michael, for herself.

Garamond sighed and took a few quick steps towards Jasmine, meeting her mid lunge. He grabbed her haloed head, side-stepping her out-thrust blade, and smashed her into the floor. Jasmine felt, even with her newly awakened strength, as if she was still just a toddler swinging a wooden sword at a wall.

"You really are determined to make this difficult, aren't you?" Garamond kicked Jasmine in the ribs. The blow sent her flying, to land next to Michael, and she coughed, struggling for breath.

"Let me make this simple for you, She-Angel, before we run out of time." Garamond advanced towards Jasmine again, taking his time as he seemed to listen out for the sirens drawing closer.

"You can leave your charge to the tender ministrations of the mortal doctors, who will be unable to help him. You can leave him to pass on and ascend, and you'll never see him again. You can

Guardian Angel by David Trebus

leave his soul for me to consume, if I am able to catch it. Or I can save his life and heal him right now."

"You…lie…you …cant heal…him." Jasmine pulled herself to her knees, struggling for strength.

"Oh, but I can Jasmine. All you have to do is make a little deal with me, and I will heal your charge, your beloved."

Jasmine looked at Michael, tears running down her cheeks and desperation warring with common sense. She guessed that Garamond was luring her into a trap, but she didn't want to lose Michael. Not now, not after all they had been through together. "What...do you want?" Jasmine asked.

Garamond's smile widened. "A simple little thing, dear Jasmine. I will heal your charge and leave him untouched here, if you willingly give yourself over to the darkness. If you willingly fall from grace."

The words hit Jasmine like a hammer blow. Falling from grace was one of the greatest fears of any angel, becoming a demon, losing oneself to base desire and evil. She almost refused immediately, but caught herself just in time. She looked down at her crumpled armour and injuries, then back at Michael. She was powerless. All her emotional suppression broke down, and all the guilt hit her at once: leaving her charge, her forbidden love, her inability to help now.

"Tick-tock Jasmine. Michael does not have long left. His life lies in your hands.

Guardian Angel by David Trebus

"So, what will it be?" Garamond knelt down next to Jasmine, and gave a cruel smile.

She remembered her promises to Michael, to herself. She remembered her vow to protect him at any cost. "At any cost." As the words replayed in her mind, Jasmine turned to face Garamond, looking directly into his eyes with all her doubt replaced by steely determination.

"Help him, and I will willingly fall. Help him, and I will join you."

"All you had to do was ask." Garamond stood up and brushed past Jasmine. He stood over Michael for agonising moments, watching as Michael's breathing became fainter and fainter, savouring the seconds as the human's life ticked away. Finally, he began to recite some infernal hymn. The words sounded discordant, random like some kind of dire modern poetry.

A red light formed over Michael and coalesced into a mist, that crept towards Michael's body and enveloped it, slowly seeping into his skin. The piece of metal jutting from his stomach rusted and corroded, falling into a brown pile of powder. Michael's wounded form reknitted itself and healed, as the infernal mist repaired the damage.

Michael's breathing eased, and Jasmine felt his life-force grow stronger as Garamond's spell took hold. She turned away, feeling a chaotic maelstrom of emotion inside. She felt relieved and terrified at the same time, knowing what was to come. She scribbled a quick note on a piece of parchment she carried, using one of her

Guardian Angel by David Trebus

own feathers and her own blood as ink. She quickly wrote out the note before Garamond could notice as he finished his spell.

"It is done Jasmine, now it is time for your part of the bargain," Garamond said. "Time for you to fall."

She looked at her charge, feeling elated that he would live, relieved that he would not miss out on all the joy that life could bring. But, she would have to pay the price now for the miracle of his life. She pressed her hand into his and kissed Michael's forehead. She gently closed Michael's hand around the scrap of parchment and stood up slowly.

Jasmine turned to face Garamond, who held out his hand to her. She placed her trembling hand in his as he began to recite blasphemous words. All her emotional barriers were stripped away in an instant. The lust she felt for her charge, the thrill of rage at attacking Garamond, and the desire to destroy, they all flared up in her. All the sins buried deep in every being came rushing up within Jasmine's soul. Her golden armour tarnished and fell away. Her burning blade spluttered and died on the floor of the train, melting into a dark patch of ooze. Her pure white wings turned jet black even as Jasmine's vision was clouded in red. Before the change consumed her soul Jasmine managed three words as her original self. Casting one last longing look at her former charge "I love you…" Jasmine whispered.

Guardian Angel by David Trebus

<u>Chapter 9: Michael's Choice</u>

Michael awoke to an unfamiliar ceiling. Small cracks had formed in the pure- white plaster surrounding a single light hanging down from its cradle. Where was he? What had happened? Then the memories began to flood back and he instinctively looked around for Jasmine.

She was nowhere to be seen, and he couldn't even feel her presence. More than that: the part of him that used to feel their connection was dull and vacant. Like a bruise upon his soul, it left him unnerved and shaken. Tilting his head around, all Michael could see was a plain room with a single window. Perhaps he was in hospital again.

Something was wrong? The injury to his abdomen had disappeared. There was no jutting piece of metal, not even a twinge of pain as he flexed his muscles and twisted in bed, only a small, star-shaped burn scar where the wound had been. His injuries were gone. But how?

He sat himself up and swung his legs out of the bed. Standing, he found his footing firm and strong, and walked slowly over to the window. Maybe Jasmine was outside? But instead he saw nothing but a road. He un-clenched his fists, which he'd been subconsciously holding clamped shut, and a small piece of parchment slipped to the floor.

Michael stooped down and grabbed it. He uncrumpled it and his heart leapt a beat as he read the flowing, red lettering.

Dear Michael

I don't have much time left so I'll keep this short.
You're badly hurt, and I only have one way to help you.
So I'm going to do what I have to, to keep you safe.
I'm so sorry...sorry for everything. I hope you can forgive me.
Know that I will always love you, and I pray you find happiness

Jasmine

Michael read the words, and it was as if he had been physically struck. He staggered back, to fetch up against the bed. Something bad had happened, and Jasmine had given up something important.

Guardian Angel by David Trebus

He knew that she was gone, that he had lost her. The vacant feeling, the void in his soul, made sense now, and he buried his head in his hands and cried.

Michael sat with his head in his hands, until a nurse came in to check up on him. She helped him into his bed, looking worried. "Mr Andrews. Michael are you ok? You've had quite a shock, I'm sure. Do you need anything?" She checked Michael's pulse and looked him over.

Michael simply shook his head, still wrapped up in the news of what had happened. He felt truly alone for the first time in his life. "Well, you've had quite a lucky escape, coming out of that accident with nary a bruise on you. I would say someone's looking out for you, young man." The nurse's smile was warm and kind, but did nothing to melt how Michael felt.

"Not any more," he muttered.

The nurse gave Michael a funny look, ignoring the comment, and went about helping him get more comfortable. She fetched a small tray of food from outside, and set it by his bed.

"Well," the nurse continued, " the doctors gave you a good looking over yesterday but decided to keep you in for observation, just to be safe. I was also told to tell you that you may get a visit from the police, just to take a statement about what happened."

"Right...thanks, I will keep that in mind," Michael replied absent mindedly.

The nurse nodded and smiled again. Under normal

circumstances, Michael would have felt bad for being so rude, but in his current mood he just didn't care. Maybe not about anything anymore. For the first time in his life he felt true despair for the future.

"A young lady came in to ask about you earlier," said the nurse. Michael's hopes flamed, until she added. "She said her name was Claire. She seemed very worried; in fact she stayed downstairs in the waiting room all night when she was told she couldn't see you yet. Is she your girlfriend? She's awfully pretty."

He was being stupid to think she meant Jasmine. After all, she couldn't even see guardians. He sighed and leaned back against his pillow.

"She's just a friend," he said flatly.

"Oh well, she's still downstairs if you want her to come up and see you."

"No it's ok. You said I could go soon? Can I go now?" Michael picked himself up out of the bed.

"Well, uh...I … yes, certainly, we could definitely use the bed. You just need to sign some discharge papers before you leave, and a doctor will come in to give you one last check over. I will get her to come in ASAP. Until then stay put." The nurse headed towards the door..

Michael nodded, pulling the food tray over and tentatively taking a few bites of a sandwich. He didn't have any appetite but ate out of habit, washing down his few mouthfuls with some watery

Guardian Angel by David Trebus

orange juice. He still wasn't sure what to do; all he knew was that Jasmine was gone and he felt lost.

The last few weeks since his accident had been a rollercoaster of strange events and new experiences. Everything had happened so fast, and even during the frightening moments, facing demons, learning about the supernatural, he had Jasmine by his side. They had grown close, very close…and in spite of the difficulties he had felt happy.

Something felt wrong with the way things were ending. Michael couldn't bring himself to accept that Jasmine had gone and he would have to return to a mundane life. He had to know what had happened to her, had to find out whether he could do anything.

Michael clenched his fists in frustration, trying to kindle the small flame of determination inside. He refused to give up now, even when events seemed the worst they could possibly get. All his experiences, even the bad ones he had got through and come out winning. He wasn't going to stop trying now.

Michael dressed and waited patiently for the Doctor to come in. After a long wait, a young lady with a short blond guardian, came in and checked him over. She remarked on how miraculous his lack of injuries was and how lucky he had been, before giving him a clean bill of health and asking him to sign out at reception. Michael thanked her and left the room soon after, walked down the halls, determined to do something but unsure as to what.

Worried guardians hovered or stood next to their charges' beds,

Guardian Angel by David Trebus

and a pang of envy struck before he could catch himself. These people were suffering, it wasn't right to feel this way. Michael fixed his sight dead ahead, trying to ignore everything but the lift at the end of the corridor.

He reached his destination and pressed the call button impatiently. He didn't have to wait long, and he stepped inside to come face to face with Claire, who gave him sharp slap. The door shut, sealing him in to face the wrath of his co-worker.

"You're up and about I see, Michael." Her face was pale and her voice level. "And you didn't have the decency to let me know. I've been so worried about you, you bastard," She added, colour flushing into her cheeks, her feelings showing.

Michael was shocked, either from the slap or how much Claire cared about him. He stood dumbfounded for a moment, before Claire leaned in and hugged him, wrapping her arms tightly around his waist. "I'm so glad you're ok," she breathed into his ear. "When I heard about the accident, I didn't know what to think."

A hospital orderly stood in the corner of the lift, smirking and shifting from foot to foot. Claire turned and gave him an accusing glance, before releasing Michael and standing a little step away from him in the lift.

Jazen wasn't present with Claire, presumably he was on high, or else close by. Another unwelcome pang of envy struck Michael. The orderly's guardian gave Michael an odd look as she stood staring at him. Michael ignored her and focused his attentions on

Guardian Angel by David Trebus

Claire.

"I'm sorry, Claire. It's just a lot has…" Michael was interrupted by the chiming of the lift reaching the ground floor. Claire ushered him out into the foyer and stood with her hand on his shoulder. "It's OK, I was just mad at you for a moment, let's go back to mine so we can talk if it's ok with you?"

Was it OK? He had to do something to find out about Jasmine, but what? He focused on Claire's face, ignoring the people and their Guardians all around him. In her eyes he could see a glint of understanding. That look made up his mind; it was not as if he had anywhere better to go or any other plan.
"Fine," he said.

They left the hospital, pausing only to sign out of reception and Claire called them a cab. Michael turned round to glance at the hospital. Another hospital in another place. Michael silently thanked the staff and prayed he had seen the last of hospitals for a good long while. He was getting bored of waking up in them.

***

Gabriel did not like to be kept waiting at the best of times, least of all, in times of crisis. Train accidents were usually insignificant in the comic design. However in this case had caused a disruption to the symphony. Gabriel had felt it even from the highest plane, a clash of noise that had shaken Heaven itself. The accident was clearly never meant to happen and had been caused by infernal designs.

The thought made the righteous fire in Gabriel burn brighter, and his hand strayed to his belt, nearly manifesting his sword before he caught himself. Recent events had him worried. The Pit was clearly making a major play in the eternal game, and that mortal was a key component in it. What was worse was that his guardian had fallen from grace, leaving the mortal undefended.

How could an angel willingly choose to fall? He hadn't been able to comprehend it during the rebellion in Heaven, and he couldn't now. Being corrupted through mortals sins, yes but even if Michael had died, he would have been elevated on High, to exist for eternity in peace. What had she been thinking?

Gabriel's Throne attendant stayed a cautious distance from the Archangel, feeling Gabriel's mood through the notes playing in his spirit. Gabriel was a strong sound at the best of times, but now the music his soul played was like the climax to a dramatic piece, full of cymbal crashes and strong notes.

Eventually, the great doors to the Metatron's chamber swung wide. Metatron emerged and walked towards Gabriel, his wings fully manifest and spread out behind him. He'd clearly just finished his communion with the Almighty and come straight out to speak to Gabriel.

Guardian Angel by David Trebus

"So." Gabriel bowed. "What news does the Voice of God bring from our father?"

"Not news that you will like, I'm afraid old friend." Metatron sighed, looking deflated.

Gabriel frowned, waiting to hear what he had to say.

"We are not to interfere with the situation on Earth." Metatron's voice was full of authority. "Even though dark powers have moved against us and the symphony is under attack, we have no basis to alter the destiny of mortals. Hell may trifle with fate and attempt to counter free will, but we will not. The Eternal Symphony will continue as it has always continued." Metatron held up his hand to indicate he had not finished.

"Michael's fate is in his own hands. It is up to him to decide what to do in his time of trials. However we are to prepare, should the symphony weaken or the Pit decide to attack."

"His will be done, Metatron, although I hope for us this does not end badly."

"Me too my friend, me too." Metatron replied tapping his chin. A small smirk formed on his face as he waved Gabriel goodbye. Gabriel ignored it, turning away to make preparations for a battle he felt was inevitable.

"What is an angel at heart but a guide and messenger of God?" Gabriel heard Metatron say to himself before he shut the door behind him.

Guardian Angel by David Trebus

***

Garamond had left Jasmine alone straight after they had entered the Pit. 'Probably to report his pathetic little schemes,' she mused waiting impatiently. A lost soul crawled and jabbered several paces from her. It was supposed to be bringing her a drink but it was making a big deal of it. Its limbs had been broken in several places, just as it had done to its victims during life, and a large plate had been attached to its back to act as a serving tray.

Jasmine detested the lost soul. It seemed pathetic and weak. She sighed and cast her barbed lash over the creature to hasten its efforts. It cried in pain, but she just lashed it again until it moved faster. She grinned as the soul finally came close enough for her to stoop down and take a tarnished goblet from the tray. She waved the broken soul away dismissively as she took a sip.

She stood in a broken chapel, long since decayed and corrupted. Its roof had wide gaps, through which shone the ruddy light of a sky alight with flame. The walls had crumbled in places, and the altar had been defiled with graven images of debasement. The windows had been smashed, leaving glass shards on the floor as torment for the damned.

Cries of pain and wails of despair made up the Pit's chorus. Unlike the soft notes, well- formed music and order of the

Guardian Angel by David Trebus

Heavens, Hell's music was chaotic, discordant and, to Jasmine now a lot more exciting. She watched, as a procession of the damned filed into the chapel, shackled at their ankles and hounded by lesser imps who prodded and jabbed at them. The pitchforks spiking into exposed buttocks reminded Jasmine for a moment of a comedy show she had seen on Earth. The image brought a small sense of amusement to Jasmine and she smiled mirthlessly.

The image expanded into a memory; a memory of her time on Earth with her former charge. A pang of something built in her gut; it pained her to focus on it. She felt regret, she felt guilt, and she felt love. Unbidden, a tear rolled down her cheek as memories of her time with Michael flooded back. Jasmine focused on her new freedom and her hatred for Michael to try and suppress them.

Being a guardian had been a boring duty, looking after a dull man. He had just been another pathetic human, and a weak one at that. His accident had been the only thing that had made Michael special. It had awakened his abilities, and made him an asset to Hell. A pang of pain made Jasmine furrow her brow. *'He may have been boring, but he was also caring and kind.'* A voice called out in Jasmines mind, her own but softer, kinder.

Michael had always been awkward and difficult, even before they had been able to interact. The human was constantly unable to express his own feelings due to insecurities and fear. Jasmine wondered how she had managed to feel anything apart from contempt for him during their time together. *'He also put other*

Guardian Angel by David Trebus

people's feelings first, and showed affection in his own gawky way.' The voice retorted.

Jasmine was beginning to get annoyed with her inner monologue and focused hard on her contempt for her former charge. Michael was pathetic, he had no ambition and never followed his dreams. He always settled. Hell, he even fell into the oldest trap in the book.

'But he never gave up, and always tried his hardest,' the irritating voice retorted.

"SHUT UP!" Jasmine cried out.

The moment passed as her new demonic self re-asserted control, silencing the voice inside. She lashed out at the nearest damned in the procession, rewarding her with a wail of pain and cries of anger. The imps jabbered and laughed, redoubling their efforts to herd the damned into the chapel. Jasmine enjoyed the pain she had inflicted. It felt good to do as she pleased. It was time to begin the latest round of tortures on this rabble of lost souls. The souls of murderers and rapists. Jasmine felt vindicated in her new duties as a demon. She had true freedom now, no longer shackled by petty rules and regulations, no longer shackled by him.

"That existence is gone now. It's not me any more, not ever me again." A single black feather fell from her wing to burn on the parched ground.

Guardian Angel by David Trebus

***

Michael had never been to Claire's house before, yet when the cab pulled up outside he had a sense of déjà vu. He had grown up in Hertfordshire but had moved to London a good few years back, probably why he had the odd feeling. Claire lived in a small commuter town called Ware. Compared to London it seemed like a very green and rural setting.

Her house was larger than Michael had imagined on the kind of salary she was getting, but probably a lot cheaper to rent or buy than anywhere in London. It had a short drive that the taxi travelled up to drop them off, and made Michael feel he was visiting some private estate.

Michael tried to pay, but Claire waved her hand dismissively and got out her wallet. Knowing better than to argue, he got out of the taxi and glanced around. The house had a small garden to the left of the drive, which seemed badly maintained. Wild flowers and small weeds grew out of the small lawn, while the flowerbeds were filled with flowers of many colours. Some patches were bare, as if the flowers had been picked.

Claire finished paying the driver, thanked him and gestured for Michael to follow her in. For the third time since he had met Claire at the hospital, he wondered where Jazen was, hoping nothing bad had happened. Claire fumbled in her handbag for her keys, taking ages to finally locate them in its bottomless pit.

Deftly opening the door, she again gestured wordlessly for Michael to go inside. She followed him in, shutting the door behind them.

The first thing that hit Michael about Claire's home was the smell. A wave of scents and aromas buffeted his nose, as his mind struggled to make sense of them all. He could pick out several different types of incense, several perfumes and a myriad other smells. It made him feel dizzy and a little nauseous.

The second thing was how brightly lit the place was. Claire had mirrors located everywhere that reflected the light, giving her entry hall a faint glow.

"Make yourself at home. The toilet is just there to the left, and the lounge is the door after that. Kitchen's down the end on the right next to the door to the garden. I won't be long, just need to freshen up a little." Claire said skipped up a flight of stairs out of sight.

Michael hesitated for a moment, before deciding to wait in the living room. In contrast to the hall, Claire's living room was dimly lit. The curtains were still drawn, and a table at the far end had been set up with plates, cutlery and now burned-down candles. She must have come straight to see him when she heard about his accident. He felt he owed her an apology for how curt he had been.

The living room was laid out much like any lounge, a TV in the corner near the window, a pair of small sofas, and a coffee table in the middle. The big difference Michael noted was the huge quantity of books and trinkets arranged on shelves all around the sides of the room. Almost all the books related to the occult, many on angels and spirits.

Michael's musings were interrupted by a flash of light behind him. He turned, assuming that Claire had come in and turned the lights on, and stared up at the most majestic being he had ever seen. Floating in the air, an angel with huge white wings and a burning golden halo smiled at him warmly. The angel's wingspan was so large that the tips merged with the wall.

"Greetings, Michael"

Despite all his experience with the supernatural, despite all the angels he had seen, Michael was left awestruck by this being. The angel seemed to emanate power in a palpable aura, but Michael did not feel threatened. If anything, he felt at peace. Everything was going to be all right.

"My name is Metatron. I don't have much time, Michael since your friend will soon return, as will her guardian. So I must keep this brief." Metatron's voice was a choir all singing the words at once.

"The Voice of God?" Michael stammered. He had seen something about it in a movie.

"Indeed, but let's put that aside for now, shall we?" Metatron sank to the floor, but the portal above him remained open.

Guardian Angel by David Trebus

"I know you have lost someone precious to you, Michael." Metatron's voice lowered in solemnity. "Jasmine has fallen from grace, become a demon. I presume you read her letter to you. That was what she was speaking of."

"A demon?" Michael stammered. That couldn't be possible could it? He wanted it to be a lie, but somehow knew that Metatron was telling the truth.

"We believe she made the choice to save you."

Michael slammed his fist down onto the table in anger. He felt anger at himself, at Jasmine and even at Metatron.

"Why didn't you stop her?" He shouted before he could stop himself. "Why didn't God help me? Why the Hell is all this happening to me?"

Instead of reacting angrily, as he expected, the angel sighed.

"Because, Michael, God gave you all free will. He is not a puppet master, pulling at the strings of the universe. He is a guardian, the ultimate guardian of all we hold dear. If God interfered every time something bad happened, or every time a human wished it due to selfish desire, then you would have no will, you would not grow and you would have no responsibility for your own actions."

Metatron paused, as if listening. He flicked his wrist and the door locked itself.

"At any rate, Michael, we do not have time for a philosophical discussion. I am not supposed to be here at all and do not have the time. I can sense the despair radiating off you like waves of

Guardian Angel by David Trebus

darkness, Michael. Don't be foolish. Embrace the little embers of hope every time they stir in your soul, because they will keep you aloft, away from the depths where you don't belong."

"What can I do?" Michael stammered. "I feel like I should do something, but I have no idea what?"

"You are already following the right path by coming here, Michael. Life is like a book being read. The future pages are already written but are yet to be seen. But, as you are a human, there's nothing stopping you from adding your own little notes and changing the outcome." Metatron gave a half smile before again cocking his head to listen.

"Free will…?"

"Precisely. You answer to no master, no rules bind you, you have the power to do whatever you set your mind and will upon doing. Even rescuing someone when no one else believes it is possible."

"But how?" The embers in his soul flared up.

"Again, you are following the right path. You are in the place you need to be. Now all you need to do is realise your potential and the resources and strength all around you."

The door-knob rattled, and Michael looked at it with a start.

"We are out of time," said Metatron. "I wish you well, Michael and I hope not to see you too soon."

"Thank…" Michael had made half his reply before Metatron was gone, vanishing through the portal of light in an instant, just as the door to the living room opened to show Claire standing there,

Guardian Angel by David Trebus

looking quizzical.

"You…" Michael finished.

"What for?" Claire asked, with a bemused expression on her face.

***

Michael stood looking at Claire for a moment, dumbfounded by what had just happened. The little spark that Metatron's words had relit burned brightly, and waves of hope washed through him. Was it possible to bring Jasmine back? Could he save her?

"What for?" Claire repeated, tapping her foot.

"Oh…for coming to the hospital, for caring about me." Michael was caught on the hop, replying with the first thing that came to mind.

Claire blushed, a side of her Michael had seldom seen.

"Uh…well…I, uh… couldn't just leave a friend and co-worker in hospital alone…." After a moment, she added."You're welcome."

Michael smiled in reply and Claire blushed even more.

"So, would you like anything, can I get you a drink?"

"Sure, a glass of water or juice would be great."

"No problems," Claire said and went out to the kitchen.

Michael was glad for the time to think. He sat down heavily on one of her sofas and sank into a deep slouch. Metatron's words kept playing over and over in his mind, but he couldn't work out exactly what they had meant, although surely the answer was right in front of him.

The thought of Jasmine as a demon disturbed him so much he felt physically sick with anxiety. His mind kept coming up with twisted and horrible visions, distorting memories of Jasmine, of her beautiful face and cute little wings. He remembered how small her wings had been when they had first met, and how they seemed to grow in the weeks since then. Was it due to her growing stronger and maturing? But even thinking about this brought his thoughts back to Jasmine as a Demon. Would she be too strong to help?

Claire returned, her face back to its normal pale complexion. and Jazen was now behind her. He gave Michael an odd look, a mix of compassion and caution. Claire leaned down to put a glass on the coffee table, and Michael had to look away to avoid glancing down her top. Jazen gave an approving nod.

Claire, who had changed into a loose-fitting black top with black jeans, sat across from Michael on the opposite sofa, putting a cup of tea on the table in front of her. Jazen stood behind her, shaking his head every time Michael looked at him directly, as if reminding him to stay focused on Claire.

"A lot has happened lately." Claire said. She exhaled deeply and, following Michael's lead, relaxed into a deep slouch.

"It sure has." Michael replied, wondering if Claire had read

Guardian Angel by David Trebus

anything more into his reply.

Claire's expression changed from tired to serious as she sat up and stared at Michael. She narrowed her eyes, as if straining to see something, then looked directly at him.

"I see your blonde angel isn't with you today." The statement was flat and her face carefully neutral.

Michael's heart raced, and anxiety stabbed stomach as if his guts had tied themselves in a knot. He made an unsuccessful attempt to sit up casually from his slouching position and ended up feeling even more awkward as he struggled upright. Jazen's expression showed his own suprise as he looked from Claire, to Michael and back.

"Uh...uhm, you could see her?" Michael managed. He was too tired to try and make up excuses.

"I knew it!" Claire yelled.

"I couldn't actually see her, but I felt someone there with us all the time down by the Thames. And that whole thing with the hobo, I knew something dodgy was going on! You were the last person I expected to be involved in this kind of thing, Michael."

Claire seemed to grow more excited and anxious before Michael. Her breathing quickened, and her face drained of colour. She was clearly struggling with it and Michael felt sympathy for her situation. He knew how bad anxiety could be, especially with the way his life had been going lately.

Jazen began humming a soft soothing song to help her relax.

Guardian Angel by David Trebus

Claire seemed to be stamping on her anxiety, as if it were an annoying bug. His song tapered off and as he ceased humming, Claire turned round to face him, looking directly at him.

"I can't see you, angel, but I know you're there. I have always known you were with me, seen your aura…I've heard you sing and hum to me in my dreams so many times when I've felt…well like I just felt a moment ago. Thank you for being there for me."

Jazen stood dumbfounded, looking like a teenager who'd just been told his popular girl- crush cared for him. He managed to mouth "you're welcome," but no words came out. His lips moved silently as he stood like a gaping fish. All this time she had known he was there, all this time she had been breaking the rules.

"But the rules don't apply to humans," he finally managed to say, regaining some composure.

Michael, staring blankly, a moment of clarity, brought about by Jazen's words. "The rules don't apply to humans." He replayed the words in his mind, managing a small laugh as he realised what Metatron had meant. There was nothing stopping him from looking for a way to save Jasmine. There had to be a way to do it! He also had help sitting right in front of him, if he needed it: help he had had for weeks and been too blind to see.

"What are you laughing about, joke boy?" Claire demanded, returning to her usual, overly composed self.

"Nothing, not you. Just how stupid all this is, how stupid I have been." Michael looked straight into Claire's eyes as his confidence

Guardian Angel by David Trebus

returned.

Claire took a sip of tea to quiet the last of her nerves and to avoid Michael's stare. It gave her goose bumps.

"That angel behind you," said Michael. "His name is Jazen."

Jazen again pulled a shocked face and waved his arms frantically. It was what Jazen had always wanted, Michael knew, to be acknowledged by his charge, and be closer to her, but he also feared breaking the rules and being separated from her. He, as a mortal, was not bound by those rules however.

"You mean you can see him as well?" Claire spluttered, trying to gulp down some tea.

"Michael, what the He…heck are you doing?" Jazen demanded, but Michael ignored him, focusing on Claire instead.

"I can…I can see all of them, every person's Guardian Angel. Ever since the accident."

"Blimey…," was all Claire managed in reply.

"That word sums it up about as well as any. I may as well tell you the whole story, if you're willing to listen? I'm sure Jazen will find some bits interesting as well." Michael was hoping beyond hope that Claire would say yes and not think he was nuts.

"Of course. It's what I've been hoping for ever since I had that dream about your accident. Tell me all of it, me and Jazen are all ears." Claire replied smiled back in Jazen's general direction.

Michael took a gulp from his cup, and tried to sit comfortably. A part of him rebelled against telling Claire everything; he was used to hiding it from everyone except Jasmine. Another part, though was glad for the chance to finally confide in someone, finally share everything he had been through and hopefully get a little advice on what to do next. 'No turning back now,' he thought.

Leaning back again, Michael told Claire and Jazen everything. How he had woken up in a hospital to find Jasmine there with him. How he could see every guardian of every person he met. About the demons he had encountered, his ability to sing. Lastly, he told them about the train accident and Jasmine's letter to him. Michael told them about Metatron's message, but decided not to reveal who had actually told him. It was probably better to keep that information to himself.

***

"Bloody Blimey," Claire exclaimed Michael finished telling his story.

"Yup, again that about sums it all up." Michael took a deep breath. "I always knew…I mean, sensed that someone was looking out for me, but I never dreamed we actually all had real, guardian angels looking after us." Claire's gaze returned to where Michael had previously indicated Jazen, although, the angel had moved to sit next to her half way through Michael's story.

Guardian Angel by David Trebus

"We do. Every single human being on this planet has one looking out for them - well, except for me right now." Michael felt melancholy, he missed Jasmine so much.

 "What you've been through…what you've seen, Michael, I can't begin to imagine what all of this has been like for you," Claire said, leaning forward and placing a hand on the table. "Part of me wants to say you're lucky, that it's such a singular thing, but from what you have told me..., told us, it doesn't sound like much of a blessing."

 "In a way, I do feel lucky. I mean, if it wasn't for all that's happened, I never would have even met Jasmine, never known she was there with me all this time. I never would have fallen in.." Michael found himself unable to say the final word.

 Claire sighed, looking round the room as if searching for the source of a noise. Michael wondered if she were trying to look for Jazen.

"Jazen..," she said, "I know you're there now, so you may as well reveal yourself. I doubt if it's going to be breaking any rules, now I know you're about. Let me see you, my silent guardian, after so long."

***

Guardian Angel by David Trebus

Jazen was caught off guard. For all his time with Claire he had wished for this moment, prayed for this moment. She had acknowledged him, knew he was there. His wings trembled as his feelings slipped their leash and sought an outlet. Sweat formed on his brow.

What should he do? His heart told him to reveal himself but he still remembered the choir's verdict and the rules. But Claire already knew of him, and not through his own design, so revealing himself at this stage would not break any edicts. In any case the situation was exceptional and he very much wanted to help Michael.

The war in his mind settled, Jazen took a deep breath and stood up next to the door. He bowed his head and let his wings spread. Pressing his hands together, Jazen gave voice to a song seldom sung by any guardian: the song that would allow his charge to see him. The last time Jazen had heard of an angel using this song was in the time of the Grigori, before the rules became so strict.

A bright light engulfed the room as the song reached its climax. Jazen emerged from the light, hoping he looked suitably impressive for Claire. Then, without warning, the light was gone, and before a very surprised Claire stood her guardian, the angel Jazen, in all his glory and for once not at all sullen. He smiled at Claire, trying his best to make a good first impression.

"Hello..,Claire," was all he could manage.

"Jazen…" Claire seemed equally lost for words. She never

Guardian Angel by David Trebus

imagined her Guardian would be so attractive. In fact, Jazen's appearance was just like her perfect man. Slim, bright eyed, intense: she knew she was facing the man she had been waiting for. It was like some cheesy romance novel or mushy film but, for once, the thought didn't make her feel ill.

The thought brought her up short, though, as she remembered the man sitting across from her. Michael had made this possible. He had been the small force for change that had turned her life upside down, and now he needed her help. Romance and angel dating could wait until later. Gesturing for Jazen to sit next to her, Claire turned her attention on Michael.

"So…now you've turned my life into a supernatural romance, what can I…we do to help you?"

***

Michael couldn't help but smile. The chemistry between the two radiating across the table, reminded him of the chemistry he and Jasmine had shared. Claire's straightforward manner was charming, and he had no doubt if Jasmine had not come along he could have been with Claire happily, if she'd put up with him and his sometimes sullen personality.

"Well…that's the bit I'm stuck on," he replied. "I don't know what to do, I'm kind of playing this all as it comes right now."

Claire glanced over at Jazen who met her eyes briefly then looked away, clearly unused to the attention. She looked back at Michael, tapping her finger against her bottom lip in thought. "Ok then, Michael." She said. "What do you want to do? Forget what you feel you can't do, what do you want to do?"

"I want to bring Jasmine back." Michael's instant reply brought a wide smile from Claire.

"Well, now we know what you want to do, we just have to find a way to make it possible, don't we?" Claire tapped Jazen on the shoulder and gave him an expectant look.

"I hate to put a downer on this," said Jazen. "But I'm not sure there is any way we can help. There is no record of angels being turned back once they have fallen to darkness. The only way to stop the fallen is to banish them back to the Pit, or to destroy them utterly. I'm sorry, Michael."

"But what about on the Thames, Jazen, when Michael sung for that girl? Surely her angel was dark?"

"That angel had not fallen. He was close, but his chains hadn't dragged him down into darkness. Michael's unique gift only saved him because it influenced the angel's charge and helped her heal, as well as him."

"But you yourself said his gift is unique," Claire pointed out. "So how do you know it wouldn't redeem a fallen angel?" Michael sat silent, letting Claire finish her chain of thought.

Guardian Angel by David Trebus

"In truth, I don't… It's possible…but if it didn't work." Jazen was clearly unsure of himself.

 "It's possible…" Michael murmured.

"Huh?" Claire said.

Michael ignored her, recalling again what Metatron had told him: that he had the power he needed to save Jasmine. Michael strained, to push through the fog of his depression and feeling of powerlessness. He remembered that little spark inside him that said "Never give up," trying to rekindle it into a fire.

Then his mind ignited, and everything clicked into place. He knew what he had to do. Metatron had been right; he was exactly where he needed to be, and he had all the resources he required to save Jasmine. All he had to do was believe in himself and his own strength; he could and would save Jasmine, no matter what it took. Hope and self-confidence flooded back into Michael, as he turned to Claire and then at Jazen.

"It's possible," Michael repeated.

"How can you be so sure?" Jazen demanded.

"Because I have faith in myself. I can do it, I can bring her back to me."

Claire grinned, "So how can we help, Michael?"

"Help me get to her. Help me get down into Hell."

***

Guardian Angel by David Trebus

"You can't simply just walk into Hell. It's not like the UK border."

"There must be a way, Jazen," Michael insisted. "If anyone knows, it would be you. You're the only angel here."

"Hell is a spiritual realm, for a start. Only your soul can manifest there; your body remains here on the physical plain. If you want the easiest way to get there, a life of sin and evil is a sure-fire way of gaining access, followed by death, of course. I seriously doubt you're capable of that, Michael."

Michael shook his head in frustration. Jazen was holding something back, probably to protect Claire and maybe even himself. But Michael was determined now. Nothing was going to stop him from getting to Jasmine and at least trying to save her. His whole life had been leading up to this moment, and even the fear that knotted deep in his gut only leant strength to his determination.

Claire stood up abruptly and left the room without word. Michael looked on after her with a puzzled expression but didn't have to wait long until she returned. Claire held an old book in her hands. The cover was cracked and the leather binding worn, but somehow it held together as if the book was determined to keep its form. Jazen gave a look of disgust when he saw it.

"I've never been one for demonology or any dark magic stuff. But I found this book in a dusty corner of a charity shop in

Cambridge a few years ago. It's pretty dark reading, all dark ritual and demon summoning stuff, no idea why anyone would be stupid enough to try anything like that though." she sat down, looking pointedly at Jazen. "I must admit I have only ever looked over it a couple of times, but I swear I remember seeing a reference to gaining access to Hell."

Jazen said nothing, but his expression spoke volumes. Michael leaned forward to get a better look, his expression hopeful at a possible way to get to Jasmine. Claire thumbed through the pages, then stopped, putting her thumb over an interesting passage. Red spots dotted the page, and Michael didn't want to think what they were made of.

"Ah, here we are. "*A ritual to gain access to the infernal realm.*" All it requires is that me and Michael," she read out deliberately, "shed blood while engaging in a carnal act within an unholy circle in a church. It should take us right into the center of hell without a problem." Michael, thoroughly confused, was about to protest when Claire gave him a "shut up" look.

"No!" Jazen yelled. "I will not allow it, damnit!" He put his hand over his mouth, realising his blasphemy. When he spoke again, he seemed defeated. "There is a way…."

"Oh?" Claire raised an eyebrow, placing the book on the table. "What do we need to do?"

"Through your dreams."

"Spit it out, Jazen," exclaimed Michael.

Guardian Angel by David Trebus

"Sometimes, in exceptional cases, mortal souls have been brought on High through a special song." Jazen said before continuing. "This is to guide them, for us to give them a message. Hell can do much the same, and the same principle applies to getting there. The song is sung while the mortal is asleep, temporarily separating the soul from the body to travel in dreams. However... I have never attempted to get to Hell before. I don't think any angel has; it would be...wait a moment." Jazen looked down at the book on the table, his face turning white.

The pages contained pictures of various erotic positions and poses, and the red spots were clearly ink that had run. Jazen's face turned pale. Claire had tricked him into revealing what he knew. He pointed his finger at her, looking indignant.

"I'm sorry, Jazen. We don't have much time, and I had to trick you into telling us." She smiled warmly. "I know you're far too devoted to my safety to willingly tell me how to go to such a dangerous place. Please forgive me, but I am determined to help Michael, and I hope you will help me."

"Please, help me get to Jasmine." Michael pleaded. "I will go alone. You and Claire don't have to come, just help me get there."

"Oh no you don't." Claire jumped in before Jazen could speak. "I.... we're coming too. I'm not letting you go somewhere like that alone" She looked at Jazen determinedly, "and I'm certain Jazen won't let me go unescorted, either. Whether you like it or not, you're stuck with us. So get used to it, buster. You won't be fighting this battle on your own."

Jazen raised his hands, his expression defeated. "Fine! You two win. I'll help you. I owe Jasmine for all she has done for me in the past, and I suppose I owe you for finally letting Claire see me," "So what do we do?" Asked Claire.

"Clear the coffee table out of the way and lie down on the floor next to each other. But don't get any ideas. I need to sit over you and have physical contact while I sing." Jazen helped Michael and Claire move the coffee table out of the way, before turning back to them. He swallowed nervously. "I'm going to take us to the elemental plane of fire, to Hell's gate. It would be too dangerous to take us right in as they'd sense us instantly."

"Heaven wouldn't be too happy if I delivered what Hell has been after ever since this stupidity started."

Michael and Claire lay down on the cleared space between the sofas. Claire's breathing became erratic and Michael wondered if she was having another panic attack. He reached his hand over to hers and squeezed it, trying to reassure her.

"How can you be so calm at a time like this?" Claire asked, her voice broken and on edge.

"Because I know it will be ok." Michael was keeping his own fear tightly bottled up "I know we can do this."

"I need you both to close your eyes and try to relax now. "Jazen said, pressing his palms together." I'm going to send you both to sleep and then begin the song. If all goes to plan, when I ask you to open your eyes it will all be done."

"Light has embraced you
Hope has empowered you
Spirits will guide you
Angels beckon you
Beyond the mortal realm…"

Jazen's voice was strong and resonant. He placed his hands on their foreheads and continued to sing, but the song became distant and fuzzy. The light of Jazen's wings seeped through Michael's eyelids, he resisted the temptation to open them. Then the light's consistency changed to a red hue.

Michael opened his eyes to find himself standing next to Claire and Jazen. They stood on the edge of a rocky cliff with a sea of fire stretching out before them. Molten lava and uncontrolled flames flowed and danced freely. In the distance, Michael caught sight of a huge red door wreathed in darkness. He knew instantly that was his destination. Straight into the gates of Hell.

Guardian Angel by David Trebus

Chapter 10: Through the Gates of Hell

Gabriel stood before Heaven's gate, looking over the white fields that stretched out before him. The fields weren't really fields, as Heaven was a spiritual realm, but the perceptions of the viewer gave them form. The threat of storm clouds on the horizon, however, was very real and represented extreme danger, whatever perception one chose.

He'd often stood on the battlements above Heaven's gate, but only once before ready to defend them from the fallen. Usually he'd climb up and look out over the calm landscape, watching the many souls living in peace. The sight always relaxed him, when he allowed himself the emotional freedom.

Today, though, he was anything but relaxed. Metatron had gone missing, and that idiot guardian Jazen had tapped into the symphony and transported the mortal Michael right outside the gates of Hell. There would be a reckoning, if Jazen ever returned on High assuming his infatuation with his charge hadn't already made him fall from grace.

Gabriel paced up and down the battlement over the gate, watching preparations being made. The weapons looked like crossbows and fortifications from a mortal perspective, but were spiritual defenses and potently bound songs designed to slay and banish demons. He nodded to his fellow angels as they worked and stopped a couple of times to assist.

As he bent down to assist with attaching a ward seal, he saw the soul of a small child staring up at him. He caught the little girl's scrutiny. She smiled at him and, before he could catch himself, he smiled back at her and managed a small wave.

"They say one's true nature is reflected in the souls of children." A familiar voice spoke from behind.

"Where in the seven planes have you been?" Gabriel turned to face Metatron.

"I had to run an urgent errand. How are the preparations progressing?" Metatron too waved at the little girl.

Gabriel grunted before replying. It wasn't hard to guess what the errand was.

"The preparations progress well. We will be ready, should the worst come to pass and the symphony be corrupted. I'd have thought the Metatron would be at his post in such a time of crisis, not putting outlandish ideas in the minds of mortals."

"I have no idea what you are talking about." Metatron continued to humour the child below, by waving.

"Don't play dumb with me, Metatron." Gabriel warned. "I have known you for centuries. Your grasp of the rules has always been flexible. Our father allows you too much latitude."

"I merely advise. Mortals possess free will, and make their own choices. As for Jazen, he was coerced into his position, he couldn't abandon his charge, after all. Leave his punishment to me, should he return."

Gabriel grunted in annoyance, and moved off down the battlement to help his comrades. Sometimes, he really envied Metatron's outlook.

***

Michael glanced at his two companions. Jazen looked worn, his wings fully manifest but glowing only faintly. A nimbus of light played around Claire's form, flickering white against the red backdrop. They both looked surprised, but clearly not at the change in scenery. They stared straight at him with confused faces.

Michael looked around him, ducking and turning; expecting an attack any moment. A faint outline of wings loomed behind him. For a moment he squirmed, trying to escape the outlines behind him, until he realised they grew from his own back.

"Wha?"

"Well," said Jazen, his voice tired, "that explains why you can tap into the symphony. Seems like you have a little of the divine in you. We are seeing the manifestation of your soul here. It's why we can see your wings, even if they are very faded."

"So..you're saying I'm part Angel?" Michael looked over his

Guardian Angel by David Trebus

shoulder again, trying to make out the faint outline of his wings. "Something like that. Somewhere in your distant past. Angelic blood entered your line. It's not going to be much use here, though in the plane of fire, we can barely tap into the symphony. When we enter Hell, we will be totally cut off from it. The only thing I can do is manifest my armour and weapon. Perhaps you can too, but I doubt it will be very strong." Jazen stooped to run black sand through his hands.

"Well, well, well, I always knew you were a special one," Claire remarked, turning away from the awful vista all around them.

"Metatron did say…" Michael murmured to himself. He remembered his brief meeting with the Archangel.

"Huh? Metatron?" Jazen's head bolted up to face Michael.

"Oh, no, nothing. It's all just a bit confusing…I mean, jeese," Michael managed weakly. He had never been very good at lying. Jazen's eyes narrowed in suspicion.

"So, how do we get in….there?" Michael gestured to the red gate in the distance.

"We cross the plains over the fire and slip through somehow. You ever see that film where the little men try to slip into that dark land? It's not going to be that easy."

"Won't you be detected easily?" Claire asked. "I mean being an angel?"

"Cut off from the symphony, my presence is vastly reduced, and I can mask myself so I look like a human soul, at least for a while.

Guardian Angel by David Trebus

The only way we're going to pull this off is if we enter Hell with one of the processions of the damned. Bind ourselves to their chains and shuffle in with the rest of the dark souls."

"It seems like we have a plan, then," Michael said, trying to move his apparitional wings.

"We do, but those," Jazen said, gesturing to Michaels faded wings, "could be a problem. They want you, Michael. and those are a big giveaway as to who you are. You need to suppress them, like I do mine."

"How do I go about doing that?"

"It's all down to willpower. concentrate on them and will them to be hidden. Focus all your energy on them and imagine them invisible. Then keep that thought in the back of your mind at all times. If you let it slip for more than a moment, they will begin to return." Jazen paused. "Before I forget, manifesting armour and a flaming weapon is much the same. If we get into trouble, you should try it. It may save your soul."

"I'm beginning to feel rather mundane here, I must say," Claire remarked.

"Claire, you are anything but mundane. You are the most special..." Jazen was interrupted by Claire putting a finger over his mouth.

"I was joking, Jazen. But thank you."

"Two other things, before we set out," said Michael, unable to take his eyes off the red gate." Once I find and save Jasmine, how do we get out? And thank you both, I owe you so much."

"Getting out..." Jazen frowned. "To be honest, I hadn't thought about that. I guess we'll cross that bridge when we come to it. If we can get back to the plains, I can return us, but from within Hell we are stuck. As for your thanks, save them for when we're safely back on Earth with Jasmine."

"There's no need to thank me, Michael." Claire added. she gestured into the distance. "Let's get this done so we can all go back."

Michael nodded. He followed Jazen's instructions and, after a few attempts, his wings disappeared. He could still feel them there, but they were invisible. Should he try to manifest armour and a weapon? No, it best to not push it. With any luck, he wouldn't need them, though considering he was entering most human's worst nightmare, he probably would.

They set off across the fire plains, Jazen leading the way. He explained that, although they weren't physically present, the flames could still burn away their souls and cause irreparable harm. The unlikely trio picked a path across rivers of lava, seas of flame and forests of fire. Time slowed to a crawl as they stepped carefully on small black stones or narrow pathways of obsidian, sometimes mere inches away from the blistering fires. With every passing moment, the ominous red gates drew closer.

***

Guardian Angel by David Trebus

After what seemed like an eternity of walking, but was mere moments, Michael stood staring up at the red gates of Hell. Jazen had cheerfully (for once) explained that time didn't exist, and causality moved in a different way in the non-material plains. Michael had felt like telling him to cram it with the way he felt, but kept his cool.

Michael, Claire and Jazen huddled behind a large obsidian rock. Perhaps it had once been a statue; still vaguely retained the shape of wings, but now was just another black, crudely shaped mass, battered by merciless fires. Michael glanced at the gate ,as Jazen spoke softly to Claire, her anxiety attacking her again. The sight before him filled Michael with the same fear and panic he could see on her face.

A huge crimson door stood alone a few hundred meters from where Michael peered over his hiding place. The door was huge, towering above Michael even from such a distance. Shadows blurred its edges, flowing around the frame in a constant stream of motion. No carvings decorated the door's solid crimson slabs except for one, a huge, leering skull with horns jutting from its temple. The skull's sockets burned orange and, as Michael let his eyes drift over it, he felt the skull staring back at him. He ducked his head back into cover.

Claire seemed to have calmed down again and looked up at him, smiling.

"Well, looks like I'm taking a big step towards facing my anxieties today." Her voice was a little shaky.

"You didn't have to come, Claire. You've done enough," Michael told her, pushing down his own fear.

"Don't be so silly. You need me and Jazen, and I'm not going to let a little thing like fear stop me now, not now I'm finally doing something worthwhile. No, Michael." Claire's voice gained strength. "I...we are with you until this is done."

He turned his attention to Jazen and looked the angel up and down. In his suppressed form, Michael would have pegged him as just another average person he'd meet on the street, if he didn't know better.

"So, what now?" Michael asked.

"We wait until another bunch of souls descend. When an evil soul dies, the guardian either ascends or descends, dependant on circumstance. The guardian ends up in Hell, while the evil soul is dumped here outside its gates, to be herded in like cattle. That's how we are going to get in. When the next lot get deposited we slip in with them. I just hope Cerberus doesn't sniff us out."

"Wha? Cerberus, I thought that was Greek mythology?" Claire's interest perked up.

Jazen smiled. "A lot of it is one in the same. Most religions and beliefs share the same constants. Cerberus is a very real Guardian of Hell. He was born from the souls of millions of slaughtered

Guardian Angel by David Trebus

animals, killed for sport or fun. But enough history. He has a keen nose, so I hope we blend in with the rest of the damned."

"Great…!" Claire looked disgusted. "I finally face my fears, only to be eaten by a three- headed dog."

Michael got lost in thought. All those souls they were about to use as camouflage were people, living people who, for whatever reason, turned to a path that led them down here. The thought was sobering and left Michael feeling faintly sick. He pushed it aside to focus on Jasmine. Nothing else mattered, apart from saving her.

They didn't have to wait long before a bright flash of crimson lightning crept across the sky above the gate. The crack it left began to widen with a loud grinding, the sky was splitting open. Small dots of red light fell from the hole like rain, streaking down towards the parched ground.

Michael watched in morbid fascination as each red dot grew closer, discerning shapes within the rain of light. He gulped hard as the shapes became more distinct; within each large drop was a human form, writhing as if in great pain, trying to escape the crimson prison of light as it fell mercilessly downwards.

The huge drops hit the ground hard and splashed open in a display of crimson pyrotechnics, hurling glowing red liquid in all directions. The forms within, clearly hurt by the impact, stood and looked around at their surroundings. More and more fell, until hundreds of forms milled about in confusion and pain. It was then the wailing and screaming began, as the dark souls of the fallen

Guardian Angel by David Trebus

finally realised where they were. It was a sound that would haunt Michael in his dreams for years to come.

Claire looked gob smacked and terrified by the sight. She gripped Jazen's hand tightly and her face contorted into a look of pure pain. She seemed to realise, like Michael, that each and every form before them was a human soul, about to enter a place they would never leave, a place where they would suffer for eternity. She gulped and looked at Jazen, who managed a weak smile to try and comfort her, but restrained himself, knowing it would get them caught.

"It's time," Jazen said, although Michael and Claire had to read his lips. The noise of the damned was too loud to be heard over.

The crack in the sky was closing as the last souls fell to the ground. There were so many, the souls at the edge of the group almost touched the rock that Michael, Jazen and Claire hid behind. Jazen led the way into the crowd, darting out and joining the mass, Michael trying his best not to lose his footing. They held hands so as not to be separated and moved their way into the center of the group.

The damned included people from all walks of life. Michael saw old men, young women, middle aged, even a few teenagers, all milling about aimlessly, crying out in pain or screaming in fear. Some crouched on the ground, rocking back and forth, pleading that they didn't belong here; others stood stoically, their fear turned inwards. Michael noticed that all the red glowing liquid had

Guardian Angel by David Trebus

disappeared, and the people looked as they had on Earth. Michael wanted to ask Jazen why, but didn't dare say anything.

The crimson doors swung open as Michael found a spot to stand in the centre of the group, as far from Cerberus's keen nose as possible. The giant dog loomed over them, large as a house. Michael could feel the heat radiating from the great beast's heads. Cerberus had sat silently as the souls had been deposited, raising only one head casually to sniff them before lowering it again as if indifferent; tainted souls being deposited outside the gates must have become boring for the giant hound.

Orange light spilled out from the crimson doorway, and a blast of heat smothered the waiting damned. Michael didn't so much feel it as sense it washing over him. The pain was intense but passed as quickly as it had begun. Others in the crowd wailed, realising that small wave was a taste of things to come. The fact that a blast of heat from Hell felt hotter than the fire plain made Michael shiver in fear, despite how hot he felt.

A small host of demons leapt from the portal. Many were small, shadowy imps or lesser creatures. A Few towered over the humans, their wings casting shadows over the assembled throng; surely these were the true fallen. The smaller demons scuttled around the damned, attaching copper manacles to one foot of each, the other end trailing along the ground.

Claire flinched as a small, orange-coloured creature attached a copper link to her. He paused to leer up at Claire and licked her leg

Guardian Angel by David Trebus

with a long forked tongue before continuing on to fetter Jazen and Michael. The imp hesitated as he placed the bonds on the two men, but then moved on as if nothing had bothered him. Michael let out a breath they hadn't known they had been holding as the danger passed.

"What are these?" Michael risked whispering in Jazen's ear.

"Shackles and marks of bondage. They keep the damned in line and mark them as lost souls. Some, you may notice, are weaker than others. Some souls after serving a time here will be allowed into ascend back through the planes up to Heaven, their punishment served. Others" Jazen indicated a woman, "will be here for eternity."

"Can we get them off?" Claire asked, looking worried.

"Oh yes, I can do that easily. I don't know how we got away with that though. The Imp surely must have noticed something odd about us, the lack of sins on our soul, but he passed us by."

"Well, let's not complain about good luck," Michael said. Looking around, he saw the lesser demons finishing their work.

Three fallen remained to supervise them, while the others filed through the gate, looking bored with the crop of new arrivals. One stepped forward, a true brute of a demon with purple skin like a bad bruise. He leered at the assembled mass and spat on the ground, his spit melting through the rock like acid.

"Welcome, scum. I am Barlan. You are the latest herd of degenerate souls fallen from Earth to fuel the forges of Hell. There is no escape, there is no mercy, and there is only punishment and pain." He barked the words out in a guttural voice.

"Prepare them!" he yelled to his two companion fallen as he turned away to march back in through the gate.

The other two fallen stepped forward and bellowed at the assembled mass. The sound was a shockwave of energy. It felt like the angels songs, but more primal, direct, corrupted. This must be how the fallen used their abilities. The energy passed through the mass and, as it touched the shackles, chains of flame formed between them.

The lesser demons herded the assembled mass into two columns, using pitchforks and small swords to elicit cooperation from anyone too stubborn to move. Several souls were skewered repeatedly and cried in pain, only to be stabbed more until they stood up. It seemed they couldn't be incapacitated, but the pain of each injury was very real.

Once the throng had been herded into two lines, the fallen turned on their heels and marched back through the gates. The mass was goaded into movement by the lesser creatures and shuffled forward after them. As they moved, Cerberus perked up; two of his heads rose and sniffed the air.

Michael suppressed a shudder of fear as he passed the great dog who, turned one of his heads to look directly at him. Michael dared not even breathe as the moment seemed to go on forever. Cerberus sniffed in his direction and a deep growl issued from his throat,

Guardian Angel by David Trebus

rising into a rumble. Any moment, Michael thought the great dog would bark and reveal them.

Then a feral-looking man stumbled right in front of the great dog, cursing and thumping his fist into the beasts face by accident. Cerberus immediately seemed to forget Michael and rounded on the man, biting into him with two of his heads. By the time Cerberus had finished only a faint scrap of clothing remained. The little imps and demons jumped around, giggling and laughing at the display.

"Big dog got himself a snack!" one imp yelled gleefully. "Good for him. Bad for the poor damned when he gets shit out the other end in pieces. Hahaha,."

Cerberus again turned his attention to the source of the noise, Michael forgotten. He snapped at the lesser demon, biting off his pitchfork and sending the creature scurrying away with a trail of burning urine behind him. His compatriots laughed loudly at the display, as the procession, Michael with it, shuffled out of sight of the huge hound.

As Michael passed through the huge doorway and into Hell, a passage he had read from Dante's Inferno surfaced in his mind. It was a famous line that was supposed to be written over the gates of Hell. "Abandon Hope, all ye who enter here."

Michael looked up to see if it was there. The inscription had been scrawled in black paint on the doorway, probably by one of the lesser demons to mock the newly arrived damned. A pang of despair ran right through his soul. Surely he'd made a big mistake. He had no chance of saving Jasmine; he was just a small man trying to act like a hero.

The moment passed, and something deep within Michael rebelled against his despair. A little light refused to dim or to give up within him. Michael fanned that little light until it grew again and his despair was banished.

"I will save you Jasmine," Michael promised through gritted teeth, as the huge, crimson gates closed behind him.

Guardian Angel by David Trebus

Chapter 11: Hell

Hell was everything Michael had feared and worse. Pools of lava overflowed across obsidian coloured pathways where the damned were forced to tread. Work-gangs of souls toiled, mining rock with bare hands, the only purpose the suffering it caused them. Every sin was punished in kind, and Michael struggling to keep up with the column, could only spare glances, at the torments being inflicted upon the damned.

Every step Michael took was painful, his feet searing on the burning ground. Claire squeezed his and Jazen's hands, looking strained and clearly suffering. Michael gritted his teeth, focusing on his determination to keep himself on track.

The column passed fields in which people were laid out on racks as if they were crops. Demonic farmers plucked the people from them as they worked. The column passed giant pits filled with emaciated people, left there to suffer. They passed giant mountains made up of souls all bonded together in lustful embrace, but contorted in painful positions and made to repeat the same acts over and over in agonising monotony by their demonic overlords.

As terrifying as the visions of Hell were, the screams of agony, and wails of pain that permeated the air around them, were much worse.. They rose and fell like discordant music, as if the demons were trying to create a sound in mocking parody of the heavenly symphony. The stench was unbearable; sulphur, effluent and rotting meat were the only odours Michael could detect, and he had to fight himself to not retch or cover his mouth.

As they shuffled past, demons stopped their ministrations to jeer and taunt them, shouting promises of pain and suffering and the torments they'd to inflict on the newly arrived souls. Several people in front of Michael, including an old man and a rough looking woman, broke down in tears. The demonic overseers goaded them on with whips and clubs. Michael kept looking round, desperately hoping to catch a glimpse of Jasmine, so they could rescue her, and escape this horror. She was nowhere to be seen, but they'd find her soon. He was sure of it.

He tried to take in his surroundings, Michael noticed the sky was a giant whirlpool of angry red clouds. The clouds flowed around in a never ending tempest, dizzying to look upon. As he tore his eyes away from the sky, he made out in the distance a huge bronze throne with a huge demonic figure sat upon it. The creatures wings, cast a large shadow over the landscape and a palpable aura of terror surrounded him. Michael shivered, he unconsciously figured out who that figure was, but dared not speak his name.

Claire squeezed Michael's hand, and he turned to see her eyes had followed his.. He managed a weak smile in return, silently

Guardian Angel by David Trebus

thanking her for the small gesture of support. She had started off as an acquaintance, but with all she had done for him now he couldn't help but see her as a close friend; after all, who but the most devoted of friends would go into Hell to help you?

The lesser demons jumped about, shouting abuse, and throwing less than savoury excretions at the lost souls, but, although some stopped to look at Michael, they soon moved on without a word or even a jibe. Every time one was about to say or do something to him or his companions, a blank look would cross its face and it moved on to someone else.

Was this some innate ability of his, or something that Jazen was doing? Maybe, but he couldn't shake the feeling they were being left alone on purpose, although why would that be? He shook his head, he shouldn't be focusing so much on questions he couldn't answer.

The procession marched onwards. The right-hand column was herded off down a side path leading towards a castle made entirely of flame.

"Time ta be put ta work you lazy shits." the demons jibed. "You're gonna be repairing the Masters castle of flame with yer bare hands. That's what laziness gets ya." Claire let out an involuntary sound in sympathy for those poor souls; surely no one deserved this kind of punishment?

While they moved on, the other group disappeared from sight, consigned to their fate. The left hand group continued shuffling forwards up the hill towards an abandoned building. From a distance, it could have once been a chapel, but its stone walls had long since crumbled and the roof fallen in. Graffiti sprawled all over its sides in various fluids, that Michael didn't want to know the origin of.

The hill was covered in blank gravestones, with no names or inscriptions to indicate to who lay beneath them. Faint wisps of smoke rose from the graves forming into figures, which sang in chorus, laughing mirthlessly as the processions passed by:

"Welcome, welcome damned ones, welcome to your new abode.
Never to be free, never to know peace
Forever to suffer, no hope of release."

The group shuffled into the chapel, passing by doors that hung open, broken on their hinges. The fallen leading them ran to the back. One paused before Michael and gave a wide, sharp-toothed grin before continuing. The lesser demons also left, some congregating at the doorway to throw more excrement or rocks at the lost souls, before the doors shut with a resounding boom.

Michael was left standing with the other damned, in line between broken pews and refuse. Broken shards of glass lay all over the floor, making every step Michael took agonising, the glass cutting into his feet. The lost souls wandered, hindered by their chains but with enough liberty to mill around.

Guardian Angel by David Trebus

"What's happening?" Someone cried.

"What do we do now?" A woman near the shut door yelled.

"I don't belong here." A teenager pleaded.

"Please help me!" Many voices cried out.

They pleaded with each other for help but each was so wrapped up in his or her own torment they just ignored each other's words and kept talking without listening. Several approached Michael, and he felt compassion warring with common sense. There was nothing he could do. It was too late for them.

"Time to get these shackles off," said Jazen, trying to ignore the pleas of the damned. Michael could tell he was worried, the angel's own metal control must have been tested to its limits.

"Is it safe to do that? I mean, wont they notice?" Claire asked, looking around nervously for any demons. For now, it seemed, they had been left alone.

"They shouldn't notice; it's barely even a flare of power to undo them. That's assuming they don't already know we are here. This has been far too easy." Jazen bent down to touch his bonds. They opened with a loud click and fell to the floor.

Jazen's words mirrored Michael's fears; the demons had pointedly avoided challenging them. Something felt wrong, but Michael pushed his misgivings aside. *"I'll deal with the future when it happens."* He thought. If the demons had seen through their disguises, there must be a good reason why they hadn't attacked. He'd find out their intentions eventually.

Guardian Angel by David Trebus

Jazen touched Claire's bond, releasing it onto the ground, before moving onto Michael. When the metal left his ankle, the shackles' oppression lifted, and he felt stronger . He had to catch himself before, in his relief, his concentration slipped and his wings reappeared behind him. Claire rubbed her ankle tentatively where the metal had chafed her.

The relief was short lived, as a shadow passed over the red light cast from the stormy sky. Two figures landed on the far side of the chapel, behind a debased and corrupted altar. Michael recognised Garamond, although he had only ever seen the demon in human form. The other, took a few moments, and then his heart sank. Jasmine the Fallen.

***

Jasmine's hair had turned jet black, while her beautiful blue eyes now glowed the red of hot coals at the base of a fire. Her wings, still full of feathers, were now as dark as a ravens, and were now at least double the size they had been when Michael first met her. He pushed down rising nausea when Jasmine turned to look directly at him, blue tinged lips twisting into a smile.

Michael was transfixed by Jasmine's new form. He couldn't avert his gaze no matter how much it pained him. He had come prepared for the worst, but the truth of Jasmine's transformation hit him like a hammer blow. Claire put her hand on his shoulder to try and comfort him, while Jazen stood motionless, looking similarly affected by Jasmine's new appearance.

Garamond also looked imposing, his wing span huge and his skin the colour of slate. His eyes, in contrast to Jasmine's, were jet black and pupil less. He radiated malevolence, leering down at the assembled throng, clapping his hands twice he bellowed a word at the crowd of the lost.

"*Scatter.*"

The power of his voice blasted the lost souls in all directions, some flying into the air, others through the broken walls and smashed windows. Some careered into walls, smacking hard against them and slumping to the ground in agony. The spell left only Michael, Claire and Jazen standing in the centre of the room, unaffected but feeling dangerously exposed.

"Welcome, Michael. I was going to pay you a visit up on Earth, but I see you have saved me the trouble. So good of you to enter the pit of your own accord." Garamond's voice was like the combined motion of a nest of vipers.

"Garamond…" Jazen hissed through clenched teeth.

"That's my name, angel filth." Garamond pointed a finger at him. "Feel free to repeat it as much as you like, for it will do you no good when you're my pet footstool."

A bolt of dark energy leapt from his outstretched hand and hit

Jazen square in the chest. The guardian doubled over, retching up black bile as he struggled to breath. Claire leant down to help him, stroking his back. Jazen struggled back up to his feet with Claire's help, letting loose the song to manifesting his wings and armour. "Oh, the angel bares his fangs, for all the good it will do him." Garamond taunted. "How pathetic having your mortal support you, but then it is to be expected from a lowly guardian."

During the altercation between Jazen and Garamond, Jasmine never once took her eyes off Michael. He felt the hatred, anger and guilt directed at him through Jasmine's gaze and it took an effort of will to keep his eyes fixed on her. He let his concentration slip, and Jasmine's lips twisted into a smile. Realising what had happened, Michael turned. He saw the faint outline of his own Grigori wings behind him.

"Oh …soo," Garamond said, gesturing theatrically. "That explains why you can tap into the Symphony, young Michael. You have a little of the divine in you. Those horny Grigori! But then, if it weren't for them, I wouldn't have the precious opportunity to lay the Heavens low once and for all."

"I won't help you, Garamond. I'm only here for one reason." Michael's reply was defiant, although inside he felt his guts were about to run away.

"Such a hero aren't you Michael? But let's face it…you're not. You're just a normal little man with a little angel blood in him trying to save the world. It's pathetic, you stand no chance. You only got this far because I allowed you too," Garamond replied.

"I won't know until I try." Michael stared straight into Jasmine's eyes, as he spoke. She looked away and, for the faintest moment Michael thought her features softened, the red glow dimming just a fraction. The moment passed, though, and she stared back at him again with the same fixed mirthless grin.

"I don't want to be saved, Michael. I like it here; I like the freedom I have now. I'm not chained to you or your stupid whims, and I don't have to listen to that awful, boring music anymore either." Her voice was harsh yet seductive, a voice that promised ecstasy, but at the price of suffering.

"I don't believe that. I know I can save you. I love you." Michael tried to ignore what she'd said. He knew this wasn't really her. He knew he could get through to her. A faint outline of gleaming silver armour formed over his clothing. That must be all the divine protection his thin angelic blood could muster in such a place.

"Oh but you can save her, Michael, or at least be with her." Garamond's voice was full of passion. "All I ask in return is that you join me. Think of it. You could help me bring the stagnation and oppression of Heaven's dominance to an end. Imagine the power you could wield. Think of all you could achieve. And all of it with the woman you love by your side."

For a fleeting moment the thought crossed his mind, could he be right, could he really be with Jasmine that way? What did he care about the great battle between good and evil, as long as he could get what he wanted: Jasmine?

No, siding with Garamond wouldn't get him what he wanted anyway. He could be with Jasmine, but she wouldn't be the woman he fell in love with. Besides, in doing so he would serve as a tool to undo all the good he had believed in since he was a kid. Even when he was little Michael had dreamed of being a hero like in the movies, saving the Earth and getting the girl.

Now finally Michael had his chance, and being the big man didn't matter to him. He wasn't interested in power or glory, or anything so naïve. The situation would have made him laugh had it not been so serious, his life turned totally upside down. All he wanted was to somehow save Jasmine, and even if he failed, he was determined at least to try.

"Don't listen to him, Michael," Jazen coughed out the words through his pain.

"You have free will, little man," Garamond persisted. "So what's it going to be? Join with me and be with your beloved, or watch her flay your little friends alive before I send her after you?"

"I do have free will…and there's not a chance in *HELL* I would ever join you," Michael bunched up his fists and stood his ground; He wasn't prepared to give in to anyone.

"Harsh words, Michael, but very well. In a way, I was hoping you would need some convincing. It's always fun to watch." Garamond nodded to Jasmine, who grinned wickedly.

She beat her wings once to gain some lift, stepping onto the

Guardian Angel by David Trebus

chapel's altar, and stooped down suggestively to scoop up a long-bladed dagger before standing up to her full height again. The dagger burst into purple flame at her touch, and Jasmine traced her tongue along its edge, the flames having no effect.

Jazen raised his flaming sword and stepped in front of Claire. "She's too far gone. The best you can do for her now is put her out of her misery."

"Yes, listen to your little friend, Michael." Garamond's taunting voice grated on Michael's nerves. "Your only chance to be with her now is to join me. However I can't have your minions interfering with our fun, now can I?"

He raised his arm again and uttered a single word *"Requiem"*

The word rebounded around the chapel, shaking its foundations, and dust flew from the walls. Jazen looked around urgently, but caught Garamond's attack, a moment too late. A giant hammer slammed into his side, sending him sprawling across the floor to fetch up against the wall.

Jazen lay prone, his wings losing their glow and his armour vanishing as his will and strength waned. Claire ran to kneel by his side, cradling his head in her lap. He didn't move and Claire shot Michael a worried glance. She began to shake, then cry. She stroked Jazen's brow as tears ran down her cheeks.

"We shouldn't have come here," she forced out between sobs. "What were we thinking?"

Jasmine stepped casually off the altar and walked towards Claire.

Guardian Angel by David Trebus

Her dagger of flame distended, extending and twisting into a long coil of razor-sharp barbed wire. Michael watched in horror as she casually approached Claire. If he didn't do something, Jasmine would kill her.

***

He looked at Jasmine and again thought he saw that little shimmer in her features. He leapt in front of Claire and Jazen to block Jasmine's path and turned to face her, grim determination fuelling his actions. It was all or nothing now, there was no way he was going to fail. A certainty spread through his soul; he looked into his former guardian's eyes and didn't flinch.

"Don't think I'm going to stop just because you're in my way, Michael," said Jasmine. "You're nothing to me now. Our life together is over, unless you join that braggart over there." She tilted her head to indicate Garamond.

"I know you're still in there, Jasmine." Michael said, pleading with Jasmine in desperation to come back to her senses. "Please just remember and try to fight it."

Garamond watched the scene unfolding from behind the altar. He made no move to intervene, deciding to wait and see things play out. He obviously thought he had nothing to worry about; Michael

Guardian Angel by David Trebus

was determined to prove him wrong.

Jasmine walked slowly towards Michael, coiling the lash and snapping it across the ground, the same fixed grin on her face. She walked so slowly, that time itself seemed to crawl. He stood his ground in front of Claire and straightened his back. It was going to be all or nothing.

"What are you doing, Michael?" Claire demanded. "We need to get out of here!"

Michael smiled and glanced round. "What I have to, Claire. Trust me." Michael put all the conviction he could into his voice to reassure Claire. It seemed to work as Claire's face softened. She managed a weak smile back and nodded, turning back to Jazen.

Michael took one step towards Jasmine and stopped. She continued to advance on him, coiling and uncoiling her weapon. Her grin was fading, though, turning into a scowl as if she were in pain. The faint shimmer caught Michael's eye; he could bring her back.

"Get out of my way, Michael, or I will damn you just as Garamond wishes." Jasmine lashed her barbed weapon at Michael's chest, scoring an angry red groove across his body. The pain was excruciating, and he felt his very soul seared from the weapons touch.

Michael said nothing, taking one slow step at a time towards her. He focused on her eyes to keep himself from crying out in pain or falling down from the ravages of her barbed flames. Jasmine's

Guardian Angel by David Trebus

features twisted into pure rage as again she lashed the flaming whip at Michael, a searing pain burning across his cheek.

"Back off, human, you're nothing to me!" Jasmine's voice seemed to carry an edge of desperation. Michael swore he could hear a faint whisper of Jasmines voice speak in his ear *'You're everything to me.'*

Michael kept walking towards her, and Jasmine stopped in her tracks. She hit Michael repeatedly with her weapon, cutting into him again and again as the barbs hit their mark. Michael flinched, but kept on walking despite the agony he was in.

"Please ... just stop ... just get out of my way. I don't want to hurt you." Jasmine pleaded, letting the whip fall to her side. Again Jasmine's whisper spoke in his ear *'I don't want to be hurt.'*

Tears of blood formed around Jasmine's eyes, running down her pallid cheeks as she stood motionless in front of Michael. He staggered towards her, crossing the final few feet between them. He ignored the pain flowing through him and threw his arms around Jasmine to embrace her, his head falling against her ear. "How could I walk away from the person I care about most?" He whispered. "I will never give up on you, Jasmine. I love you." His soul's strength finally gave out, and he fell against his former love.

"I...*I love you too,*" Jasmine whispered this time the whisper and her own voice joining as one.

Michael felt warmth around him. Not the searing heat of Hell, but the comforting warmth of a lovers embrace. Pure white light

Guardian Angel by David Trebus

almost blinded him, making him shut his eyes against its intensity. When he opened them again, the sight made his heart race and his soul sing.

Jasmine's feathers turned white from centre to tip in a rolling wave. Her black hair returned to blonde, as armour of polished gold, formed around her body. The red glow faded from her eyes, and they returned to normal as the waves of light flowed around her.

Jasmine was stood before him in all her former glory, and she had never looked more radiant and beautiful. Michael scarcely dared believe it, he had won. All the pain and effort leading up to the moment melted away as he embraced her, nothing else mattered. He laughed, unable to contain his joy and could see from the smile on Jasmine's face she felt the same. He leaned in and kissed her, pouring all his love into the gesture. All his strength spent, Michael collapsed against Jasmine, too weak to even stand.

Jasmine after a long moment pulled away, supporting him against her. *"Thank you, Michael."* She breathed. *"Now it's my turn to save you."*

Her soul restored to her, in the split second of her redemption, Jasmine allowed herself to feel again. She still remembered how she had felt as a fallen angel, and how she had thought during those dark moments. She had felt like being without responsibility was liberating, that doing what she wanted was the best feeling in the world. But that freedom had come at a cost. She had given up the very things that made her, her. She had given up on everything that made her existence worthwhile.

Michael's love had restored her, tapped into that small part of Jasmine's soul that had refused to give up on him, refused to give up hope. Michael had tapped into that part of her that loved him. Now she had to repay the gift he had restored to her.

Jasmine leapt over to Jazen and Claire, carrying Michael effortlessly in her arms. She focused her will on returning them to Earth and reversing Jazen's song. Normally, such a feat would have been impossible but, empowered as she was, Jasmine felt she could do anything.

"Ascension!" Jasmine yelled as the last of the demonic taint left her.

A crack of blue and red lighting intertwined hit Jasmine, Michael, Jazen and Claire in a blinding flash. When the light faded, they were gone.

Garamond stood dumbfounded for a moment before pure rage overtook him. He screamed at the roiling, red sky in impotent fury.

***

Returning to Earth through the elemental planes felt like falling to Michael. His senses were reversed and his soul, battered and

Guardian Angel by David Trebus

bruised as it was, distorted his perceptions. Michael knew that when he returned to Earth, the injuries inflicted upon his spirit would be there waiting for him on his body. His Grigori blood sang in his veins, telling him things he couldn't possibly have known as human.

But he didn't care. He'd brought Jasmine back. Held in her small but strong arms, he felt carefree. The future didn't matter, and at this moment he was exactly where he wanted to be, by the side of the woman he loved.

"You know that was stupid." Jasmine turned her head to Michael. "I gave it all up to keep you safe, and you go and risk it all.

Jasmine was so beautiful. He had even found the demonic version of her attractive; not that he would ever admit that to Jasmine. But as she was now, Jasmine was divine. She was perfect. "Yeah, it was stupid," he agreed, "but being human I'm allowed. I couldn't leave you down there. I wanted you back, and I knew I could do it."

Jasmine didn't take her eyes of Michael as they flew towards the mortal plane. She leant down and placed a soft kiss on his forehead. "Well…stupid as it was, I'm glad you did it, even though it's supposed to be me protecting you." Was that guilt in her expression?

"Why can't I look out for you as well? You're so used to carrying it all on your own shoulders; why not share the burden with me? We are together now, and together we can do anything, Jasmine."

Guardian Angel by David Trebus

Michael replied. Was that a bit corny? He didn't care.

It was funny. For all this talk of his Angelic heritage, special powers and new found abilities. What had saved them both were traits that every single person was capable of: love, hope and determination. He wanted to laugh, not out of irony, but for pure joy. He and every other person had so much potential if they just realised it.

Jasmine's serious expression faded as they neared Earth, and for a moment the air-head he had met back in hospital returned. As Michael returned to his body, Jasmine disrupted her perfectly timed landing in Claire's living room by tripping on the edge of the carpet. He laughed inside as he opened his living body's eyes to the sight of her trying to right herself.

Michael still held Claire's hand when she awoke; she released it quickly and looked around for Jazen, who knelt behind them. She stood up and caught him just before he fell.

"Are you ok, Jazen?"

"Yes, I don't know how we did it, but we won. "We got her back."

He gently pushed her away and stood.

"Welcome back to the light side, Jasmine."

Michael looked at Claire, the stress of events finally breaking as he burst out laughing. She stared at him for a moment, before she cracked a smile, and the laughter swept her away too. Jazen gave them an odd looking as if to ask what was so funny, but it only made them laugh even harder. Michael felt a stab of pain, as the

Guardian Angel by David Trebus

small cuts, large bruises and welts, from Jasmine's demonic lash made themselves apparent. But he still laughed, relieved beyond belief.

"What's so funny?" Jazen demanded.

Between deep breaths and laughing, Claire managed a reply.

"Sorry, Jazen, it's just you sounded like someone out of an old sci-fi movie with that line. It was hilarious,"

"Well…uh…I didn't know it was so..." Before Jazen could say any more, Claire put a finger on his lip and kissed him on the cheek. Jazen blushed bright red.

"It's finally over." Michael breathed.

"*Not yet,*" a voice boomed from below.

***

Garamond shot up through the Planes like a comet. All his carefully laid plans had been undone by the love of two pathetic little beings. He had laid it out all so carefully. He'd pictured how it was all supposed to turn out, Michael, his willing slave, leading him straight into the gates of Heaven with an army of newly corrupted souls at his back.

It was all going to be so glorious.

He had pictured that day ever since his fall. Ever since he had appeared before the gates of Hell, with the feathers still dropping from his wings. He had imagined destroying the Heavens and claiming them for his own. He had crawled his way through Hell's ranks, one depraved act at a time. He had built himself up to the very pinnacle of power and achieved so much.

It disgusted him how now he had failed, not once but twice, to corrupt the mortal. Michael's Guardian had been redeemed somehow and, to compound matters, they had all actually escaped from Hell right under his nose. Jasmine had even used the powers she'd gained from her demonic transformation to facilitate it. Lucifer must have been watching from his throne of bronze, seeing his failure in its entirety.

"*Love!*" Garamond spat the word out.

"Well, we will see how long love lasts when they are corpses and slaves being crushed under my boot." He sneered smashing his fist into the rock as he ascended.

If he couldn't corrupt the mortal, he would enslave him, destroy everything Michael held dear and then bring his soul back in chains to be a personal plaything. He would break Michael, crush him utterly and make the boy regret ever daring to defy his plans. Garamond reached Earth hot on the heels of the escapee's and heard Michael speak as he burst from the ground.

"It's finally over..." Garamond heard with his superior senses.

"*Not yet!*" Garamond bellowed.

Guardian Angel by David Trebus

***

Michael saw Garamond burst from the ground in a huge pillar of fire through Claire's patio window.. The garden around him was instantly charred and blackened. In his rage, Garamond cast the flames all around him, burning plants, animals and anything else that got in the way.

He wore his full obsidian armour and grasped his demonic hammer *Requiem* in his both hands, flexing his grip in anticipation of the slaughter he was about to reap.

Michael ran to the door to see what had happened, closely followed by the others. They stood shocked, gazing out at Garamond in his full demonic glory. Claire began to hyperventilate, while Michael gripped Jasmine's hand tightly, even as Jazen struggled to re-manifest his armour, despite his spiritual injuries.

"Didn't think you could get away from me so easily, now, did you?" Garamond sneered.

Jasmine looked over at Jazen "Can you fight?"

"I think so." Jazen's silver armour was reforming, and a brightly glowing spear formed in his hands. "The dark energy is fading, now I can hear the symphony again, and my strength is returning."

Jasmine nodded and turned to Michael. "This isn't something you can help with Michael. Although I know you're not going to listen anyway, so just stay behind me ok?"

"You read my mind," Michael replied. He could felt symphony again; his experiences down in Hell had attuned him to it. His wounds were healing quickly.

Jasmine and Jazen passed straight through the patio doors as if they weren't there. Claire had to go and find the key to open them, while Michael waited impatiently. He wanted to dive through the glass but thought better of it.

Jasmine and Jazen circled Garamond, flanking him. Garamond stood his ground, leering at them both and waiting. He looked like he was in no rush to finish the exchange and considering all his plans had failed he was likely looking to extend the fight, and create as much fear as possible. "*Probably wants to make us suffer.*" Michael thought.

Michael and Claire ran outside after she found the keys. Michael desperately tried to manifest armour and wings, but in the mortal world he couldn't, feeling frustrated as he failed to bring them into being. Through his efforts, he un-intentionally tapped into the symphony and healed himself. But beyond that he wasn't sure how he could help in this battle. Desperation flooded Michael's mind and he did the only thing he could think of to help. He closed his eyes, raised his head, and uttered a silent song to the symphony.

Though I walk through the valley of the shadow of death.

Guardian Angel by David Trebus

I shall fear no evil. For hope walks with me.
Wherever I may be.
For you are always with me.
Forever my Guardian, unto my final breath.

He didn't know where the words came from, and they seemed a mix of different prayers, songs and poems he had heard that came to his mind unbidden. Realising that he had successfully tapped into the Symphony, a faint beam of light rose through the Heavens to contact someone on High.

Jazen glanced at Claire and nodded. He ran forward, his spear held in front of him. Jasmine swept in from the opposite side to exploit an opening, as Garamond defended himself against Jazen. Jazen's spear struck Garamond directly on the chest, while Jasmine's flame-wreathed gladius hit in above the thigh. Both weapons glanced off Garamond's armour harmlessly, leaving no more than small scratches.

"Finished? Now it's my turn." He brought *Requiem* round in a wide arc, and knocked both angels back into the brick wall. Jasmine staggered to her feet, helping Jazen up next to her. Their armour crumpled and broken, but weapons still in hand.

"Do you see how futile it all is?" Garamond walked towards them. "All that effort, all that...love...for nothing. It isn't going to stop me crushing your spirits."

Michael, stood his ground, unflinching. Garamond seemed

Guardian Angel by David Trebus

unstoppable and, if it was going to end, he knew all four of them shared the same view: they would go out together, standing tall with hope in their hearts. Garamond sneered at the small display of bravado and swung his huge hammer around in practice arcs.

"Well, looks like I couldn't save you, after all." Michael said.

"You did," Jasmine replied. "You've saved me more times than you know."

"Isn't this the moment we are supposed to hear inspirational music and somehow beat him, like in the movies?" Claire said from behind Jazen.

"Sadly, this isn't the movies." Jazen replied stoically.

"Hun?" Claire gave a wry smile. "I don't consider myself a hun kinda girl, thank you. You should learn that about me if you want to be with me." Claire replied with a wry smile as Jazen stood dumbfounded.

Michael in reality was terrified. He knew everyone else felt the same, they were just all trying to hide it through light-heartedness. Still, he had done the impossible: he had brought Jasmine back. That was enough for him.

"If your quite finished," snarled Garamond, "it's time for you to die." Garamond stepped forward, raising his hammer to strike.

***

Guardian Angel by David Trebus

Before Garamond could land the final blow, a deafening horn note sounded from the sky. A bright pillar of light erupted, parting the clouds, and two figures came careering down from inside it, huge white wings curved behind them in a dive.

At the last moment, they flapped their wings once to land softly on the ground. One Michael recognised as Metatron, the angel he had spoken to in Claire's living room, the other he guessed at from descriptions in books and artwork. From the sheer strength pulsing from the being, it had to be Gabriel, Heaven's messenger.

"Seems we are all rule-breakers now. Those two are starting a bad trend," Gabriel remarked, his tone serious.

"I can't see any rule breaking here," Metatron retorted "Garamond crossed the line; we were simply paying a visit to give guidance when we heard a prayer and found a demon in full battle armour on the mortal plane about to slay innocents."

Gabriel grunted in reply and managed a small smile. "It's been a while since we have had the chance to fight like this together."

"I know, it should be fun. Although I think our opponent is getting impatient." Metatron replied, ducking as Garamond swung at him.

"Requiem." He bellowed, as he launched another attack in an overhead strike designed to crush Gabriel. Garamond seemed to be growing more and more frustrated. He didn't pause one moment in attacking the two new arrivals, even knowing how powerful they were.

Gabriel flung up his own weapon; a flaming sword, in a two-

Guardian Angel by David Trebus

handed grip above his head. The blades met with a thunderclap, and Gabriel's feet were driven into the ground from the sheer force of the impact. Metatron took guard in front of Michael and his companions, his two-pronged spear wreathed in blue flame, ready to defend them.

As Garamond withdrew his hammer for a second strike, Gabriel moved so fast he blurred, swinging his sword across Garamond's midriff. The blade cut through the armour and scored a line across his stomach. Garamond staggered back, bellowing in pain.

The demon turned to Metatron, advancing on him in an attempt to get to Michael and the others. He muttered some dark curse and disappeared in a cloud of black mist, only to reappear above Metatron, with his hammer poised to strike.

The angel shifted the grip on his spear, moving it to block Garamond. The demon's hammer hit home, and shattered Metatron's weapon into two halves, causing Garamond to laugh in satisfaction. His joy was short lived however, as the angel thrust both blue tipped spear heads into Garamond's chest.

The demon staggered back, his rage and frustration only building. He pulled the two blessed spear hafts from his chest and flung them to the ground in disgust. He was wounded but he was not beaten yet, he could still at least take vengeance on the mortal if he could just get past the two Archangels.

He advanced on Metatron again, hoping to take advantage of the angel losing his weapon. But Gabriel got in the way, slicing at

Guardian Angel by David Trebus

Garamond with his flaming sword and pushing him further and further away from his objective.

The ground shook and both Gabriel and Garamond, so focused on the fighting almost lost their footing.

"Get back! Gabriel, quickly!" Metatron shouted.

Gabriel leapt back, beating his wings to help propel him, and landed next to Metatron.

"Coward!" Garamond yelled.

"What's going on?" Michael asked, struggling to keep his footing..

"Someone is a little displeased at how Garamond has conducted himself." Metatron explained. "Hell doesn't like failures."

The ground shook more violently and split underneath Garamond. Flames erupted from the rent as it widened, and a huge, bronze claw thrust upward. It grabbed Garamond and held him fast in its powerful grip. He struggled but, unable to escape, bellowed in impotent rage.

"*Enough, Garamond,*" a booming voice echoed out. *"Your continued incompetence is beginning to wear on me. It's time for you to be…re-educated in your duties."*

"No, lord, please! I can still win, I can bring you Heaven's ruin, please, just let me…" Garamond's protest was cut off, as the huge claw dragged him down into the flames and back to Hell. The rent in the ground closed, leaving only the scorch marks of the flames to show it had ever been there. A long silence fell over the assembled beings, before Michael broke it with a sigh of relief.

Guardian Angel by David Trebus

***

Michael felt the angels' choir was taking forever. After the battle, Gabriel had demanded that both Jasmine and Jazen return to Heaven with him. Michael had tried to protest, but Gabriel made it clear the decision was not open to debate. Metatron hadn't been much help either, commenting cryptically, "Have faith," before they left. Now Michael sat in Claire's living room, perched on the edge of her sofa, with little to do but wait.

Police, fire crews, and an ambulance had arrived soon after Garamond's demise, and remained for most of the day, putting out the fires and taking statements. According to the firemen, someone had reported a lightning strike, others a gas explosion. Thankfully, no one had actually seen what actually happened.

"What do you think will happen to them?" Claire asked, sitting on the sofa next to him.

"I really don't know." Michael was wondering the same. "Gabriel didn't look too happy when he took them."

"Heaven can't blame Jasmine and Jazen for what happened can they?" Claire sounded desperate. She was clearly missing Jazen, and the toll of recent events was showing.

Guardian Angel by David Trebus

"I hope not," Michael replied, trying to think positively. "I'm sure it'll all be Okay. We did nothing wrong, and they're our Guardians. They can't exactly take that away from us."

Michael lapsed into silence. What more could he say? He fidgeted nervously, shifting position constantly on the sofa. How would Heaven handle Jasmine becoming a demon? . What if they decided to banish her to hell? Or, worse imprison her for her transgressions? Did they even imprison angels?

A loud clap of thunder made him jump, shocking him out of his thoughts. Was it Garamond? Surely he couldn't have returned. There was no portal, no bright light: just a loud noise, and Jazen lay on the floor, with Jasmine standing over him. Michael immediately noticed something about the Guardians was different. His eyes widened as he noticed what it was. Where were the angels' wings?

Claire had leapt from the sofa, but she regained her composure quickly. She knelt down on the floor next to Jazen, while Jasmine helped him stand.

"Jazen!" Claire looked him up and down, clearly noticing his missing wings. "What happened?"

"Are you ok?" Michael asked Jasmine, and she gave him a quick nod. Jazen brushed himself down, looking sheepish. He glanced behind him, where his wings used to be. "I'm fine." He paused. "Can I sit down? I feel a little dizzy. Jasmine can explain things."

"Of course!" Claire stood again, looking a little confused, but helped Jasmine taken Jazen over to the sofa.

Michael couldn't help himself. Before Jasmine could take a seat he pulled her into his arms, hugging her tightly. He kissed her cheek before letting her go, eager to hear what had happened.

"We were brought before a full choir of angels to answer for our actions," Jasmine explained. "Metatron spoke in our defence and all charges but one were dropped. We were found guilty of breaking a cardinal rule" Jasmine paused, taking a deep breath. "No angel shall ever enter Hell. And for it we were made mortal."

"Made mortal?" Michael felt a shock run down his spine. "As in human?"

"Yes," Jazen said. "It was Metatron who suggested the punishment."

"Considering all that happened, we got off very lightly," Jasmine added. "We could have been banished, or worse."

"Does that mean we can stay together?" Michael's voice trembled. What would he have done had Jasmine been banished?

"Yes." Jasmine smiled. "I think Metatron planned it this way. It was the only way to appease Gabriel, yet still allow us to remain with you. I may have lost my powers, but I think," Jasmine looked over to where Jazen sat, "Jazen will agree, we have both gained something far more precious."

Michael knew what Jasmine had meant, but he wanted to hear her say it, to make it feel more real. "What have you gained?" he asked softly.

Guardian Angel by David Trebus

"Love, of course, silly." Jasmine embraced her former charge, now her lover.

***

Garamond sat at the feet of the great bronze throne; every moment agony in the fires of the raging inferno. The pain steeled his spirit and fuelled his rage. He still had a few cards left to play on Earth. The Lilith sisters ran amuck on the mortal plane, having escaped the great one's notice and his mortal agents still remained, watching, waiting.

"I will return to Earth." Garamond whispered to himself. "I will have my vengeance, and I will have the head of the mortal who defied me mounted on a stick outside Hell's gates."

Guardian Angel by David Trebus

Guardian Angel by David Trebus